CORVID WHISPERS

CORVID WHISPERS

THE AMETHYST WRATH
BOOK ONE

DEE MANNINE

CONTENT WARNING

This story contains mature themes and sexual content that may not be suitable for all readers.

<u>Content warnings include, but are not limited to:</u>

Explicit brutal abuse, character death, graphic miscarriage, profanity, infertility, references to sexual assault (chapter 10 specifically), gore, depictions of bullying, and violence toward a parental figure.
Additionally, this book contains cruel and discriminatory language directed at people with albinism. These depictions are included to illustrate the impact of cruelty and prejudice, not to condone such behavior, and to give depth to the character's experience.

Although I tried to avoid going into too much detail about specific triggers mentioned above, they are present, and I recommend that those who are sensitive to these topics take caution.

Chapter ten has an asterisk at the top as a warning for sexual assault of a main character.

DEDICATION

For those who feel trapped by the rules others impose.

For those who've had their light taken from them and found the strength to shine again.

For those who know they're capable of achieving more.

Especially for those who've been hurt or betrayed by the people they trusted the most.

I hope you love how this series takes you to the stars.

CONTENTS

GLOSSARY

Locations

- **Amanita Copse:** The giant mushroom forest where the Vatte live
- **Barrio:** The slums of Joro and the location of the Murkway
- **Camp:** A rehabilitation center where humans are sent when they are chosen from a Wyrd or for misbehavior
- **Cascade:** The high-class section of Joro and the location of Joro Hall
- **Dracamora:** Unknown
- **Dunes:** The vast dunes outside of the Camp
- **Gardvord:** Plant science division
- **Heath Forest:** The Hailec-infected forest northeast of the Camp
- **Joro:** The human city enclosed under a dome
- **Joro Hall:** Government building where meetings are held
- **Mt. Ebenveil:** The mountain where the Wisps reside
- **Murkway:** Sewers of Joro
- **Noctrya:** Unknown
- **Orience:** Farmlands of Joro and location of the Gardvord
- **Palatium:** The central building of Joro
- **Tuath:** The Lycanthrope realm
- **Umbrea (um-bree-uh):** The Fae realm
- **Umbrea Castle:** The castle within Umbrea
- **Willow Grove:** The willow forest where the Jotnar reside
- **Xyberus:** The world

Beings

- **Corvid:** Ravens with invisibility magic that transform into humans
- **Dragor:** Non-magical lizard humanoids employed by the Monster King
- **Fae:** Beings with mist magic who reside in Umbrea
- **Gnashing Flora:** Non-magical man-eating plants
- **Hailec:** Magical, zombie-like monsters that transform themselves to attract their prey
- **Human:** Non-magical beings
- **Jotnar:** Non-magical giants
- **Lionne:** A creature that is half lion, half dragon
- **Lycanthrope (lie-can-thrope):** Animal shape shifters who live in Tuath
- **Mother Goddess:** The divine creator
- **Mungder:** Non-magical, octopus-like monsters that inhabit bodies of water
- **Solios (so-lee-oh-s):** Sun god
- **Vatte:** Beings with earth magic who live in the Amanita Copse
- **Wisps:** Magical beings of the Mother Goddess

Roles

- **Advisor:** A person who works under Lord Mordred
- **Rozzer:** The guards of Joro and the Camp
- **Rozzer Captain:** The captain of the Rozzers
- **The Rising:** A rebel group of Joro.
- **Traverser:** Humans whose job is to venture outside of the city
- **Umbrea Council:** The Fae who serve as counselors to King Ael

Characters

- **Ael (eye-el):** King of the Fae
- **Alexi:** Joro Rozzer
- **Askold (as-cold):** Joro Rozzer
- **Benny:** Seda's brother
- **Cahir (cuh-hear):** Seda's best friend
- **Chief Vidar (vi-dar):** Vatte chief
- **Elco:** Lionne
- **Esper:** Seda's co-worker
- **Ferona (fer-oh-nuh):** Roya's Corvid sister
- **Feich:** Roya's Corvid brother
- **Fran:** Head Housekeeper at Umbrea Castle
- **High Gravemara:** Jotnar queen
- **Jason:** Seda's father
- **Kalon (kuh-lawn):** Joro Traverser
- **Lucja (luke-juh):** Daughter of Chief Vidar
- **Luelle:** Umbrea council member and spy
- **Meir (mare):** Umbrea council member
- **Michael:** Joro Rozzer
- **Mogthud:** Jotnar prince
- **Mordred:** Lord of Umbrea
- **Neoma:** Daughter of a Fae lord
- **Orion:** Son of Lucja
- **Ojore (uh-JOR-ray):** Citizen of Joro and friend of Jason
- **Praxis:** Umbrea counsel member and captain of the Umbrea guard
- **Roya:** Warden of the Corvids
- **Ruel (ru-el):** Joro Traverser
- **Sara:** Seda's mother
- **Seda (say-duh):** Citizen of Joro and main character
- **Seren:** Joro Traverser
- **Suza:** Maid at Umbrea Castle
- **Somnium (som-nee-um):** Unknown
- **Tahti (tah-tee):** Fae witch
- **Teivel (tee-vul):** Joro Advisor
- **The Monster King:** Ruler of monsters

CORVID WHISPERS

TUATH
MT. EBENVEIL
AMANITA COPSE
WILLOW GROVE
JORO
DUNES
THE CAMP

XYBERUS
NOCTRYA
UMBREA
HEATH FOREST
DRACAMORA

BEFORE

*In a long-forgotten dungeon, a creature gave up hope of earning its
freedom.*

*It remembered songs from their past, sung over a thousand years
ago, with premonitions of yanantin, the balance of opposing sides.*

The creature sighed and closed its eyes; there would be no balance.

*The gods were now forgotten, their savior nowhere to be found,
the scales now tipped too heavily on one side.*

Darkness filled the room, and its heart turned to stone.

NOW

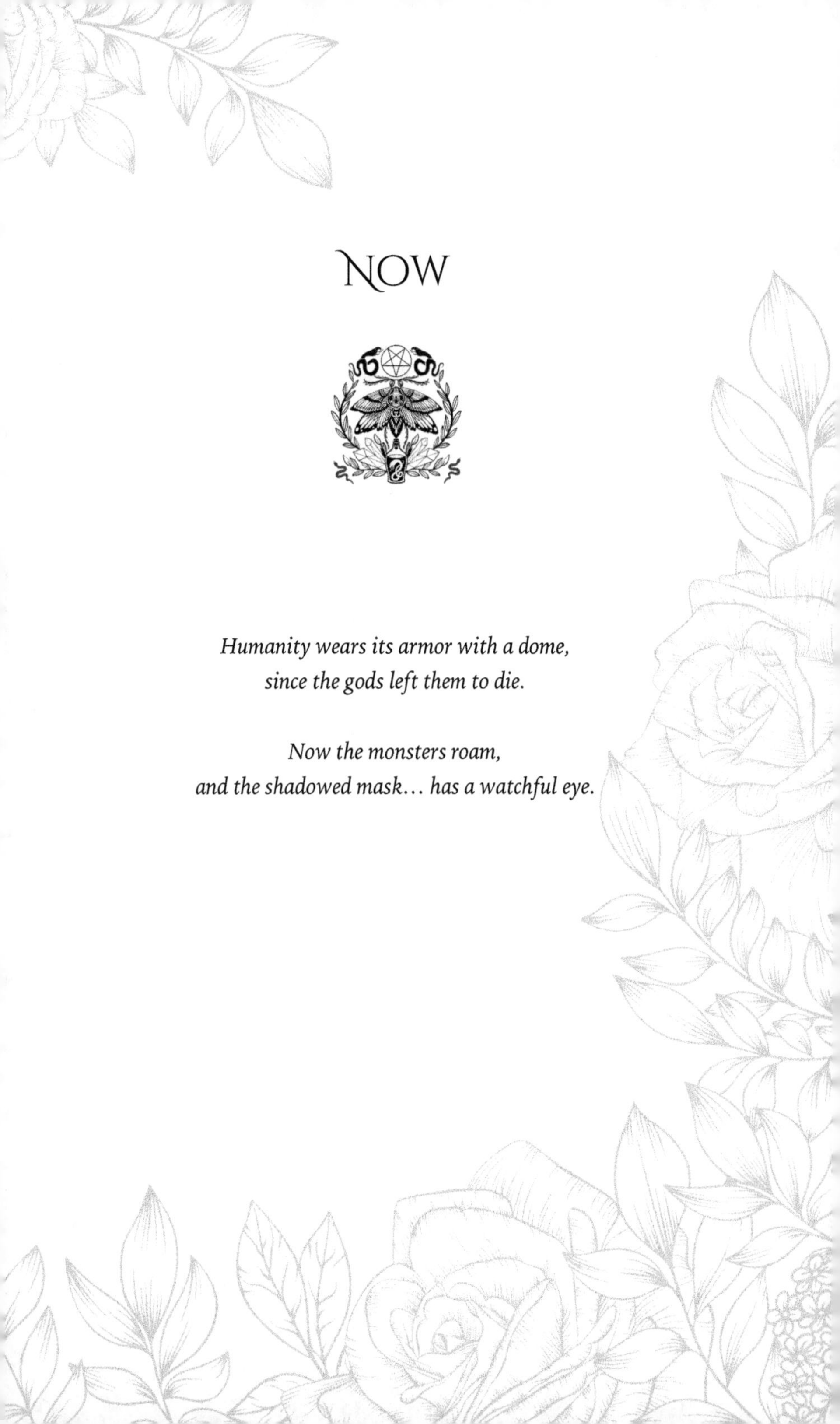

Humanity wears its armor with a dome,
since the gods left them to die.

Now the monsters roam,
and the shadowed mask… has a watchful eye.

PART ONE
THE CITY OF JORO

CHAPTER 1

<u>Seda</u>

Today was the first day of the sixth month, and the Wyrd alarms hadn't gone off yet. Seda's anxious heart fluttered as if it were a trapped moth, its pattering wings thrashing against the confines of her chest.

As the soft hum of the computer vibrated beneath her fingers, she stared at the screen with trembling hands, the words in front of her blurring together as she read.

For the third time in the last minute, she anxiously checked the clock and saw it was noon. The alarms could go off at any moment, and she needed to be ready. Her gaze moved from the clock to her friend, Cahir, noticing he had fallen asleep.

He was constantly nodding off at work, and she *usually* fought the urge to throw something at him, but this time she gave in. She grabbed her last mandarin and threw it, hitting him square in the forehead, then watched as it ricocheted across the empty room before finally landing with a soft thud in the far corner.

Cahir stirred and looked up at her with a lazy, dimpled smile. "You actually got me that time."

"Wake up! You're going to get us in trouble!" she snapped, jumping up from her uncomfortable seat and glaring at him.

Cahir chuckled as he rubbed his forehead. He looked up at the harsh fluorescent lights and let out an annoyed groan. His gaze shifted back to Seda, and his smile returned, lighting up his face.

"Not if I'm caught up," he replied, his emerald-colored eyes sparkling with mischief.

Seda sat back down and tapped a random key on her keyboard, the letter multiplying across the screen. "What if we get selected today?"

"I won't let that happen."

She bit her nail. That sounded reassuring, but what could he really do? Their names were now in the selection queue.

As Cahir stood and walked around their shared desk, he gently placed his hands on her shoulders and began massaging them. She closed her eyes, feeling her tension ease as she sank into his warmth, exhaling slowly through her nose.

She smiled at herself as she thought about how the mandarin struck his head. She really did get him good that time. Usually, he caught the objects she threw before they made contact.

Several heartbeats passed in silence as they listened to the subtle ticking of the clock.

But, as always, the piercing Wyrd alarm shattered their peace, jolting both of them from their thoughts and pulling them back to the present.

Seda's smile faded as her anxiety returned, making her feel like she was walking a tightrope with hope just out of reach.

BY THE TIME they arrived at the Palatium, sweat clung to Seda's shirt from the scorching sun shining down through the city's protective dome. She panted from their brisk walk and caught the smell of the stale air, as if the crumbling Palatium walls were exhaling from years of repetitive, painful memories.

Unease filled Seda's vision as she scanned the crowd that had packed into the stadium. Her eyes softened as she spotted children quietly whimpering in the scorching sun, their fragile skin battling the heat.

Growing up in Joro, citizen learned from an early age to keep their complaints to themselves, as misbehavior often led to severe consequences.

Her gaze landed on the banner proudly displayed across the Palatium tower, showcasing the years since the victory. It had been nearly a thousand years since the gods abandoned their planet, Xyberus, forcing everyone to find refuge beneath the dome.

Just as the sirens were in the middle of their song, they suddenly stopped, and the entire crowd fell eerily silent. Seda froze with her hand trembling as it linked with Cahir's.

"Everything's going to be okay, Sed," Cahir whispered, gently squeezing her hand. His wavy, chestnut hair clung to his forehead, and his brows furrowed as he gazed down at her.

A line of Rozzers surrounded the stadium walls, backed by brown, dried moss that had died years ago, stuck between the large, sand-colored bricks of the Palatium. The Rozzers stood rigidly, their dark red uniforms crisp, and their eyes methodically sweeping the crowd for any signs of misbehavior.

A few minutes of silence elapsed before the creak of a door echoed throughout the area, revealing a short, stout man who stepped out from the Palatium doorway. He wildly clapped his hands as he moved toward the podium positioned in the middle of the stage.

"Attention, all!" he announced into the microphone, his

voice reverberating with a sharp echo through the speakers. "As you all know, I'm Advisor Teivel, and I am *thrilled* to kick off today's events." His piercing, beady eyes scanned the crowd, and a slight smile curled his lips. "Let us begin!"

A Rozzer stepped out of the doorway, forcefully shoving a man from behind. A rope had been tied around the man's wrists, and blood trickled from a wound on his forehead. The man, struggling with an injured leg, stumbled forward and fell. A cry of pain echoed through the stadium as the Rozzer holding him captive kicked him in frustration.

Seda's eyes widened, and she instinctively bit her fingernail with her free hand. The sight of blood and pain on the man's face was too much to bear, and she quickly looked away.

She wished everyone would follow the rules. When you followed the rules, you didn't get hurt.

A wave of fear washed over her as she remembered that, for the first time in her adult life, she had broken the rules today. It wasn't because she didn't try hard enough, but the regulations in Joro didn't account for 'trying'.

"And what do we have here?" Teivel asked, his grin widening. "An absentee from today's festivities?"

The man cried as he lay on the floor. "I'm no absentee, sir," he slurred, blood dripping down his chin. "I was making my way to the stadium from the Murkway, but the sirens stopped before I could arrive in time."

"You see..." Teivel started, his eyes sparkling with delight. "You're considered an absentee if you don't make it inside these walls *before* the sirens stop. That's one of our many important rules."

When the Wyrd's sirens sounded, everyone was expected to stop what they were doing and attend. Sometimes the sirens went off right after the morning prayer, sometimes in the middle of the afternoon, and other times a few hours before curfew, which was the scariest time for Seda to hear them. Hearing the alarm then left little time to return home before the Rozzers rounded up those still out.

"You're today's first rehabilitation member." Teivel's smile resembled a wolf scenting its prey.

"I've had two children before turning thirty! My babies, please, sir. My wife!" the man cried out hoarsely as he pleaded for himself.

With a roll of his eyes, Tievel said, "Rozzer, please process this man and bring him into the cell."

The Rozzer seized the man by the tightly bound ropes and dragged him across the platform. He snatched his ID card and tossed his injured body into the cell, slamming the door shut.

A woman in the crowd let out a piercing cry and rushed forward, pushing through other citizens. Seda's eyes quickly shifted back to Teivel, her stomach tightening as anxiety swept through her.

"My husband!" the woman screamed. "He was coming!"

The woman dropped to her knees, sobbing as she clasped her hands together, and pointing them toward the stage. Two young girls ran up behind her and hugged her, their cries blending with hers.

Please don't hurt her. Please don't take her, too, Seda thought.

Seda's mind flooded with memories of her coworker, Esper, who was sent to the Camp for a similar reason. Esper's loved one, Diantha, was collected during the Wyrd, and Esper resisted, calling Joro a tyrannical society.

It was the first time Seda had ever heard those terms, and when Cahir explained what they meant, she disagreed, but that was before their time ran out, before she also broke the rules.

Seda wiped away a tear that slipped free from her memory, and Cahir gave her hand another comforting squeeze.

"These are not my rules. I'd highly suggest you pull yourself together before the same fate comes to you," replied Teivel as his eyes slightly softened. "I'd hate to see you end up in the

Camp, as you seem to have proven yourself valuable to society."
He looked at her daughters and back to her. "Your husband has
an opportunity to prove himself loyal to us for this disagreeable
behavior."

For Seda, the Camp was a terrifying prospect. She knew it
was her one shot at proving she was worthy of rejoining Joro's
society if selected, but the truth was, nobody really knew what
went on there. And Seda had no desire to find out firsthand.

She was mostly happy with her life in Joro, by Cahir's side.
She simply yearned to have a child to share their life with.

Teivel looked away from the woman, a sneer of disgust on
his face, and back to the crowd. "We cannot tolerate absentees
or misbehavior. Those are the rules." He waved his hand to the
Rozzers, telling them not to interfere with the woman or her
children.

The Rozzers, who had begun to step toward the woman from
their spot on the wall, moved back to their original position,
their swords falling back to their sides.

The woman remained kneeling on the ground with her
daughters, their cries softening into sniffles. A few bystanders
helped lift them off the rocky ground. Dirty streaks now marked
the girls' faces as they brushed away tears, dust now covering
their worn-out dresses.

"Now, for the important part," said Teivel with a dramatic
pause to ensure that all were listening. "But first, our prayer in
honor of our lord, Lord Mordred." Teivel nodded his head to the
Rozzers on the landing above. The Rozzers turned around and
flipped the switch to play the song.

The seraphic voice of the same prayer they heard each
morning began to fill the speakers across the city, the music an
eerie reminder of why everyone was still alive.

Oh, our lord, Mordred,
protects us from these evils that consume,

and prevents the Monsters who dwell,
from us meeting our gloom.
The gods wished us farewell,
but his love allows Joro to bloom.

When the prayer ended, Teivel perked up once more. "And now..." He paused before raising his voice, "Lord Mordred!"

Teivel extended his short arm toward the doorway, and the lord stepped out. Lord Mordred's hooded black robe billowed behind him, flowing like wind through the darkness.

Lord Mordred walked across the stage, threw his hood back, and smiled broadly, showing noticeable gaps in his teeth. His scarred, lifeless skin didn't detract from his imposing presence as he glided to the podium on his long legs.

The entire crowd knelt in a gesture of respect. Soft murmurs of love and gratitude spread among the majority. Seda and Cahir joined them, pressing their hands against the rough ground, and watched the shadows of birds flying overhead.

The crowd chanted, "Our lord, we serve. Our lord, we love."

"Thank you all for coming. Please rise," his sonorous voice sounded through the speakers.

Lord Mordred gestured broadly with a theatrical display of his arms. "We're here to celebrate the nine-hundred-and-ninety-ninth-and-a-half Wyrd with two gifts for everyone who remains after today's events. Only those who consistently demonstrate their love and dedication to our society each day will receive these tokens of appreciation."

Each Wyrd typically came with a single gift. Sometimes it was an extra day off work; other times, it was a silver token. Many in the crowd looked up in surprise and excitement at the mention of two gifts, with children jumping and clapping.

Lord Mordred responded with a broad smile. "Everyone will receive three additional food tokens for extra rations upon the completion of today's Wyrd. Please remember not to spend all of it at once and to save some for a rainy day."

Rain never fell on Joro soil with the dome high in the sky. The aquifer, flowing from the ground, moved through the city and was the only source of water and relief. Seda could only see the rain patter against the dome on the stormiest days, a gentle reminder of their safety.

She had always yearned to feel the gentle touch of rain in her palms and on her cheeks, but the idea of leaving the safety of the city was too terrifying to even consider. It just wasn't worth the risk.

For whatever reason, animals and people could pass through the glittering barrier, but neither rain nor monsters could. For safety reasons, no one was allowed to leave without prior approval. A large, heavily protected wall surrounded the city, with only a few exits allowing passage beyond.

Lord Mordred continued, "I want to thank everyone for your dedication to our society. Your efforts have helped us sustain ourselves. As we approach the one thousandth year of our victory over the monsters, we have repeatedly improved our education, allowing us to offer stronger protections for our families."

Lord Mordred scanned the crowd and pointed at a man with a young child. "You, sir, are a prime example of why we succeed!" He bared his jagged grin once more.

A light applause echoed through the stadium, and Seda rose onto her tiptoes to get a better view of the man in the crowd. The man had dark hair, and a small boy, about seven years old, stood with him. The man bowed deeply, then stood, revealing a proud smile and reddened cheeks as he looked at his young son.

"As for our second gift, this Wyrd, we will select forty individuals instead of fifty who have not been committed to Joro's success. These forty have been given more than fifteen years to secure their place in our society by bearing children, but have failed to do so. They will be sent to the Camp as a final effort to redeem themselves, where our doctors will do everything possible to ensure successful reproduction." Lord Mordred slowly scanned the crowd.

Everyone stood there in silence, watching those around them.

"Teivel, please bring the list of names," he demanded.

Teivel hurried over to him, his robe slipping loosely over his small shoulders, and handed Lord Mordred a rolled piece of paper tied with a red ribbon. The ribbon's color accentuated the shine of the lord's thick bracelets, catching Seda's eye.

Please don't call us. Please don't call us.

Lord Mordred looked over the crowd. "Rozzers, be on standby. The following people must come up to the podium for processing. Ensure a smooth transition." The Rozzers all gave a firm salute in unison.

Conflicts during selection were rare, as Joro citizens were well-versed in the Wyrd and its rules. Everyone was aware of the risks. Having a child by age thirty guaranteed a sense of security.

Reproduction rates had dropped significantly over the past two centuries, and now only one in fifty could bear children. Nobody understood why the decline had occurred, or why it was worsening. For Joro to survive, their community had to flourish, and the drop in birth rates was a significant concern.

"Derek Howell, Margarite Powers, Ruthette Winters." Citizens watched as Lord Mordred read off the list of names.

Seda continued to hold tightly to Cahir's hand as the selected individuals turned to their loved ones and shared somber embraces before taking their first steps toward their rehabilitation.

"Cahir, I'm so scared of the Camp. What will happen to us if we get chosen?" Seda whispered nervously. "What do we do if only one of us gets called?"

Cahir pulled Seda into a hug, and his familiar, cedar scent

surrounded her. He reassuringly ran his hand up and down her back. "We will always have each other, Seda. *Always.*"

Before each Wyrd, every adult without a child registered their age and birthing registration. Registration, like the Wyrd, was mandatory. If you or your partner confirmed a pregnancy, you both received a stamped pregnancy certificate, which gave you additional time before signing up for the selection queue.

When the child was born, you received a birth certificate confirming your continued loyalty to Joro. But if you were over thirty and didn't have a certificate, your name was submitted for selection.

Cahir and Seda registered five days earlier for the selection, despite their ongoing efforts to conceive through artificial insemination.

"Brad Merguee. Xavier Ruppert." Lord Mordred continued calling names with a hint of nonchalance as more people solemnly walked to the stage to be processed.

The Rozzers remained alert, holding various weapons and blocking all escape routes.

A loud, crashing sound erupted against the dome, shaking the ground violently and echoing through the sky. Seda fell away from Cahir, and she braced herself against the trembling earth, feeling fear crawl up her spine.

Black birds screeched as they swooped down frantically, one scratching Seda's shoulder and causing a sharp pain.

She raised her hands to shield her face.

Cahir struggled to find his footing and crawled over to her, pulling her close. He wrapped his arms around her protectively, shielding her from the bird.

"We have to get up!" he shouted over the terrified screams ringing out through the stadium. Seda stayed frozen in Cahir's arms, her body refusing to move as she watched people around her desperately searching for their loved ones.

Over the past few months, the Jotnar's attacks on the dome

had intensified, with each subsequent attempt to breach the barrier growing stronger. The Jotnar were the worst of the monsters in Xyberus, towering over twenty feet tall. They were colossal creatures that ate humans for both entertainment and delicacy, and were known to hunt anyone who wandered outside.

"Look at me, Seda, please." Cahir pulled her face to his. "I've got you." His steady gaze fixed on hers, and gradually, Seda's fear began to fade as she was drawn into the familiar comfort of his eyes.

"Okay," she responded weakly. "I see you."

He wrapped her in a tight hug and helped her to her feet, off the rough ground. "Don't let go," he said, as she clung to him.

The rumbling earth gradually quieted.

"Calm!" Mordred called over the crowd. "Everyone, calm yourselves. This dome has never faltered. We're *safe*! They cannot get in."

As the dome's resonance died down, a profound silence descended upon them. People slowly got to their feet and glanced around nervously.

"Where were we?" Mordred asked into the mic as he adjusted it. "Ah, yes... Now that the little display from the Jotnar is over, we can move on."

He resumed calling the names from his list.

Seda took a deep breath and tried her hardest to refocus her attention on the Wyrd.

"... Gavin Smith," the lord continued. "You're our final Wyrd selectee."

The crowd, still timid from the attack on the dome, clapped quietly.

"Our names weren't selected," Seda whispered as a small smile crested her lips. "We have another chance."

"And that concludes our Wy..." Seda was staring at Cahir as

Lord Mordred paused. She looked back at the man in front of the podium, and her eyes widened.

Lord Mordred's fierce crimson gaze sliced through the nervous crowd, locking onto her with a disturbing intensity.

She didn't know what to do or how to respond, so she quickly looked away from him.

Was he aware that she and Cahir had registered this Wyrd without a certificate?

"Excuse me." He cleared his throat, looked away, and then resumed in an overly cheerful tone, "What an eventful day we've had. I want to thank everyone for their dedication to our success and survival. Please don't forget to collect your tokens on the way out."

CHAPTER 2

Seda had to fight the urge to smile as she walked beside Cahir. Being safe this Wyrd was a huge relief, as if she had found a beacon of light in the darkness.

"Are you okay, Sed?" Cahir asked as they joined the crowd heading toward the stadium's east exit.

"Oh, Cahir. Yes! I'm so happy we have another chance!" she exclaimed, her smile finally slipping free. "We'll be successful and conceive this time, I know it."

She longed for the deep connection that comes with being a mom, wanting someone to love and care for, and someone who would love her back just as much. She also desperately wanted them to be safe from the Wyrd.

Cahir hummed thoughtfully, his gaze shifting from the birds soaring above to Seda's shoulder. "I meant your scratches. Did something happen when she scratched you?"

She looked down at her shoulder, the sharp pain overshadowed by the happiness in her heart.

"No, the bird just came out of nowhere." She hadn't done

anything to deserve the scratches, and it wasn't the first time a bird had come too close. The birds were always around, watching them, watching *her*. At least it felt that way, anyway. Until today, they had always been harmless.

She considered the black ravens annoying, similar to the meat bees that sometimes tried to steal her lunch when she ate outside.

"Was Lord Mordred watching me?" she wondered out loud, the rocks crunching under her leather shoes with every step. She recalled the way his eyes seemed to penetrate her, and the memory sent a chill down her spine.

Cahir's face was unreadable. "It seemed that way. Have you ever met him in person before?" They both paused, letting others pass.

Throughout her life, she had only ever seen Lord Mordred at the Wyrds or in the numerous portraits of him around Joro.

The only reason he would have stared at her like that is if he knew she registered for selection. What other reason could there be?

"No—ow!" A woman bumped into her, and her shoulder flared in pain. The woman apologized and quickly moved around them toward the exit.

"We need to get you to the medical wing to check that out," Cahir suggested.

"Maybe later," Seda replied, thinking she could get another insemination if they went, but exhaustion overwhelmed her nerves, and she was eager to head home first.

The crowd led them to a long line, where people were collecting their food tokens from the Rozzers.

"Maybe we can actually get some decent food this time. I'm tired of chicken and rice," she mumbled as she walked in front of Cahir in line.

The air was thick and heavy as they made their way to the exit. The Rozzers were watching people, making sure they stayed in an orderly, single-file line at the door. The closer people got to the exit, the quieter they became.

Seda and Cahir moved to the front of the line, and the Rozzers shifted their attention to them.

"What about some fermented eggs this time?" Cahir whispered into her ear from behind, tickling it with his breath. She grimaced. He knew how much she hated those, something often handed out at the food dispensaries.

"Shhh," she silently scolded. "We have to remain quiet."

Cahir tickled her side, and she shot him a warning look over her uninjured shoulder, struggling to hide her smile. Cahir chuckled and made a hand gesture signaling he was sealing his lips and keeping his hands to himself.

"No child, I see?" the Rozzer at the counter asked her as she stepped forward, his eyes suggestively roaming over her from head to toe. "What's your name, darling?"

"S-Seda Arbor." Her heart pounded fiercely at his leering gaze, but she felt a surge of gratitude and pride that her voice mostly stayed steady, something she often struggled with.

The Rozzer looked through the files, checked off her name, and handed her three copper food tokens, giving her a slight smirk and a wink.

As Seda stepped out, she grabbed the tokens and slipped them into her pocket, along with her apartment key and ID, then paused to wait for Cahir on the other side, nervously biting her nails.

The Rozzer's eyes tracked her as she walked out and then looked back at Cahir.

"Name?" the Rozzer asked sternly, as if disgusted he was there.

"Cahir Cutlass." Cahir's voice showed no hint of fear or hesitation. He stood tall, reaching out to take the tokens, but not before giving the Rozzer a sharp glare.

As they left the stadium, the eastern and southern parts of

the city came into view. Joro consisted of three main sections, with the Palatium at its center.

To the south was Barrio, where lower-class residents and most of Joro's population lived. The people of Barrio were usually the laborers in the Murkway, their clothing stained with a map of the city's filth. Barrio consisted of dilapidated, shared homes, with doors that barely held on to their hinges. Falling rooftops, peeling paint, and dirty streets defined the area: the slums.

Seda and Cahir lived in the northeast region called Orience, which featured farmland and the Gardvord. Many apartment complexes were built in Orience to house both scientists and farmworkers.

Out of view to the northwest was Cascade. Cascade's population was small, comprising the wealthiest and most influential members of Joro's society. People from Cascade worked inside the Palatium as advisors or were among the city's top scientists and medical professionals. Their homes were luxurious, and they received priority in food distribution due to the importance of their roles in society.

"I want to hurt that Rozzer for the way he looked at you," Cahir seethed, his fist curling and uncurling with each step.

Cahir always responded that way when someone stared at Seda for too long.

Seda forced a smile. "I hate all of them. They could have been something else in Joro and decided to go into the one field where they hurt people."

"While I'd love to tear apart the ones who look at you like that, I don't think that is always the case, Sed." He sighed. "They can't all be bad."

"I doubt that," she retorted snidely. She truly hated each and every one of them.

Cahir looked at her and furrowed his brows together. "Some people don't have a choice in what they want to do to make a living. This society has its way of bestowing fortune on some while keeping others stuck in the lowest depths of despair."

That was true. The laborers certainly didn't have an advantage because of their limited education. If a child performed well in primary school and their test scores indicated they had the potential to move into a higher section of Joro, they could advance.

It was difficult, but not impossible; her father was a testament to that.

The Rozzers paid well and lived within the Palatium. They also didn't require high testing scores. As a result, many people from the Barrio chose to join.

She disagreed with their decision, though. To her, violence was just violence.

They traveled down the road in silence as Seda lost herself in thought. The streets of Orience were neat but dusty from the nearby fields, and the birds flying overhead stirred up dust in the air.

Seda coughed when one of them flew too close, and she narrowed her eyes at it. "You dang things are always causing chaos!"

She pointed her finger at it.

Cahir laughed and looked at the feathered troublemaker. The bird had landed in a nearby tree and watched, cawing loudly as they walked past. "If I didn't know any better, I'd think she understood you."

"I don't care," Seda huffed and continued walking. "My shoulder hurts from one of them. Let's get back home."

"No can do. We have a date with the food dispenser and three solid copper coins to spend, *each*." He flashed the coins in the sunlight and smiled brightly.

Her eyes landed on his dimples, and she couldn't help but smile back.

"Here, take mine. No fermented eggs! I'd rather *starve*. Can you see if they have any bananas this time, please?" She handed him her coins, and he placed them alongside the others in his palm, closing it tightly.

"Are you sure you'll be alright? What if the Jotnar attack again?"

"They never attack so quickly after. I'm heading straight home—no other stops. I really want to shower." She desperately needed to wash herself after how that Rozzer looked at her.

"Okay… no yummy eggs for you," Cahir teased as they reached the split in the road. "I'll be back home before you know it."

He hugged her tightly before they parted ways.

Seda carried on alone through a maze of apartment complexes to their building and ascended the winding stairs to the top floor, where she and Cahir lived. She dug her key out of her pocket and unlocked the door. The soft, citrus scent surrounded her, the familiar smell of safety. She turned around and made sure to lock the door behind her.

Seda paused at the portrait of Lord Mordred in the entryway and pressed her palms together. "Thank you for your protection," she said as she bowed at the waist.

It was customary to offer a prayer. All citizens kept a portrait of the lord within their homes and paid tribute when they left or returned.

The memory of his searing eyes watching her made the hair on her neck stand, and she shivered. She tried to recall if he might have been looking at her or someone nearby, but even Cahir admitted it seemed likely.

She walked through their tiny apartment into the bathroom and turned on the shower, watching the cool water sputter and trickle out.

Looks like a cold shower today, she groaned to herself.

She undressed, grabbed the slim bar of soap, and stepped into the chilled trickle.

Her shoulder flared in pain as she lathered up the soap and rubbed it into her scratches. The slow flow of water was a challenge, but she managed to lather enough shampoo into her hair and wash all the dust from her body.

She felt dirty and disgusting, thinking that perhaps if she cleaned herself more, she would finally feel truly clean.

She scrubbed herself until her skin turned red.

A loud noise from outside the bathroom caused Seda to jump and nearly slip in the soapy water.

"C-Cahir, is that you?" she hesitantly called out, a knot twisting in her stomach. She did lock the door. What if someone broke it down? *What if it was that Rozzer?*

She felt her heartbeat thunder in her throat, but all she could hear was the gentle drip of water.

She tried again, "Cahir?"

For the second time since arriving home, her neck hairs prickled. She took a deep breath and summoned the courage to turn the knob, her hand trembling as she did. With heightened senses, she heard the water dripping, the shower curtain rustling as she stepped out slowly, and the sound of her uneven, shaky breathing.

She forced herself to breathe steadily and carefully grabbed a worn towel, slowly wrapping it around her body.

She cracked open the bathroom door and peeked out.

There was no sound or movement in the main room.

She gently pushed the door open, wincing as the hinges squeaked, and took a cautious look into the small living room.

"Cahir?" she asked once more as she stepped further out of the doorway.

The sound of shattering glass made Seda jump against the wall behind her. A wave of panic surged, hitting her chest and freezing her limbs.

CAW! CAW!

Seda didn't think to protect herself as a bird flew in through a broken window and over her, barely missing her head. It effortlessly swooped around the room and perched atop a cabinet, staring down at her with seeing eyes.

These damn birds! Why are they after me today?

"Get out!" she yelled, her anger flaring, causing the slightest bit of vibration to echo in her chest. She grabbed a pillow off the couch and threw it at the bird in the kitchen. Its azure-tipped beak let out another caw as it averted her pillow.

The bird danced around her attacks as she tried to direct it back out of the window. With some yelling, lots of pillow-throwing, and a lost towel, she managed to get the nuisance out of the apartment.

She grabbed her towel and wrapped it around her again, eyeing the broken window in its fullness for the first time.

That was going to cost a lot to fix.

"What the hell's wrong with these damn birds?!" She now had a mess to clean and a broken window to repair.

The door lock clicked, and Cahir stepped inside, carrying a paper bag of food, his body freezing when he saw the chaos in the room.

"What happened? Are you okay?" He looked around at the pillows scattered across the apartment, the cabinet doors left open, and the broken window. He quickly set the bag down and rushed to her, looking over her body for injuries.

"A bird broke the window and came in! Why do they follow me around?"

He looked down at her towel, as if only now realizing she was wearing it, and his cheeks flushed with warmth.

He cleared his throat and turned away from her. "I'm glad you're okay. We'll get this fixed and cleaned, don't worry." His voice was soft as he spoke. When he looked back at her, his eyes fixed on hers. "Something happened when I was grabbing the food."

He gently released her and went back to the portrait to pay his respects.

She waited for him to finish his prayer before she asked, "What?"

He sighed and ran his hands over his face before answering, "They were starting to run low as I got our food, and the line had backed up pretty long behind me. A fight broke out, and they arrested roughly thirty people, including children."

Seda's jaw dropped. Thirty? Children, too? When had the Rozzers started taking children? All the punishments she had seen and been part of for kids involved public displays, with the kids always returning to their parents afterward. Only after a child finished primary school at age fifteen were they considered adults and sent to the Camp if they misbehaved

She winced as she thought about children being taken away. There was simply no way they were actually collecting them. Her nerves twisted into a tight knot. There had to be a reason.

"I don't know, Sed. I know I've said this before, but we should leave this place." He walked over to the broken window and gazed out.

Cahir always talked about leaving, like there was some safe haven waiting outside the dome, and the suggestion made her frustrated every time.

"And go where?" she huffed, throwing her hands in the air. Her towel almost slipped, and she grabbed onto it quickly. "I'm sure it's a misunderstanding. Maybe they just removed the kids from the scene and are finding their homes now."

"Yeah, maybe." He glanced at where she held the towel before quickly looking away. "We could go anywhere. There's a whole world out there." He extended his arm toward the window.

"A world full of nothing but monsters, remember?" she sighed. "We've talked about this."

He didn't reply.

"Did something else happen?" she asked as she approached him, taking a deep breath to calm her agitation, and gently placing her hand on his shoulder.

"No." He turned back to her. "I managed to get bananas, oatmeal, and some milk as well. We only have two food tokens left."

"Thank you for going. I'll clean this mess." She started picking up the items she had thrown around the room, having to hold the towel tightly so it wouldn't slip free.

"You should probably get dressed. Why don't you let me clean this time?"

She glanced at him, smirking. "Fine." She shook her head and headed to the bedroom. Cahir always left a mess, but she could clean up behind him later.

After making sure the bedroom door was completely closed, she took off her towel and hung it to dry. She paused at her dresser and looked at her reflection, gazing at the moon-shaped stone that hung from a long chain around her neck. It cast a shimmering light around her.

There's no way they collected children, she told herself.

She put on comfortable pajamas, a bit worn but still usable, and then brushed out her long, white hair, braiding it back as her mom had taught her. When she finished, she walked back out into the living room.

Cahir sat in the chair, facing away from her, staring sorrowfully at a crumpled piece of paper. He heard the floor creak and quickly tucked the paper into his shirt pocket, then looked up to Seda with a quick smile.

"What was that?" she asked.

"Oh, just something for the work I need to finish." He dismissed it and glanced at her shoulder. "Your injury's already looking a bit better." He stood from the chair. "I'm going to take a shower, too."

Cahir often had small papers, which Seda was told were

about work. He never told her what they were for, though. They both worked at Gardvord, in the plant science division. Although they worked in the same department, Cahir's role was slightly different from hers, requiring him to attend meetings quite often.

She and Cahir met there a few years ago and quickly became friends. At the time, both were single and approaching twenty-five, with no plans to have children, so they chose to enter into a mutual friendship to conceive, which was common in Joro.

"The water's cold and slow today," she mumbled, lightly touching her shoulder and feeling the lingering pain.

"Perfect. It was hot out there anyway," Cahir replied, and slipped into the bathroom, softly closing the door behind him.

CHAPTER 3

<u>Seda</u>
(26 years prior)

"I finally found you," whispered a voice.

The little girl opened her sensitive eyes to the glaring sun and watched a cerulean butterfly flutter across the dusty road. She followed it and bent down when she noticed a twinkle, picking up a white gemstone and examining it as if for the first time.

What a pretty rock, she thought.

She cradled the rock in her hand, loving how it sparkled in the sunlight and reflected the light onto her and the surrounding ground. She slowly raised her head and looked into the distance, where a massive tower rose toward a radiant glow in the sky. It was so beautiful.

"Hi there, sweetie, are you lost? Where's your family?" a woman asked as she approached the little girl, carrying a baby on her hip and a bag slung over her shoulder.

The girl looked up at the woman. She regarded her brown hair, perfectly braided back, and her kind eyes staring down at her. The baby pulled at his mother's earring, and she softly brushed his hand to the side.

"What's your name?" the woman asked her.

"I don't know," she replied in a weak voice.

The woman reached into her bag and held out a piece of bread for the girl. "Are you hungry?"

The little girl took the bread and munched on it. The soft fluffiness and taste of flour and yeast were heaven on her tongue. She smacked her rosy lips in delight.

"Yummy!" She held out her hand and asked for another.

The woman tittered. "I'll have more for you back at the Gardvord. Will you come with me so we can try to find your family?"

The girl nodded and placed the pretty, shiny rock into her dress pocket. She accepted the woman's offered hand, and they walked up the long road, opposite the tall tower, toward a cluster of buildings and distant farmlands.

She heard the cawing of black birds in the sky and gazed up to count them. Three birds flew high above, weaving in and out of the shimmering dome overhead.

They reached a tall brick building and stopped at a glass doorway. The woman dug into her pocket, pulled out a card, and pressed it against a small gray box beside the door. It clicked, and the glass doors opened. She followed the woman inside, wondering when she'd get another slice of soft bread.

They walked down a long hallway and entered another doorway, where the woman scanned her card again. The door opened into a large greenhouse filled with trees, and the fresh scent hit the girl in the nose.

"This smells like home," the girl said. She noted the sunlight filtering through the branches and the earthy smell of dirt.

"Oh, that's good to hear. Your family must be close then. Why don't you wait here with Benny for a moment while I go to call my husband?" The woman pointed to a large cushion placed on the ground.

The little girl sat down on the cushion, and the woman positioned the baby beside her. She walked over to a nearby wall, picked up a phone, and looked back at the girl with a gentle smile.

Benny giggled and reached for the girl's dress, trying to put the ends of it in his mouth. She looked around, noticing the trees were unlike the ones she was used to.

What did they look like before? She couldn't remember.

"Hi sweetie, my husband should be here soon, and we'll try to find your family, okay?" The woman sat next to the girl and Benny on the cushion. She opened her bag again, this time pulling out a banana. She offered it to the girl, who accepted, then broke off a small piece for Benny.

The banana was soft and sweet, helping to fill her hungry belly. When she finished, she asked for another piece of bread, and the woman tore off a chunk and handed it to her. She chewed happily as she stared at the pretty trees.

"Will you help me water while we wait?" asked the woman.

"Oh yes, miss! I'd love to." The girl's voice was muffled, stuffed full.

Watering the plants excited the little girl.

"Please, call me Sara." Sara looked at the girl, taking in her fair, shimmering hair, amethyst eyes, the oversized dress, and the eager anticipation on her face as she waited to water the plants. She had never seen anyone with her complexion before. "Follow me, sweetie. The hose is this way."

Sara picked up Benny and then led the girl to the garden hose, where she turned on the faucet. A stream of cool water flowed out, and she handed it to the girl, who accepted it with a bright smile.

"While we wait, do you remember anything about where

your family might be? What color is your apartment?" Sara asked while showing her where to point the hose.

"Hmmm... no." The girl furrowed her brow and tried hard to think back to what happened before the dusty road. "I can't remember, but I did find this pretty rock."

She handed the sparkling rock to Sara, who held it up to her face to get a closer look.

Sara squinted, observing the shape and the brilliant sparkle surrounding it.

"This rock reminds me of a story my mom used to tell me when I was little. Would you like to hear it?" She flipped the rock over in her palm to see the other side.

The little girl looked up at her and nodded. She hadn't heard a story before; this was exciting!

Sara took a deep breath and began, "Once upon a time, there was a magical Fae who wished to be more. He made a deal with a beast, and his life was no more."

"What's a Fae?" the girl interrupted, watching the woman with rapt attention and quickly forgetting she was holding the hose.

The woman smiled warmly. "They're mythical beings, believed to be filled with *magic*." She raised her brows and twirled her fingers in the air as she held the rock with her thumb pressed into her palm.

The girl giggled and cheerfully jumped up and down, splashing water all around with the hose. She had never heard of magic before, and Sara was funny!

Sara laughed as the water splashed on her and Benny, then continued her story, "The beast tore through the lands and ensnared all the men. When the Fae tried to fight back, his magic was stolen then. Four crystals had the power to shield the beast from his plunder. But the crystals went missing, hidden hither and yonder."

"Like my rock?" the little girl asked with excitement.

Sara nodded. "It does look quite magical." She took a breath before continuing, "Only a key placed perfectly into the lock could stop the beast's torment and his murderous aftershock. The Fae's never-ending love for mankind allowed him to create one final act of love for the four of a kind. Only with friendship could the key succeed, and the beast was forced to secede. But now that the beast's plunder was no more, the Fae went back to wishing for more."

Sara looked down at the girl and noted her furrowed brow.

"That sounds so sad." Her lips pursed into a pout. "Why would he still wish for more after that?"

Sara laughed again. "That's a good catch. That's the moral of the story, though. Greed brings ruin, and the Fae didn't learn from his mistakes. It's a good lesson, though." Sara sighed. "We must learn to be content and find happiness in the things that we are given and appreciate the things that we have."

The little girl responded with a bright smile, saying, "I like the things I have. I like my rock!"

Sara handed the sparkling rock back to the girl. "That's the spirit, sweetie. You should hold on to that tightly. Don't let it go. It looks very special."

The girl put the rock back into her pocket and smiled up at the woman, eager to tend to the trees and continue playing with the cool water.

As she watered the plants and waited for Sara's husband to arrive, the little girl's thoughts drifted back to the voice that had woken her up.

Who was that?

CHAPTER 4

<u>Seda</u>

"Wake up, sleepyheads!" Benny burst through the bedroom door and jumped onto Seda's bed, knocking the air out of her. He ruffled her hair, which had come undone from the braid overnight while she slept. Seda roughly pushed him off the bed and threw the blankets over her face with a loud groan. Even though they were both adults, Benny was still a few years younger than Seda and just as annoying as when they were kids.

"Why did you give him a key again?" complained Cahir from his side of the room. He slowly rolled over and rubbed his eyes. "The guy has no sense of time. Why are you here so damn early?"

"Oh, you know, a little of this, a little of that, but mostly I was awake and wanted to show you guys this." Benny held a newspaper. "It's actually a little concerning."

As the haunting prayer resonated through the apartment walls, they waited in silence for the song to end.

"Welp, it's six AM," Benny said when it finally finished. "I almost got this to you before the morning call."

"Let me see." Cahir reached out to take the paper from Benny, his hair a messy tangle on top of his head. He shifted on the bed and looked at the paper, his brows furrowing.

"This isn't what I saw yesterday," he said as he bit his lower lip.

"What does it say?" Seda asked, sitting up with her interest now piqued. She stretched her arms over her head and yawned.

Cahir remained quiet as he reread the paper before finally sighing and saying, "It says that because of recent Jotnar attacks, our food supply is now limited. Which roughly matches what I saw yesterday. But—"

"Why would Jotnar attacks affect our food supply?" Seda interrupted. "They're outside the dome."

"It doesn't, and it also doesn't say. But it does say that a couple of people were taken to the Camp for misbehavior in the food lines. They're encouraging everyone to stay calm and follow the rules, especially the curfew. It mentions they collected a few people, but I clearly saw thirty people loaded into cells. Even the kids. The paper doesn't mention anything about them." Cahir bit his lip again, and Seda noticed how his hand reached over his shirt pocket, possibly fiddling with the piece of paper beneath it that he had brushed off from the night before.

"You saw kids taken, Cahir?" Benny asked as his leg began to jump up and down, a nervous tic he had since childhood, his Gardvord uniform pants rustling with the movement. "I came here wanting to tell you about the food. I had no idea you were there yesterday, and I'm glad you're okay. Seda, were you there too?"

She shook her head. "I came home right after the Wyrd. Cahir went to grab the food with the tokens before too many others arrived. Seems everyone had the same idea." She rubbed her shoulder, expecting there to be pain. When she looked down, the scratches were gone; no pain, no sign that the bird had scratched her yesterday at all.

"I want to understand why the Jotnar attacks are impacting our food supply. We've been making significant progress lately in the Gardvord. I knew we had limits on how much we could distribute, but I didn't realize that the Jotnar attacks were related to it," said Benny.

Both Cahir and Seda nodded in response. There was no logical explanation for why the Jotnar's attack on the dome had any impact on the food.

"Do you think Dad might know more?" Seda asked Benny. "Has he said anything to you recently?"

Jason was the top scientist at Gardvord. He worked his way up from the Barrio as a child who had scored well and then moved to Orience, where he met Sara. They started a family, and Jason chose to stay in Orience, despite his career taking off, so he could be close to the office. He was the reason Seda always worked hard in her studies her entire life.

Benny shook his head. "No, and he isn't in Orience for the next few days either. He has meetings in Cascade. Maybe they're meeting about this? We can ask Mom if we see her today."

Sara worked in the Gardvord as an orchardist, one of the lower levels within Orience. She found solace in getting her hands dirty and watching the trees grow, even though her test scores suggested she was more suited for a higher-paying career.

"You two, get ready so we can walk over together," Benny said. "I'll be waiting outside."

As Benny left the room, Cahir got out of bed and looked over at Seda. "I'm concerned, Sed. What I saw last night isn't what they said in the paper. I fear things are changing." He ran his hand over his neck, then continued, "We can find a new life together outside of the dome. Just consider it for me, please?"

This was the second time Cahir had mentioned leaving Joro

in the past few hours. Where would they go? Outside the city, dangers and miles of emptiness awaited.

Seda was at a loss for words as she gazed at Cahir, her mind spinning.

Cahir grabbed some clothes and headed to the bathroom to get dressed.

"Hey, Cahir?" she asked as he was passing the doorway. He paused with his back to her. "The Wyrd was a close call with us potentially being selected. If I can get pregnant, then we wouldn't have to talk or think about leaving. I want to go twice a week now for insemination, if that's okay with you?"

He didn't turn back to look at her and said softly, "Yes, we can go again tomorrow." He stepped out of the room, the door closing gently behind him.

After they dressed and said their prayers, they met Benny downstairs and began their walk to the Gardvord. They passed multiple apartment buildings on the way out, alongside others also heading to work. They walked past a couple of people with confused looks, quietly arguing over the morning's paper. Cahir watched them as they walked by, but Seda looked away.

They made their way up the long gravel path to the entrance of the Gardvord, where each of them pulled out their ID cards. Benny scanned his and walked through the open door while Cahir and Seda waited for their turn. A new protocol was recently implemented, permitting only one person to enter at a time due to security concerns.

Cahir extended his hand, letting Seda go in first. Seda scanned her card and walked through the door, the smell of soil and chemicals hitting her nose. She slid her card back into her blue uniform pocket and stepped aside so Cahir could enter.

"Let me know if you catch Mom today. Will ya, Seda?" Benny asked over his shoulder as he walked toward his department.

"Sure thing," she responded.

He gave her a mock salute, mimicking the Rozzers, and left them as he walked down the hall.

As they made their way toward their office, Cahir slipped his arm around Seda's shoulder, and the frayed opening on her uniform from the bird scratch made her skin rub against his. They passed a few other workers wearing the same blue uniform along the way. No one said anything to them as they passed, too absorbed in their work to notice.

They approached their office and entered once more. As Seda stepped into the room, she took in the scent of paper and ink, and a sense of comfort enveloped her. Her work was her refuge, a haven of normalcy and quiet ease, a steady rhythm from the chaos outside the walls.

She and Cahir were the only workers left in this department. Their former coworker, Esper, was taken to the Camp six months ago. Like them, Esper and her partner, Diantha, had been trying to get pregnant through artificial insemination for years with no luck.

Seda sat down at her desk and turned on the computer, keying in her passcode. Cahir sat across from her, watching her intently. "Seda, there's something..." he paused as if he didn't know how to say the right words.

"What is it?" she asked as she waited for the computer to boot up.

"Well..." He moved his lips, but nothing came out. He cleared his throat. "I mean, there are things I want to tell you. Can we walk home alone tonight, and I can try?"

"Why—" Seda began.

"It's just... *something*," he interrupted her, before pausing. "Better said in privacy. I love you, Sed."

She glanced up from her computer at him, her gaze locking onto Cahir's smile once more—the same smile that had left many girls blushing. His emerald eyes seemed to plead with her to say yes.

"Of course, Cahir. I love you, too." His request didn't make sense. They usually walked home alone together.

The day mostly passed in silence as they worked, quietly entering harvest data. At lunchtime, Cahir pulled out a couple of bananas and some chips for them to share.

Around three in the afternoon, Seda stood up, stretched her legs, and looked over their workstation at Cahir.

He was asleep... again.

She threw an eraser from her desk at his head, but Cahir's hand shot up and caught it before it smacked him in the face.

Dammit! Almost had him.

He lifted his groggy face, and Seda saw the peel from the banana he had eaten earlier stuck to his cheek.

"What did I miss?" he asked, the banana peel moving as he spoke.

She fought back a smile. "Wanna go for a walk? I'd like to see if I can find my Mom. She likes going for walks around this time."

"I don't know, Sed. I'm kinda busy here with work." Cahir grinned mischievously as he got up from his chair, removed the banana peel from his face, and held out his arm for her to take.

"You really need to stop sleeping at work," she scolded.

"I was inputting calculations in my brain," he joked. "It's called discrete mathematics for a reason."

Seda rolled her eyes and accepted his outstretched arm. They left their office, walked down the long hall to the entryway, and stepped outside. They wandered around, watching the bees dance around the gardens, then headed toward the orchard's side entrance. Both Seda and Cahir scanned their cards and went inside. Sara sat on a bench near the trees, crying as she clutched a piece of paper in her hand.

"Mom! What happened?" Seda asked as she ran up to her.

"Oh, hi sweetie." Sara wiped her brown eyes with her uniform sleeve. Her hair was a bit messy, with half of it coming out of her braid. "I just got..." Sara paused, holding out the letter for Seda to take. "I just got this letter from the Palatium. It seems your father was taken to the Camp for misbehavior."

"MISBEHAVIOR?" Benny paced back and forth in the orchard between two trees, biting his nails. "Dad exemplifies the best qualities of society!"

Jason always followed the rules and encouraged his children to do the same, setting an example for them. The letter, unfortunately, said little. It was addressed to Sara and family, indicating that last night, around six in the evening, Jason Arbor had been taken into custody for misbehavior and was being transported to the Camp as soon as possible, and that they wished for a quick rehabilitation, given his status.

Seda sat on the bench next to Sara, her worry over her father growing heavier with each passing thought. Was he okay? Did they hurt him like they hurt that man at the Wyrd?

The news felt so overwhelming that the cool concrete bench was the only thing holding her steady, stopping her body from collapsing to the ground. Would this mean she would never see him again?

"What could Dad even have done? Mom, do you know why he was in Cascade?" Benny asked.

Sara shook her head as she nervously twiddled with the hem of her dress. "No, darling, he didn't tell me why he went there. Just that he had meetings with some officials and would be back in a couple of days."

Cahir was standing behind Seda, and she numbly felt him touch her shoulders, doing what little he could to offer her comfort.

"What if I go to Cascade and try to talk to someone on that side of the Palatium?" Benny suggested.

"Please, no," Sara said. "I cannot have something happen along the way, and you possibly being taken as well. I couldn't handle it. All we can do is pray to Lord Mordred for your father's rehabilitation."

Seda agreed. There really was no way to reach Cascade in time, especially with curfew approaching. Benny would definitely get caught being out after hours. He wasn't the best at being sneaky and often got into trouble as a child.

But they had to find *some* answers. The letter didn't give them any valuable information to move forward.

"What if I go?" Cahir suggested.

Seda looked up at him sharply and exclaimed, "No!"

Cahir and Seda rarely left each other's sides. The only times he wasn't near her were when he had to attend work events. She couldn't bear the thought of her best friend going to the Camp if he got caught out after curfew.

"Seda, I can help with this. Let me see if I can find some answers." Cahir's gentle eyes met hers.

"Seda's right. You shouldn't go, Cahir. You two are trying to start a family. I can make some calls and see if I can find answers," Sara suggested as she lightly patted her swollen eyes.

"I love Jason, too. He's as much my family as you are, Seda." He looked back down at her.

Seda vehemently shook her head again.

"Seda, he wants to help. Maybe he can find some answers for us," Benny pleaded as he sat beside her, nervously shaking his leg. "Please? I'm really worried about Dad. It has to be a misunderstanding. We both know they won't answer when Mom calls."

"But what about *curfew*?" she asked, her voice cracking on the last word.

"I'll arrive before curfew and find a safe place to stay overnight. Then, first thing in the morning, I'll look for answers. I'll try to meet you here tomorrow afternoon with an update.

Maybe I can arrive before he gets transferred to the Camp and see if we can work something out," Cahir offered.

Seda did *not* like the idea. She couldn't recall a time when anyone could interrupt a collection, but her father was probably scared and alone, and he was a member of high society.

Maybe rules could bend sometimes?

She stood up, spun around, and wrapped her arms tightly around him, breathing in his cedar scent. She whispered into his shoulder, "Thank you, Cahir. Please be safe, I can't do any of this without you."

He leaned in, gently kissed her forehead, and softly brushed a tear from her cheek with his thumb. "Would you mind staying with your family tonight while I'm away? What if another bird breaks through a window?"

She let out a strained laugh and nodded as she watched Cahir walk out the door, leaving her truly alone without him for the first time in five years.

"Bird?" Benny asked.

CHAPTER 5

<u>Cahir</u>

The sun was low in the shimmering sky, and the air was gradually starting to cool as Cahir sprinted off the Gardvord grounds, intent on reaching Cascade before the city's curfew alarm went off.

He wasn't sure where to find Jason, but he figured he could start at Joro Hall, where most society gatherings took place. It was a two-hour walk from the Gardvord, and he had only an hour to get there.

He had just enough time to reach the hall and find a place to hide for the night if he jogged the distance. He cut through apartment complex courtyards and leaped over fences lining the fields.

The roads in Orience twisted among themselves as buildings and farmlands were gradually constructed over the centuries, necessitating expansion to support the growing population. It ended up creating a maze of roads that made travel slower than just cutting straight through when possible.

A bird swooped down from a tree and flew alongside Cahir.

"Why did you scratch her yesterday, Roya?" Cahir huffed as he tried to quicken his pace through an alley of buildings.

As the bird soared, its dark eyes gazed back at him, mirroring his own reflection.

"I was trying to protect her and accidentally scratched her," her melodious voice replied.

"She thought you were attacking her. You can't just grab someone like that. And was that you in the apartment?"

Roya flew ahead to a tree, perched on a low-hanging branch, and let out a loud caw. Cahir ran up to the tree and stopped, catching his breath, with his arm against the stump for support.

"It's in my nature to protect. I want an easy way in." Roya ruffled her black feathers as the fading sunlight caught them, reflecting their azure hue.

"I could have just opened a window for you."

"You and I both know she wouldn't leave it open," Roya huffed.

"My time's almost up, and I haven't found it yet." He pulled the piece of paper from his shirt pocket that Roya had given him the day before and unfolded it to reveal its contents.

Twenty-five days remain...

"They've been watching," Roya warned. "You need to find a way to tell her before your time runs out."

"You know I can't. The Wisps' magic binds me, remember?" Cahir looked down at the paper and crumpled it tightly into a small ball.

The fucking Wisps.

He should have just set out to find Seda alone without their magic to help him. He hurled the crumpled paper past the tree into the tall, dry weeds and glared at Roya.

"What are you running to?" Roya changed the subject as she hopped to another branch, trying to avoid his glare, with the tree rustling from the movement.

"Her father was collected for the Camp. I want to find him and get him out before he's transported. Things are changing quickly here, Roya. The Jotnar attacks are also more frequent. I fear I won't have enough time to help with this. I need to get her out of here."

Roya tilted her head and gazed up at the sky. "The dome will crumble soon," she warned. "We've heard the conversations."

He felt a coil of dread wrap around his throat, squeezing tight like a snake around its prey. He stepped away from the tree and resumed his jog toward Cascade. Roya leaped from the branch, following him above as the setting crimson sky darkened in the distance. He ran until the gates of Cascade appeared before him, and the road changed from the crunching of pebbles to smooth, basketweave brick.

Boutiques had closed their shops for the night, their window displays showcasing their wealth, so vastly different from the other two sections of Joro. Streetlights flickered on, casting an orange glow over the street. No one was in sight except for a group of Rozzers standing in the distance.

As Cahir rounded the corner of a street, he spotted Joro Hall in the distance. The building's brick exterior and stained glass windows towered over the end of the long road.

From the sound of flapping wings above and the slight breeze in the air, Cahir knew that Roya was still with him.

The curfew siren blared throughout the city, and his chest constricted. He didn't find a safe location in time.

"Hey there!" a Rozzer called from behind. He didn't hesitate and took off running, knowing that getting caught meant being taken to the Camp. He turned the corner of a shop and searched for a place to conceal himself as the sound of boots closing in on him grew louder.

"Over here," Roya called from behind a large bush. Cahir ran to the prickly, flowering bush and ducked down. She landed on his shoulder and spread a wing over him, her magic making them both disappear from sight.

With his breath held tightly in his lungs, Cahir remained still as the sound of the Rozzers encroaching grew louder.

Two Rozzers neared the bush and stopped a few feet away, both holding their guns. A tall Rozzer with greasy, dark hair and a scarred face said, "I saw him go there. Where'd he go?"

Next to him, the Rozzer with red hair nodded toward a building, which had a narrow path running between two other buildings. "These fucking assholes. Maybe he ran that way. The Captain said we need to catch all of them. If we ever want to move up, Michael, we can't keep failing. Let's go." They both hurried away, their figures disappearing down the path.

With a sigh, Cahir finally stood, his body reemerging as Roya pulled back her wing and landed next to him on the ground.

"Thank you," he said to her.

She hopped over to the nearby green grass, dug her pointed toes into the damp earth, and looked for a bug to catch. "It's in my nature to help you, as you protect her," she replied.

Something about the two Rozzers seemed oddly familiar to Cahir.

It couldn't be them. Could it?

He shook his head, refocusing on what he needed to do. He moved stealthily around the bush and up the street, keeping an eye out for any nearby activity. Roya ascended into the air again, scanning the area. He heard a man's distant cry and the Rozzers' shouts, signaling they had found another person.

He continued sneaking up the road toward the hall when Roya flew back down and lightly advised, "Go three blocks to the west." She lifted into the air once more and flew in the direction she wanted him to go.

He turned left and crept along the building walls, down dark alleyways, making sure to keep his steps light and his body hidden as much as possible.

He navigated through the third block and spotted the stone perimeter wall surrounding the dome's base coming into view. He could hear the clanking of metal as he got closer. He stopped when he reached a large crack in the wall, hidden behind foliage, with light streaming through the vines.

He carefully peeled apart the hanging plant and peered through the crack to the other side of the wall.

Outside the city's protective wall, Cahir saw a group of Rozzers and a cell packed with people, their cries reverberating through the crack. The Rozzers were shoving three more men into the cell, their hands chained in front of them.

With cautious steps, Cahir carefully made his way through the narrow crack, the magic of the dome prickling against his skin. On the other side, he ducked behind a pile of wooden boxes haphazardly placed, staying crouched and out of sight.

"All of you have been labeled with misbehavior and will need to redeem yourselves in the Camp!" a large Rozzer with dark hair and a piercing gaze said with a serpent-like tone. He banged his baton against the cell bars, hitting someone's fingers. A wail of pain escaped from the injured person, and the Rozzer snarled at him like an animal. The remaining people inside the cell quickly shuffled away from the front bars.

"I've done nothing wrong," a brave woman begged through harsh cries. "This is a mistake. I was heading home to the Barrio after my shift in the Palatium. It was before the curfew!"

"Silence, all of you!" the Rozzer barked, striking the bars again with a loud clang that echoed through the area and bounced off the perimeter wall.

A man inside the cell caught Cahir's eye with his graying hair and long beard.

It was Jason.

Roya flew down and whispered, "You know what we need to do."

"I'll try. What's our backup plan if it doesn't work?" Cahir asked her.

"We run."

He took a deep breath before stepping out into the alleyway, fully showcasing himself to everyone at the end. A young Rozzer looked over and said, "Captain. Look!" He pointed at Cahir.

The Rozzer, who had banged on the bars, looked over his shoulder. He looked at Cahir with surprised disgust and lightly stuck out his tongue, as if to smell him like a serpent.

"Gentlemen..." Cahir said with mock confidence as the Rozzers slowly drew their guns and moved toward him. "I believe you have someone I want in your possession."

He took a step forward, and a vibrant green mist wrapped around him, turning his six-foot frame into one that was a foot taller. His canines elongated into sharpened daggers, and the tips of his ears grew pointed. As his skin began to glow with a jade glimmer, his muscles swelled, and his clothes tore during the transformation.

Everyone at the end of the alleyway gasped, and a woman in the cell screamed, "Jotnar!" Frantic chaos erupted. Those in the cell rattled the bars and screamed, desperate to break free. The Rozzers all stepped back in fear.

Cahir couldn't help but smile at the chaos and the fact that his transformation actually worked.

"What the fuck *is* that?" a Rozzer asked, warily watching Cahir approach.

"That isn't a Jotnar, you idiots!" the Captain shouted. "Get him!"

Born from cunning moonlit shadows, Roya shifted from her

Corvid form behind the wooden boxes into the graceful figure of a woman with sleek, azure-blue hair flowing down her back, slanted eyes like a feline's, sharp eyebrows, and pale skin.

She stepped beside Cahir and casually picked at her elongated, sharpened nails, poised to cut down anyone who approached.

The Rozzers surged ahead and opened fire on them. Roya dodged the bullets, bouncing out of the way with ease, and danced her way toward the cell. The bullets struck Cahir and ricocheted off his skin, clinking onto the ground in misshapen forms.

"What the fuck," a Rozzer said as he reloaded his gun.

Cahir confidently stepped forward, unfazed by the bullets raining down. A young Rozzer approached with his steel sword drawn and sliced it through the air. Cahir held out his hand, and a burst of dark green magic shot out from his palm, violently throwing the young man toward the wall.

The Rozzer collapsed to the ground, his body unmoving.

More Rozzers closed in, their swords drawn. Since guns were ineffective in this fight, they formed a circle around Cahir. He spun and used the magic from his palms to push everyone back as they closed in.

The Captain dodged Cahir's magic and charged forward, slicing his arm with a ruby-colored sword. Cahir's emerald-colored blood stained the Captain's weapon and splattered on the ground.

Hissing in pain and shock that someone had managed to hurt him, Cahir punched the man in the chest, sending him flying backward and crashing onto his side. Cahir's injured skin dulled in jade color, returning to his human shade. The Captain jumped up swiftly, and his dark brown eyes flashed crimson before shifting back.

What the fuck?

Roya approached the cell and shook the door, trying to open

it without the key. The people inside screamed as she approached and backed away, squishing themselves against the opposite side. Roya looked around for a way to bust the door open, seeing nothing.

With a swift move, Cahir cast his magic at the Captain's throat, trying to close in tightly, but the man dodged quickly, sliding his sword across his thigh. He snarled in pain and threw out another blast of magic, but the tendrils of his power started to weaken with each use.

Roya looked around the area for any sign of the keys to open the cell. A Rozzer was lying on the ground about twenty paces away, a silver set of keys strapped to his pants. She pushed away from the cell doors and ran to him, averting the bursts of green magic that were blowing past her, and slid down to snag them. She grasped the metal chain with her fingers, and the Rozzer's gray eyes flashed wide open. His hand closed around her wrist, and he quickly pressed a knife to her throat.

The Captain charged at Cahir again, and Cahir kicked him with his uninjured leg. The Captain fell with a grunt, but not before slicing another gash in his opposite leg.

He was losing his magic faster than expected due to the sword's injuries.

"Don't make another move!" someone yelled from the distance between Cahir and the cell. He turned and saw a Rozzer holding Roya in a chokehold, a knife pressed to her throat. "If you do, she's dead."

Roya had been his partner for a long time, watching over Seda when he wasn't there. She couldn't get hurt in this fight. Cahir quickly raised his hands in the air in defeat.

"I want you to back the fuck up and keep those hands in the air," the Rozzer said as he pressed the knife into Roya's throat, a trickle of scarlet blood beading around the blade.

"I'll be fine, Cahir," Roya said confidently, her eyes darting toward the dark distance behind him.

Cahir hesitated before spinning around and sprinting into the darkness. As he ran, the damp, thin air and the smell of moss and trees closed in around him.

He didn't change back to his human form until he was far enough away, allowing his ears and teeth to soften and his size to shrink back to normal.

It was going to be tough to find a way back to Seda now that he was outside the city walls.

CHAPTER 6

<u>Roya</u>

It was a cold, moonlit night when Roya awoke from the head injury she had suffered while being locked up with the others. As the horses hauling the cell lumbered down a dark trail, the wheels squeaked intermittently. She glanced down at her wrists, seeing that the Rozzers had bound them with bloodstone cuffs, an attempt to suppress her magic.

Pathetic weaklings.

She waited until the people around her quieted down and then crawled over to Jason, accidentally nudging his side a little too roughly. She needed to send a message, as best as she could, before she transformed and left this stupid cell. He lifted his head and looked at her, his beard crusted with blood from a previous bloody nose, with no sign of fear in his eyes.

Interesting, she noted.

"The world isn't as it seems," she began, "We came here to rescue you, Jason."

"I'm aware the world isn't as it seems, Corvid," he replied, looking at her knowingly. "I'm going where I need to go." He leaned his head against the bars and stared off into the distance, a mask of neutrality on his face.

The cell hit a bump in the road, and the people inside stirred. Jason shifted, adjusting his legs and clasping his hands on his knees, his fists clenched tight.

Roya sat in silence, her gaze fixed on him for a long moment.

A cricket bounced to the side, and her focus quickly fixed on it. She transformed into a Corvid; the bloodstone having no effect on her, and she broke free from the chains. She grabbed the cricket on her way out and flew between the bars into the crisp night air, causing Jason's beard to sway from the wind.

She soared high into the night sky, twirling among the glittering stars and looking down at the horses moving south toward the Camp. The dome was no longer visible on the horizon from their position. Roya could see the heavily guarded Camp, just about five miles away.

To the west, she saw endless willow trees, their long branches swaying in the cool, dry breeze. Large rock formations with caves clustered between them, and several camps had Jotnars sitting around a fire, roasting their meals over the flames.

Roya turned around and flew north. It took her hours, but she passed the dome and entered a landscape where towering trees reached for the sky. The stars above were crystal clear, casting a glow over the pink and blue hues of the rising sun.

She flew until she found a small cave hidden in the mountains, surrounded by a thick, luminous fog that clung to the branches of the trees it touched.

"Where have you been, sister?" Ferona sat in a plush, baby blue chair, reading a book. She snapped it shut and looked up at Roya. The cave was circular and warm, with a small fire at its center, illuminating the walls. The stalactites slowly dripped onto the flames, creating small mists of steam.

Roya shifted into her human form and stared at her sister. "I was out, trying to help. Seda's father was taken."

"Her father?" Ferona asked.

"Jason was taken to the Camp. We attempted to intervene."

"I see..." Ferona stood from her chair and walked to the stove, grabbing a match to light the coals from below. "I'm going to make a cup of tea, would you like some?"

Roya nodded and sat down in her chair, which matched her azure accent color. The cushion let out a squeak as it compressed under her weight. She closed her eyes and reflected on the evening's events. Cahir was out there alone. She wasn't overly concerned about his safety; he knew how to handle himself and could find his way back to Seda.

But Jason... Jason was... interesting.

He wasn't afraid to see her or to be near her, and he knew she was a Corvid. He also didn't want to be rescued.

Why does he want to go to the Camp?

"Feich should be back soon. He went out to find breakfast," Ferona said, pulling Roya from her thoughts.

Feich was their brother. They were triplets, nearly identical. Roya was the oldest of the three, so she held the title of warden. Feich was born second, and Ferona last. They had no other close family, except for their Corvid allies. Their family circle was a small murder of Corvids.

"Here, sister." Ferona held out a cup of black tea in a hand-made mug, the steam twirling out of the top like a ballerina's dance. Roya accepted the cup and hummed into it. She slowly sipped the heated liquid.

"They called upon me today," Ferona said as she sat back into her chair, holding her own cup of tea. "They want her to come to them."

"That's not as easy as it sounds. Seda isn't ready," Roya responded sharply, feeling drained from the night, and wanted to take a quick nap before heading back to watch over Seda.

Ferona let out a small sigh in response to her tone. "Give it a little more time."

"We're almost out of time." She placed her cup on a small side table. They both sat back further into their chairs, watching the fire crackle between them. "Cahir's time to help her is almost over, and she still hasn't left the dome. Not once."

Feich flew through the cave entrance with a limp squirrel tucked between his claws. He landed near the stove and shifted. "About time you're home, brother," Ferona said. "I got the coals lit for that. Do you want any help with it?" She looked down at the squirrel and licked her lips.

"We're cooking this one, Ferona." Feich shook his head. "Besides, the boss over there looks like she's already eaten. Let this one have the time to cook."

"It was only a single cricket," Roya chipped back, wanting them to know she was also hungry. Roasted squirrel did sound lovely.

Feich prepared their meal while the sisters relaxed in their chairs. The aroma of roasting meat filled the cave. Roya massaged her forehead, the bruise fading and her headache easing. She winced when she remembered how she had accidentally scratched Seda. That wasn't her intention. For years, her goal had always been to protect Seda.

The distant sound of the dome echoing reverberated into the cave. The murder all stiffened and looked toward the exit at once.

The Jotnar were attacking the dome again.

"Time's running out," the three of them said in unison as the ground trembled slightly beneath their feet.

CHAPTER 7

Seda

Seda sat at her desk, fiddling with the chain around her neck. She kept checking the clock and the door every few minutes, growing more anxious with each passing minute. It was two o'clock, and Cahir still hadn't returned.

Her hair caught on the chain as she twirled it around her fingers, and a few strands snagged. She took off the necklace, setting the white stone down on the desk as she unwound the strands from the chain.

She needed to focus on her work while also handling Cahir's responsibilities today, so no one would notice his absence. There were two piles of papers on her desk that needed to be reanalyzed and entered into the system, but her nerves prevented her from focusing.

She let out a deep sigh, picked up the top paper from the stack, and started reading the report, but the words began to run together halfway through. She set the paper back down and picked up her necklace again, watching the sparkles dance around the tabletop.

She jumped at the sound of a beep as the office door swung open. She spun around with a smile, expecting to see Cahir, but it was Benny standing there with a cup of coffee.

Her smile faded.

"Sheesh, don't look so excited to see me. It's not like you were expecting anyone else?" He laughed lightly, then winced, realizing how insensitive that came out. "Here, I brought you a drink. Not the best coffee… a little burnt. But it was leftover from some execs who came through and brewed a large pot."

She accepted the coffee with a small smile, the aroma filling the air and making her stomach growl. "Thank you."

"He'll be back," Benny offered, his eyes filled with tenderness.

"I hope so," she replied as she took a slow sip of her coffee and winced. "You weren't joking. This is a little gross."

They shared a gentle smile, both making an effort to stay positive despite the circumstances. As Benny took his seat in Cahir's chair across the desk, his leg started to bounce up and down.

She noticed his gaze drift to the mandarin on the floor, the same one she had thrown at Cahir for falling asleep the day of the Wyrd.

She hadn't picked it up yet. Picking it up felt like giving up hope. She knew that didn't make sense, but every time she glanced over at that same mandarin, she saw his dimpled, mischievous grin as he awoke from his nap.

"I'm scared for him and Dad," she admitted as she set the coffee down. "What if something happened to Cahir? There wasn't enough time to make it to Cascade when he left. Where would he even have stayed to be safe for curfew? What if Dad's already at the Camp? This was a bad idea. I can't do this without Cahir, Benny."

"Do you remember that one time when the Jotnar attacked the dome and the crowd went crazy, and a Rozzer tripped while holding his sword? Cahir caught that sword by the blade. It almost stabbed you!"

Seda did remember that. The blade hadn't actually cut Cahir's hand. He claimed it wasn't sharp and handed it back to the Rozzer, who stared at it in confusion.

"He's a lucky guy, Seda. You're also special to him. I can see it in his eyes when he looks at you. He'll be back."

She took another sip of the bitter, lukewarm coffee and nodded. Hope felt better than despair. He was right, Cahir was clever. He would return. She just needed to stay positive.

Benny stood up from the chair. "I'll be back in a bit to check on you. Mom wanted to know if you were going to stay with us tonight again?"

"No, I want to be home. Please tell her I love her when you see her." She wanted to be in her own home, where she felt secure and surrounded by their belongings, and perhaps Cahir would come back, looking for her there.

"I will. Love you," Benny replied.

Benny left the room, and Seda looked down at her desk. The conversation gave her a little confidence. Cahir *would* be back. She picked up the report once more and began reading from the first sentence again.

AT FIVE O'CLOCK, the clock chimed, and Seda put down the last report she was inputting. She had wrapped up both stacks of reports for the day and only got up to use the restroom. She stood from her desk and stretched her cramped back, nervously biting her nail as she stared at the clock.

She watched the second hand slowly move across its face.

Cahir hadn't returned yet.

It occurred to her that maybe, since the work day was almost over, he had gone home instead of coming to the office. She quickly gathered her things, cleaned up her workspace, and left the room.

Walking home felt lonely as she rushed through the streets, occasionally taking shortcuts through apartment courtyards to quickly close the distance.

A cat suddenly darted across the road in front of her. She tried to avoid it but tripped and fell, catching herself with her hands.

She worried she might have hurt the cat and called for it. It peeked its little black and white head out of a bush, gave her a dirty look, then turned away and sauntered off, as if Seda was the one at fault.

She sighed and tried to compose herself as her palms now ached from the fall. As she sat there brushing the gravel from her hands, the color red caught her attention.

Someone had stapled red pieces of paper onto a nearby wooden post. She rose and moved closer to read what they said.

> *Joro citizens,*
>
> *Expect more Jotnar attacks.*
> *We have observed them camping outside*
> *of the barrier in larger numbers.*
> *The dome is weakening, and the food*
> *supply is not running low, contrary to*
> *what is said.*
> *Ration your portions in case they do not*
> *continue to hand them out.*
> *Be prepared.*
> *We await the Darkened.*
> *—The Rising*

At the bottom of the paper was an image of a dragon. All of the pieces of paper conveyed the same message. Seda tore one from the post, shoved it into her pocket, and quickly ran the rest of the way home.

Complete silence enveloped her as she entered the apartment. She hurried to the bedroom and bathroom, searching for Cahir, but he wasn't in either room. She stifled a sob and went back to the portrait to say her usual, brief prayer, then slowly walked into the living room, feeling the heavy silence as her heart sank

Seda approached the sofa and straightened a throw pillow. Then, unsure what else to do, she grabbed a small towel and wiped the kitchen counters, removing the thin layer of dust that had settled from the opening of the shattered window. She cleaned her way around the apartment, keeping busy as she waited for Cahir's return. She kept glancing at the clock every thirty seconds and watching the door, hoping it would swing open and she would be met with his dimpled smile.

Time passed slowly as she worked. When she had nothing left to clean, she sat on the couch, cringing internally at the thought of messing up the perfectly straight fabric, and stared at a photo of her and Cahir on the table beside her.

She picked up the frame and looked at it closely, remembering the day. Cahir was looking down at her with a wide grin, his arm wrapped tightly around her shoulders. She was making a disgusted face as he held a fermented egg toward her lips. Her hair was down that day, blowing in the wind and sparkling in the sun. She noticed a raven behind her in the photo, as if it had just landed and perched on a tree. She looked more closely at the bird with an azure-tipped beak. How strange that it looked like the one who scratched her and broke the window.

She wondered how many black birds shared that peculiar coloring.

Seda felt a pinch in her pocket and pulled out the red paper, realizing she had forgotten about it.

Who are The Rising?

It couldn't have been Joro's government officials or advisors, since it addressed the food issue. And the dome was weakening? The dome was the only thing keeping them safe from the horrors outside.

If the dome falls… The thought was too overwhelming.

She set the letter on the side table beside the photo, walked into the kitchen, and grabbed a pot to make rice for dinner. While it cooked, she peeled a banana and pressed the peel to her nose, inhaling the scent. The delicate aroma reminded her of the peel stuck to Cahir's face, and she smiled at the memory, feeling her eyes sting.

After dinner, she tidied the kitchen once more and went to shower.

Curfew alarms blared out across the city.

Seda froze as a sudden feeling of loneliness washed over her, like a cold, forgotten cup of coffee left on a table. She fought to contain a sob as her hand covered her mouth. She glanced back into the living room, her gaze locked on the door, still waiting for him to walk through.

Cahir had not made it home before the curfew.

Her eyes stung as she turned on the shower, watching the cold water stream out slowly. She numbly undressed, trying to hold back the tears that threatened to fall.

She stepped into the water and began scrubbing her body until it burned.

The ground trembled violently, and Seda slipped on the wet tile. She fell, and the slippery soap flew out of her hands just like her hope had moments before.

The loud sound of the dome wailing pierced the air, and the earth shook again and again. The apartment walls quivered, and dust fell around the bathroom with each quake.

For the first time in her life, the Jotnar were attacking the dome while she was alone. She curled into herself as the cool water splashed against her red skin.

Her heart beat like a heavy drum, her body clenching tighter with each attack.

I am alone. I am alone. I am… alone

She sobbed as another violent tremor shook the room. Her lungs seized, as if grasped by invisible fists. She pressed her hands to her head, and a muffled scream echoed in the shower, the sound trapped between her clenched teeth.

The monsters were about to break down the dome at this rate, as the red paper had warned. Seda had never felt the force of their attack on her home so strongly before.

What would she do if they did? She had nowhere to go and no protection.

Gradually, the ground stopped shaking, leaving her

surrounded by the same quiet, empty space. The cold water dripped onto her, echoing off the hollow walls of her chest.

Her body began to tremble.

She stayed there, shivering but motionless, until the hard floor began to ache against her hip and her skin started to wrinkle from the splashing water.

She slowly took a deep, agonizing breath, sat up, and reached for the shower knob, turning off the water. She placed her hand back on her lap and sat there, staring down at her fingers.

Drip... Drip... Drip...

The silence consumed her, the gentle tapping of water hitting the tile floor the only sound she could hear. The noise grew louder in her mind with each passing drip, until it seemed to pound against her skull like a hammer.

Her legs felt weak as she stood. She reached for a towel, wrapped it around herself, and took her first brave step out of the shower.

She slowly made her way to the bedroom on shaky legs, her hair still wet, and the towel securely wrapped around her body. She placed her necklace on her dresser, then lay down on Cahir's bed, her damp hair soaking into his pillow. The tightly wrapped towel felt like her only protection.

She fell asleep to the scent of cedar on his pillows, sinking deeper into her loneliness.

Dark images of slithering snakes haunted her dreams.

The same snakes she often dreamed of.

CHAPTER 8

<u>The Monster King</u>

The Monster King sat back on his burgundy velvet chair and looked at the paperwork stacked on his desk in front of him. The gold-stamped, sealed envelopes were a never-ending irritation. He had a problem that needed to be dealt with quickly.

He had spent the last few days in the sun, and his skin had developed a reddish tint, something he despised. Sunburns were for those beneath him. He took a sip of blood-enriched wine from his crystal goblet, the taste metallic and fruity. A knock came on his office door, and the Monster King growled.

A Dragor peered past the doorway, his hand still on the golden knob. "We have collected an additional twenty children, Your Highness," the Dragor, who annoyingly invaded his presence, said with a hiss as he entered the room. His blue, scaled skin glittered in the candlelight, which cast faint light on the Monster King's desk.

"It's not enough! We have to deliver one hundred to Somnium soon!" the Monster King shouted and threw his goblet across the room. It hit the opposite wall and shattered the crystal, spilling the liquid over the wallpaper.

The Dragor shrank back into the dark corner of the room, too scared to move or say anything more. His long tail, tipped with spikes, shifted to cover his face for protection, and his crimson eyes peeked over the top.

"Incite more hostility. Increase the watch. We aren't producing enough to deliver. We need to collect from the city."

"It shall be done." He nervously clicked his claws together and shifted his feet. "But... There's more, Sire."

The Monster King sneered and stared at him, waiting for him to continue. The Dragor took a tentative step forward, emerging from the corner.

"The Fae are back. Two tried to intercept the collection. We caught one, but she disappeared." He knelt and presented the ruby sword, its blade coated with darkened Fae blood that crusted on the surface.

The Monster King shot up from his desk and slammed his palms upon it. "What did you say?" His voice came out low and dangerous.

"The Fae, Your Highness." His head remained low with the sword presented.

The Monster King reached for the sword's handle and ran his tongue over the flaky green blood. The Fae shouldn't be here; the Fae were banished, exiled to the very edges of the planet. The monsters were supposed to break through Joro's dome during the last attack. They had been working on these plans for nearly a thousand years, with the barrier expected to weaken significantly by the year 970 and be nearly fully ready by 999. Research showed that the barrier had been gradually weakening since its creation. Why hadn't it cracked this last time? They had been trying to break the dome for years with this knowledge, and it had never failed. And now the Fae are back? He feared that things were reaching a breaking point, and they needed to act on their plans as quickly as possible.

The Jotnar were powerful beings, throwing everything they had into destroying the dome. Their ongoing failure infuriated the Monster King. The only creatures that couldn't come and go freely from the dome were his monsters. The magical barrier was a fucking annoying creation.

"Go find someone to clean that mess." He pointed to the broken goblet and spilled wine. The Dragor quickly exited the room, shutting the heavy, metal door behind him.

He growled and slammed his fist on his desk, causing papers to scatter. The window was open, a gentle breeze drifting in, blending the cool desert air with the subtle scent of the candle. He took a deep breath and exhaled slowly, still savoring the rich taste of the Fae blood, a flavor he hadn't had in a long time. The Monster King reached into his pocket and grabbed the stone he always carried, watching its dark shimmer.

It will happen soon. The Monster King twirled the stone around his finger. *It's almost time.*

CHAPTER 9

<u>Seda</u>

Two more days passed without any sign or word from anyone about her father or Cahir. Seda felt lonely and worried for them. She barely ate, drank very little water, and kept fixating on the mandarin on the floor or on the clock and the doors, making it hard for her to focus on her work.

Benny and her mom visited daily to spend time together as a family. Her mother was struggling deeply with the loss of their father, and she worried about her just as much as she worried about him. Her mother had become increasingly dependent on Jason over the past few years, and with him gone, Seda wasn't sure how to help her, especially as she found herself in a similar situation with Cahir.

How had she allowed herself to become this way?

Seda sat back at her desk, sighed deeply, and forced herself to take a drink of water. Her workload doubled in Cahir's absence, but she somehow managed to stay ahead. Without any word from the Palatium about Cahir, she still held onto hope that he would return, so she continued her workload and only discussed his absence with her immediate family.

Her heart ached when she thought about her father.

Rumors circulated about the Camp, fueling speculation and suspicion, but no solid proof ever surfaced to clarify how individuals were truly treated inside.

All Seda knew was that people rarely came back, and when they did, they had… *changed.*

No new Jotnar attacks had occurred since the night before, and Seda felt very thankful. Her knee was still in pain from slipping in the shower.

She rested fairly well while sleeping on Cahir's bed, breathing in his pillows and cuddling under his blankets. However, she kept a close watch on the clock and constantly listened for the door to open.

She stood from her desk, tidied the papers, and went outside to get some fresh air. As she passed the rose bushes lining the entrance of the Gardvord, she noticed a bird watching her from a nearby tree. At first, she hesitated, but curiosity got the best of her, and she slowly walked closer.

Interestingly, the bird had the same azure-tipped beak.

Seda looked up at it and asked, "Are you following me, or are there more of you with that same fancy stripe?"

She quickly glanced around to make sure no one saw her talking to a bird. People would probably call the medical wing to admit her.

The bird tilted its head to the side, watching her with its small, beady eyes. Seda walked past the tree, slightly nervous that the bird might come down and scratch her, but with faux confidence, she strode into the brown, dried grass beyond.

The bird jumped off the branch and flew down onto the ground in front of her. Seda shrieked, her arms flying in front of her to protect herself, and quickly stepped back.

"I-I'm not sure what you want. I don't have any snacks to give," Seda nervously said.

The bird jumped into the air and flew a few yards away, then landed again in the grass and looked back at her.

Hesitantly, she took a step toward it. The bird watched Seda as she slowly moved closer, then took off again into the air, landing another few yards farther out, looking back at her once more and waiting for her to get closer.

Seda quickened her pace and followed. It hadn't tried to hurt her and seemed to want her to follow. Her curiosity grew, and she was eager to discover where the strange bird was leading her. The bird took her into a dark thicket of trees, past a circle in the woods where people had once gathered, and kept guiding her until she reached a large mound of vines, where the bird perched atop.

A stone slab peeked out from beneath the greenery.

The bird cawed loudly, then shifted direction and flew over the wall. Seda sighed.

What a curious creature, Seda noted.

She approached the mound and looked at the dense vines hanging over the stonework, along with the large, fuzzy leaves that matched the size of her face. She reached out and touched the vines, and they recoiled, as if expecting her arrival. She gasped at the sudden movement, but curiosity called her forward.

When the vines fully parted like a curtain, a door appeared. Thick logs of ancient wood, a crystalline handle, and a hole in the center shaped like a circular segment. The hole had an impression below it, forming a complete circle around the opening.

Standing on her tiptoes, Seda peeked through the opening, expecting to see more of the same area beyond.

She gasped as her eyes took in the view through the hole.

Through the opening was a glen, tickling her memory—a foggy fantasy that escaped her long forgotten dreams.

A slow-moving stream flowed through the area as a white deer drank from its waters. Her eyes widened at the majestic purple trees with pink tips, encircled by glowing tulips on the mossy ground. In the center of the glen was a massive stump, larger than a house. It pulsed faintly with a purplish light, surrounded by small, gleaming, white-tipped mushrooms.

She grasped the handle and twisted it, but the door wouldn't budge.

"Seda?" a male voice called from behind her, startling her. Seda jumped back, and the vines crumbled back down onto themselves. "Are you out here?"

Benny came into view as he rounded a tree, and she sighed in relief. She didn't want to be out in these woods alone with a stranger, especially a man.

"Hey, Benny! Look what I found!" She excitedly turned around and noticed the vines had returned. She quickly brushed the vines aside, expecting them to retract again with her touch, but they only moved as she brushed them away. She furrowed her brows when she saw only the stone wall behind them. The strange-looking door was gone.

"What the—" Her words came out as a whisper.

"That's strange. Why's there a random wall here?" Benny walked up and brushed the vines aside. "Who would build such a thing? It looks old."

"There was just… just…"

"Are you okay?" Benny looked at her in concern. He reached out and touched her arm.

"Yeah, I thought I saw something." Her eyebrows stayed tightly knit as she gazed at the empty stone surface and the vines.

"Have you eaten today?" he asked.

She glanced back at him. She hadn't eaten anything; actually, she hadn't had a proper meal since the night of the Jotnar attack. The thought of eating made her stomach churn.

She slowly shook her head as her eyes shifted back to the wall. Benny offered his hand for her to take. She averted her gaze from the stonework, rubbing her head, then accepted his hand.

He led her back toward the Gardvord; the walk felt much longer than when she had been following the bird.

"I saw you walk through the trees when I came outside and was concerned about you, so I followed you out here. I know the last few days have been hard. I have some extra lunch from earlier if you're interested?" Benny asked as they approached the front door. When they reached the glass entrance, they both swiped their ID cards to gain entry.

"I'm okay, Benny. I have some food back in the office," she lied. "I'll eat as I finish up my tasks." She just wanted to get back to her desk as soon as possible.

He looked at her for a moment before he nodded and gave her a tight hug. "Love you, sis. Find me if you need to talk, okay?"

They parted ways, and she quietly walked back to her department.

When she walked in, Cahir was sitting in her seat, his chestnut hair a disheveled mess, and his clothes torn across his body.

She felt her heart lurch.

"Cahir!" She ran up to him and hugged him tightly to her, afraid that he might be a figment of her imagination. "What happened? Are you okay? Are you hurt? What did you see? Is Dad okay? I was so worried!"

He tightly embraced her, pressing his nose to her shoulder and breathing deeply into her.

Her friend, her best friend, her *only* friend, was finally back, and he was *alive*. He was not in the Camp.

She let out a strangled sob, and her knees buckled. Cahir wrapped his warm arms around her and let her cry into his lap, gently brushing her hair away from her face and wiping away her tears.

"I'm back, Sed. I've missed you so much."

CHAPTER 10

<u>Seda*</u>
(15 years prior)

The only sounds in the room were pencils scratching against paper and a periodic cough from the instructor at the front of the class. The classroom was warm with the tightly packed students taking their final assessments.

Seda studied tirelessly for this day, determined to make her parents proud. She spent the last two weeks struggling to get enough sleep as she prepared for the exam, and the fatigue was beginning to take its toll. She brushed a loose strand of hair behind her ear as it fell forward and set her pencil down on the paper. She had finished. She flipped back to the first page and reread her answers from the beginning.

That was it. She was done.

Her chair loudly squeaked as she stood up from her desk. Other students looked up from their assessments and rolled their eyes.

"Albino-freak," someone snickered, and a few others laughed.

"Silence! All of you!" the instructor at the front of the class-room shouted as he slammed the table with his stick. The threat of punishment hung over his face as he stared at the remaining students.

Seda walked to the front and placed the packet into the designated basket, double-checking that she had written her name on the paper.

"Thank you, dear." He winked at her as she stepped back. "You're free to leave."

Seda smiled broadly in response, then turned to leave, but someone kicked out a leg, and she fell forward, landing hard on her knees.

The classroom erupted in laughter.

"I said *SILENCE!*" the instructor yelled again, this time taking his stick and smacking a boy in the front of the room across his shoulder with it. A loud cry erupted from the boy.

Seda got up quickly and ran out of the metal doorway, the heavy air filling her lungs as she looked up at the sky toward the glittering dome and saw the sun beginning to turn red.

Freedom, she reminded herself. She was finally free of this place.

She sat on a concrete bench, pulled out her favorite book about a love story between a brave warrior and a woman with magical powers, and opened to the last page she had read. She smiled and anxiously chewed her lip, knowing they were about to kiss soon.

The students were always mean to her that way. She never had a friend, except for Benny, but he was her brother, and he was also younger than she was. She didn't mind, though. She was officially done with this wretched school.

She had a couple of hours left before curfew and wanted to sit and relax before going home, where her family was anxiously waiting, but she didn't care. She was now officially an adult, with her test scores expected to come back within the week. They would notify her about her placement and performance.

She grabbed a sandwich from her bag and began to eat it as she slowly read through the pages of her book.

"There she is," someone said, diverting her attention from her story. She looked up at the two boys approaching her.

"The albino-freak. What are you doing here? Shouldn't you be celebrating being the first one finished?" Michael, the tall boy, asked. His greasy, dark hair clung to his face.

"Nah, my mom says girls like her like to gloat to make us feel inferior," said the shorter, second boy with red hair and freckles.

"Is that so?" Michael smirked as he slowly raked his eyes over her body.

"Leave me alone," she huffed in annoyance.

She hated them. Out of everyone in her class, these two were the worst. They constantly targeted her, making her feel insecure about her purple eyes and white hair. She knew she looked different, and they continually reminded her of it.

As she always did, she would simply leave and ignore them.

She put her sandwich back in its sack and then into her bag. She began to put her book away when Michael roughly snatched her wrist, causing her to drop it.

"Why should I?" he hissed in her face, and his rotten-smelling breath assaulted her nose. "I've spent the last ten years having to look at you... at this..." He looked down at her modestly covered breasts and smiled slowly. "And now we won't get to see this anymore. We might miss you." He paused and nodded at Alexi. "Right, Alexi?"

Alexi walked behind her and placed his clammy hands on her shoulders. He slowly moved them to her hair and gently twirled a loose strand between his fingers. "Yeah, Michael. I'll miss her and this shiny hair. I think she wants one last goodbye."

Seda's heart rate increased, and she swiftly stood up, knocking over her belongings and shoving the boys aside.

They grabbed her roughly and pulled her into the prickly bushes, the branches scratching at her skin.

Michael ripped open her dress and got on top of her, holding her legs down.

Seda started screaming as confusion and horror overwhelmed her mind. What were they doing?

Alexi swiftly placed his hands over her mouth, silencing her.

She fought back, slapping and trying to bite. She scratched Michael's face as hard as she could. Blood and skin caked under her nails, leaving behind jagged cuts down his face.

Her necklace caught on one of their hands, and they ripped it off her, throwing it aside. Her eyes filled with tears, and her vision went blurry.

"Stop fighting back, or it'll be worse," hissed Michael as blood dripped down his face onto her.

He ripped her underwear to the side.

She felt a distant sensation of tears trickling down her temple as her mind drifted into the clouds, and she thought she heard the cawing of birds.

CHAPTER II

Seda

When the clock struck five, Seda and Cahir left their office, hand in hand, and slowly made their way home. Cahir explained that he had to go outside the dome and found her father in a cell. He tried to free him but had to run when the Rozzers attacked. It took him days to find a way back in without being caught.

He assured her that no one knew who he was, and no one would come for him.

They ascended the winding stairs to their apartment and entered through the door. Seda paused to say her prayer, but Cahir walked past her and took a seat on the couch. Seda looked at him with a puzzled expression, but she didn't want to push him. She was relieved he was home and safe. He'd clearly been through a tough time and looked exhausted.

She sat on the couch beside him, her ear against his chest and her palm against his heart, listening to the gentle beat, the sound soothing her. They sat together in silence as he gently ran his fingers through her hair.

She lifted herself from his chest and said, "I saw something today." She nervously chewed on her fingernail.

He gently pulled her hand away from her lips, placing it on her thigh with his warm hand remaining over hers. There was a softness in his eyes when he said, "Tell me."

She fidgeted. "Well, I saw a bird. I think it was the same bird that scratched me and broke into the house. In fact, I think it might've been the same bird that I yelled at on our walk home after the Wyrd. I shouldn't have yelled at it. You were probably right that it could understand me."

Cahir half smiled, a singular dimple accenting his cheek, and encouraged, "Go on…"

"Well, I followed it into this grove of trees way out past the Gardvord. It led me to this hidden wall that was covered in vines."

She picked up her other hand this time to bite her nails and then set it down herself and took a deep breath. "You're going to think I'm crazy."

"Never."

She hesitated and then forced out, "I touched the vines and they moved on their own. Then I saw a door with a hole in it, so I peeked through and saw… and saw…"

Seda paused what she was saying and winced. Thinking back, how could she really know if what she saw was real? Benny was right. She hadn't eaten, and maybe her mind *was* playing tricks on her because of the stress.

Maybe she never even saw the bird.

"It's okay, Sed. Tell me what you saw."

"I don't know. Maybe I'm just tired and hungry, and maybe I didn't even see anything."

"I'd like to know."

She lingered for a long moment, discomfort creeping as her own memory resurfaced.

"Well..." She took another deep breath and continued, "I looked through the hole in the door, and I saw this giant forest with this massive stump, and when Benny found me, the whole thing disappeared."

He looked at her intently, his face showing no pretenses. His eyes flicked between hers, then he paused briefly before saying, "I believe you. There's a lot beyond the dome, and magic still exists."

"How do you know that?" she asked.

Cahir looked away from her and stared at the photo of them on the side table. "Because I have trust that there's beauty beyond this place that confines and hurts its people. I have faith and hope that one day things will change for the positive. I know magic exists because this dome exists. It's something ancient, something right, etched into the bones of this world, and I don't believe that we have learned everything there is to know yet."

Seda leaned back on the couch and pulled her legs to her chest.

"Thank you for believing me." She smiled at him and gave him a playful nudge. "That was beautiful, by the way."

Cahir smiled back at her and then stood. "Well, I'm hungry after all of this. Would you like to eat with me?"

Seda nodded as her stomach growled in response. She got up from the couch, and they headed to the small kitchen to quickly prepare a meal with the ingredients they had on hand.

After they finished dinner and cleaned up, each of them took a shower. Seda grabbed his clothes for him, and they both made their way into the bedroom when they finished.

Cahir paused at the doorway and saw his crumpled bed with Seda's bed on the opposite side in pristine condition.

"Was someone else here?" he asked, a look on his face that Seda couldn't place.

Seda blushed and fiddled with her fingernails. "No, I slept there while you were gone." She felt her nerves tighten, fearing he might be upset with her for invading his personal space.

With a sigh, Cahir rubbed his neck and stepped into the room. He settled onto the bed and patted the space beside him, inviting her to sit. She gladly complied.

"Will you lie with me tonight? I'll give you all my pillows if you'd like," he asked her, his neck slowly turning red.

A fragile laugh slipped free from her. "I can get my own pillows, and yes, I'd love to sleep here too, if that's alright? Although it'll be pretty cramped. This bed's barely big enough for you as it is."

She didn't want to leave his side, preferring to stay wrapped in his comfort and his scent for as long as possible.

"I'll survive."

She grabbed her pillows, tossed them onto the bed, and snuggled under the blankets against the wall. Cahir's weight caused the bed to shift as he climbed in, making Seda lean into him, and she caught herself with her hands on his firm chest. She quickly apologized and turned back around. He wrapped his arms around her and spooned her close.

Without saying a word, they shared each other's space, and both drifted into a deep, peaceful sleep.

SEDA WOKE and gazed at the wall as the soft orange light of sunrise streamed through the window. She felt safe and secure as Cahir's arms wrapped tightly around her and snuggled in closer, pressing her body against his. She relished the moment as if a comforting blanket was enveloping her soul. He was back and safe.

She felt the whisper of his breath in her hair, and he tenderly squeezed her hip. Cahir pressed against her backside, and she felt his firmness press into her.

Her body tensed immediately, and her heart started to race.

"I'm sorry." He quickly pulled away from her.

"I-It's okay," she replied, her voice catching.

Memories of that day flooded her, her eyes stinging as she pressed her fist over her mouth, stifling a cry. It had taken a long time, but when she finally confided in Cahir about that day, she felt relieved when he believed her.

For years, she struggled with her own memories. Her family knew something had happened when she returned home with torn clothes and blood that day, but she never explained in detail, never telling anyone who they were.

She only briefly explained their appearance to Cahir, but never shared their names.

She felt disgusted and unclean, as if she had done something wrong.

Bile burned in her throat as she thought back on it, and she let the tears fall.

"I would *never* hurt you, Seda."

He had always treated her with respect and kindness, showing no signs of romantic interest. After learning what had happened to her, he took even more care to slow things down in their friendship. They only started hugging and holding hands within the last couple of years.

She had no clue if Cahir ever felt that way about anyone. He attracted the attention of many women, but he always kept his distance. The fact that his body reacted that way to her confused her. Maybe it was just a physical thing that happens to some guys in the morning?

She rolled over and stared at him, face to face, inches apart. She pulled the blanket over her mouth and said, "I know you wouldn't."

He gently wiped away a tear that was sliding down her face, running along the ridge of her nose. "When you're ready to talk about it more, I'm here. I'd like to know who those assholes are who hurt you."

She nodded and said into the blanket, "Someday."

She looked away from him, unable to meet his eyes.

"Why do you have the blanket over your mouth?" he asked.

"Because I need to brush my teeth, and so do you." She smirked, thankful for the change of subject. She took a section of blanket and placed it over his mouth, and he grabbed onto it, holding it in place.

"What's our plan today? Isn't today a day off?" his muffled voice asked into the blanket while staring at her.

"We should catch up with Benny. I promised him and Mom I'd let them know when you returned, and I totally forgot yesterday."

"That sounds like a plan," he said.

"And…" she began, but hesitated. She chewed her lip before asking, "If you're okay with it, can we go to the medical wing, please?"

He stared at her for a long moment and then slowly nodded his head and whispered, "Yeah, we can do that."

The Prayer Song rang out over the distance.

Seda climbed out of bed, and Cahir shifted his body away from her, allowing her to pass. "I'm going to go brush my teeth," she said to him as she left the room.

She left Cahir in the room while he sat on the edge of the bed, his hair a rumpled mess, and a pillow covering his lap.

CHAPTER 12

<u>Cahir</u>

As Cahir and Seda headed out of the apartment to look for Benny and Sara, he continued to scold himself. He knew Seda struggled with a traumatic past. She didn't tell him the specifics, but he wished he knew who the fuckers were who did it so he could rip their faces apart, literally, and feast upon their agony.

But all he had were vague descriptions of them.

He always respected her boundaries, only coming close when the situation was right, and never in *that* way. He believed she was beautiful both inside and out, and he could see the real her beneath her veil of shadows. She was like the first glimpse of sunlight after a dark storm. Her kindness brought out the best in him, helping him become a better man.

He fought with himself countless times to keep his reactions in check. But that didn't stop him from catching himself watching her from behind and admiring her rounded hips, her thick thighs, or the way her loose tops would shape against her when the wind picked up just right.

He would spend the rest of his long life like this, only as close as she wanted and needed, being her friend *forever*.

He was thankful for the ability to take cold showers most days.

Lately, it had been getting harder for him to keep his emotions in check. Maybe it was due to those damn letters from the Wisps, constantly reminding him of the time he had left.

Uncertainty consumed him, and he just wanted to take Seda and head back to his home, fuck the consequences, and leave this awful place behind.

Seda had no idea who or what he really was. He was under a strict agreement not to reveal anything. The bargain he had made with the Wisps made it binding; his desire to come to her was their payment. Cahir was also not allowed to lie to Seda. Navigating his backstory to her was a never-ending challenge. She knew that he was an orphan and that he had no family within the dome, all true, but all falsified truths as well.

He dreaded the day she found out the truth about him, knowing it would crush the trust he'd worked so hard to build with her. Now that he had it, it felt like he was grasping at water and watching it slip away drop by drop.

They walked past a shouting crowd and paused, watching it swell as more people joined the chaos. Seda and Cahir pushed through to the center and saw a Rozzer beaten by a group of men.

"Let's get out of here." He quickly grabbed her hand, guiding them back through the crowd and as far away as possible.

Sirens blared in the area, and Rozzers flooded in, striking people with batons and dragging bodies away.

The crowd began fighting back fiercely.

"I-I don't like this, Cahir. Citizens of Joro don't act like this." She nervously bit her nails. They continued their walk to Benny and Sara's house. Cahir looked at her concerned expression, and worry swept through his heart. He needed to get her out of this city. What would she do if he just whisked her away without telling her? Would she forgive him?

They walked a few more blocks to another apartment complex and went in through the front door. They found apartment nine, knocked on the door, and waited for them to answer. Light footsteps approached, and the door cracked open. Sara peeked out from the crack.

"Oh, Seda and Cahir! You're back!" she exclaimed, pushing the door open wider. "Come in. Come in."

As they walked through, Seda paused at the entrance and said her prayer.

Cahir refused to fake-pray to that hideous man any longer. He walked past her into the living room. He was over this entire charade. He didn't have much time left, and his feigned loyalty was wearing thin.

"I'm so happy to see you back, Cahir. We were so worried about you. Were you able to find out about Jason?" Sara asked, anxiously fidgeting with her shirt sleeve.

For the second time, Cahir went over the story he was allowed to share, this time with Sara.

Sara wiped her eyes with the ends of her shirt. "I was worried he'd already be there," she responded.

"Where's Benny?" Seda asked.

"He went out earlier to grab some food," Sara said, trying to compose herself and wipe away her tears again as she straightened.

"We saw a mob on our way here fighting with Rozzers. I really hope Benny didn't get caught up in that," Seda said.

"A mob?" Sara paused and shook her head. "No... no... your brother knows better than to get involved with things like that."

The door opened, and Benny walked in, carrying a small paper bag.

"Cahir! You're back! Did you find Dad?" he exclaimed as he

walked to a table and set the bag down, turning to him and giving him a big hug.

Cahir explained the events another time, allowing the information to flow through him and the others to absorb. All listened with rapt attention, even though it was the third time Seda had heard it. He made sure to tell the same story each time to avoid confusion.

He did not want Seda to pick up on any inaccuracies and question further, and she would, too. The little bird was too bright for her own good.

"There really isn't much we can do at this point," Sara said. "I don't know who we can talk to, or where to go to find answers."

"I refuse to believe that," Benny said. "Father was important here in Joro. He made the most significant advancements in our city's food supply. His absence will make this whole situation even worse."

Cahir looked over at Benny, noticing for the first time a black mark on his wrist, inked in, that looked like the tail of something.

Benny noticed Cahir looking and pulled his sleeve down and shook his head, pleading with him not to mention it.

Cahir didn't care if Benny went to the Barrio black markets and got a tattoo. Cahir had plenty of them marking his Fae form.

Why would he be ashamed?

CAHIR AND SEDA left their apartment and headed to the Medical Wing for her insemination. As they waited in the lobby, Cahir saw Seda biting her nails again, clearly worried about her father and anxious about the failed attempts at conception.

He knew that she longed so deeply to get pregnant and feel secure. He only wished he could help.

"Things are going to work out, Sed. I know a lot has happened over the last few days, but I'll do everything I can to stay by your side, no matter the consequences," he said to her. "Maybe after we leave here, we could go to Cascade and find some honey cakes? I have some money saved up."

Seda perked up. Honey cakes were her favorite. They were the one thing that bridged the gap between her reluctance to befriend him. He had woken up extra early each day when they first met to go to Cascade and find them for her.

She pulled her fingers out of her mouth and smiled, causing his heart to skip a beat. His gaze settled on her full lips, and he glanced away quickly, feeling his desire surge.

"Cahir Cutlass," a short, burly woman called for him from the front desk. "Your room's ready for you."

He stood and followed the woman into a small, overly lit, sterile room, where he sat in a chair. He looked to his side and saw the picture books available for the process.

Being in this room made him feel a sense of disgust. He hated this place with its sterile smell, the used images on the table for the men, and the bright, fluorescent lights.

The woman swiped her card on the computer and entered his name into the system. "Your container." She handed him a sealed tube and then left the room, the door clicking shut behind her.

He got up and locked the door, resting his hand on the lock and his forehead against the cool metal of the door.

He really shouldn't do this. He couldn't trap Seda into pregnancy when he was bound to secrecy, and she was living in this hellhole.

He weighed the pros and cons of each, the same ones he had always grappled with whenever he stepped into this miserable place.

Pros: Seda would be safe from the next Wyrd.

Cons: Seda would never speak to him again once she had a baby and discovered who he truly was. She would be tied to Joro even more than she already is. The baby could come out with Fae qualities. And most importantly, she deserved to have a baby on her own terms, with honesty and love, and a home where safety isn't a concern.

Unease wrapped around him. If he didn't do it and Seda found out he was doing this each time he went, she would be furious, but all this worry and stress over these fucking Wyrds *could* be avoided.

His mind wandered back to them lying in bed together and how her soft body felt pressed against him, how he desperately needed to release the built-up tension from earlier, and all the times before.

That was the closest they had ever been, and he couldn't suppress his desire for her.

He thought about how he longed to touch her in ways she deserved to be touched, to make her feel relaxed and loved, to show her how much she meant to him.

His mind drifted to how her body fit perfectly against his, the soft curve of her hips in his palm, and the lilac scent of her hair as it pressed against his nose this morning.

Visions of her only wearing that towel when Roya shattered their window flashed through his mind. He thought of her beautiful amethyst eyes and how they enchanted him whenever they met his gaze, as if he were under a magical spell only she could cast.

He adjusted himself as the tension in his body built in his pants.

As he reached down and pulled his hard length out, he stared down at the silky skin that no one had touched in years. A shudder ran through his body, and it thickened in his palm.

What if he did it just this once?

He firmly squeezed his cock. A deep, rumbling groan escaped

his lips as his knees buckled from weakness, and a steady pulse beat in his palm, begging for more.

A wave of excitement rushed through his chest as his heart pounded.

He grabbed the worn book and looked at the images within. Nude photos of women lined each page.

A disgusted sneer flew from his lips as he hurled the book across the room, and was replaced with a slight smile of satisfaction as it crumpled on the floor.

He tucked his straining cock back into his pants.

He was a fraud, a liar, and she would never forgive him if she got pregnant and found out the truth.

He didn't deserve relief. He didn't deserve *her*.

He let out a deep sigh, opened the container, and spat into the cup.

CHAPTER 13

<u>Seda</u>

As Seda and Cahir walked out of the Medical Wing, he wore a stern expression and remained silent, refusing to speak when she tried to talk to him.

"That went well," she tried.

"Mhmm."

"Would you like to see the wall I found?"

"Not now," he snipped.

She had no idea what had caused his attitude to shift. She attempted to hold his hand, but he gently pulled away when her hand grazed his.

They walked home side by side, step by quiet step.

When they entered their apartment, Seda said her prayer to the portrait, and Cahir went straight to the bathroom, shutting the door roughly behind him. Why was he avoiding his prayers?

She went into the kitchen and opened the cabinet to see what food was left. A bag of rice and a can of beans were the only options left.

Great. So much for that honey cake, she grumbled to herself.

Her mood was souring like a forgotten cup of milk. She removed a pot from the cabinet and began cooking the rice, watching as the water gradually came to a boil.

She heard the bathroom door open and looked over. Cahir stepped out, freshly showered, with a towel wrapped around his waist.

She had never seen him like this before.

A warm, shameful feeling spread low in her stomach as her eyes traced down his muscular build to the area hidden beneath the tied towel, where a prominent bulge was visible.

He didn't look at her as he went to the bedroom, and guilt heated her cheeks and ears.

She shouldn't be staring at him like that. That was definitely a first.

She had spent the day thinking about what had happened this morning, hoping that maybe it was actually *something*. She felt bad for reacting the way she did this morning. He didn't deserve to be treated like that. She knew he had a tender heart and would never hurt her.

But it had to have been just a coincidence, an accident. Cahir didn't really feel for her *that* way.

She was shattered, weighed down by her own emotions and memories, and Cahir couldn't possibly want that. He wouldn't desire someone so broken and unlovable.

They were just *friends*.

Why would she even look at him like that?

She took a deep breath to calm herself and absentmindedly stirred the rice, even though she wasn't supposed to.

Her irritation slowly simmered again, matching the rice. She was angry with herself for looking at him, for hoping for something she didn't deserve, and for his silence toward her.

When he finally stepped out of the bedroom fully dressed in his pajamas, she angrily said, "Listen, I don't know what I did to deserve your silence, but I'm now frustrated. Just talk to me. What did I do wrong? Why are you so upset?"

"Not *everything* I feel is about you, Seda," he retorted.

Anger flooded her at his response, and she threw the rice spoon she was holding across the kitchen. It clinked, and the rice clinging to the spoon stuck to the wall. She didn't care. Let it be messy. She flew into a rage and stormed out of the kitchen.

"Oh, great. Now the little rice we have left in this fucking hellhole is stuck to the wall." He flung his arms up in frustration.

Seda paused at his comeback and replied curtly, "Good, I hope it dries out and crusts over, and I hope you *scrape* yourself on its sharp edges when you walk by!"

They both froze and locked eyes.

His lips curved into the beginning of a smile, and he quickly covered them with his hand, averting his gaze from her and focusing on the rice on the wall instead.

Seda thought about what she said. What a stupid comeback. Why would she even think that?

For a brief moment, the air hung heavy with silence, but then they both erupted into laughter.

"What kind of wish is that?" Cahir asked her, laughter slipping out as he fought back tears.

"I don't even know. Who even gets cut up from rice? Not you. You don't even get cut up by swords."

Cahir's laughter died, and he looked at her in confusion. "How did you know that?"

"Because that one time you caught the sword from that stupid Rozzer who tripped."

"Oh, right. I forgot that happened," he softly replied.

They both quieted down. Cahir opened his arms to her. "Come here. I'm sorry I've been in a bad mood. I really don't like that place. I'm not upset with you."

She stepped forward and wrapped him in a tight embrace, feeling the warmth of his arms around her.

She reminded herself that they were friends, and he was her *best* friend.

Wyrd sirens blared out, their pulsing beat reverberating through the air. For a moment, the tension between Seda and Cahir was palpable as they locked eyes, their faces a mix of confusion and shock.

"I-It can't be," she gasped, her mouth falling open, her heart pounding as if it had missed too many beats.

"It is…"

"But it hasn't been six months, and the curfew's about to start!"

The alarms continued blaring.

With Seda's nerves on edge, she rushed back into the kitchen and immediately forgot why she'd gone there in the first place. She spotted the stove's flames and quickly turned them off. Cahir promptly returned to the bedroom and changed out of his pajamas.

Seda paced around the room while she waited for Cahir to finish, which was only about thirty seconds, but felt like an eternity.

They immediately headed toward the Palatium, forgetting to say their prayers as they walked as quickly as they could. Anxiety crept through Seda's spine like static electricity gripping her nerves. Everyone else around them was moving in the same direction, their faces mirroring the confusion.

Birds flew high in the sky, cawing loudly amid the pulsating alarm, an eerie warning of what was to come. The garnet sun was low on the horizon, and the sky was darkening rapidly. They quickened their pace and started jogging.

As they walked through the gates, more and more people gathered inside the stadium, with confused conversations echoing through the crowd. Seda and Cahir found a safe place to stand and waited for the alarms to stop.

Ten minutes of ear-splitting alarms finally ceased. The stadium lights flicked on, illuminating the stage. The Palatium door swung open, and Teivel stepped out, wearing a nervous expression. His robes were disheveled, and his usually clean-shaven face now had a bit of a beard. He hurried on his short legs toward the podium.

Seda watched with anxious curiosity as she bit her nails.

"Thank you all for coming on short notice," he said. "We have a special event for you tonight. Due to recent events, Lord Mordred would like to speak with everyone collectively." He extended his arm toward the Palatium door and bowed at the waist.

Lord Mordred stepped out, his scarred face looking stern under the bright stadium lights against the darkening sky.

Everyone in the crowd dropped to the floor and bowed.

Silence ensued.

"Rise," he commanded as he waited for the crowd to settle. "As you all know, we've seen increasing Jotnar attacks lately, and because of that, our food supply has decreased significantly."

Someone in the crowd yelled, "Stop lying! We've seen the papers around the city."

Lord Mordred nodded to the nearest Rozzer. The Rozzer stepped forward and struck his baton against the man's head, knocking him to the floor and dragging his body into the cell. Everyone else stayed silent, watching in stillness.

"Would anyone else like to interrupt me and spew lies?" His words hung in the air, and the eerie silence of the crowd echoed around the stadium. "There's been an increase in misbehavior and people going to the Camp as a result. We've kindly asked for your cooperation in this matter as we work to resolve these issues. But..." He paused and looked over the crowd.

Ten seconds, fifteen seconds.

"As punishment for these recent acts, we have decided to host a very special series of Wyrds—a reminder as to why we're here to begin with. Our continued growth is essential to our survival," he said.

Seda's heart sank, and the crowd all murmured at once.

"Now, now. Do not fret. This Wyrd will be smaller. We'll host these events *weekly* until we see a change in behavior around the city. Teivel, bring me the list."

Teivel rushed forward and nearly tripped on his robe as he handed the scroll to the lord.

"Today and all the Wyrds moving forward, until we get full cooperation from everyone, we'll select ten citizens who have yet to complete their duty and prove their love for our society. These ten will have a chance to redeem themselves with our specialists at the Camp." Lord Mordred looked back over the crowd.

This can't be happening. Please, please, please, Seda silently pleaded, feeling her legs give out. She fell into Cahir's side, and he quickly wrapped his arm around her, stabilizing her.

"Mary Jones. Jessica Blue," Lord Mordred called.

Both women slowly walked forward and registered for placement in the cell. The lord continued calling names until he reached the last one. "And last but *especially* not least..."

As Lord Mordred's eyes blazed a deep red, he locked his gaze on Seda. Seda's heart plummeted into her stomach, and her vision faded to black.

"Seda Arbor."

The birds attacked.

They swooped through the air and attacked the Rozzers; they cawed loudly and scratched at Lord Mordred, their focus entirely on the people in charge. The Rozzers fired their guns at them, and black bundles of feathers fell from the sky.

"She's over there! Get her!" someone yelled at the Rozzers.

With a swift move, Cahir grabbed Seda, hoisting her over his shoulder, and sprinted toward the nearest exit. The panicked crowd all rushed in the same direction. Birds plummeted from the sky and crashed into people as they fled. Two Rozzers stepped in and tripped Cahir, yanking Seda from his grasp.

She spun around to face them, and fear seized her chest.

Michael and Alexi had her in a tight, painful grip, and memories of that day came flooding back to her.

"Not again. Not again. Don't hurt me!" she shrieked as she clawed at them. "Please don't hurt me. Please, please, please."

As Seda broke free, Michael and Alexi pounced, tackling her to the ground. She shook with fear and let out a blood-curdling scream.

"Shut up! Call off these fucking birds. The last time they almost killed us!" Michael shouted as his rancid spit hit her in the face.

CHAPTER 14

<u>Cahir</u>

People trampled Cahir after he fell, but he rolled to the side and jumped up. He saw and heard the Rozzers with Seda, and rage clouded his vision.

The scars on one and the red hair on the other… Just as Seda described them. These were the fuckers who had hurt her, and they were the same ones who had tried to capture him before he left the dome the other night.

Anger surged through him like an erupting volcano, spewing burning lava that destroyed everything in its path.

Magic smoked from his nostrils.

He ran forward and ripped the red-haired Rozzer off violently, throwing him to the side with such force that the man slid across the gravel and cried out, clutching his arm to his chest. He plowed into the dark-haired one, releasing Seda from his grasp, and bit his grotesque, scarred face on the way down. His bite tore his cheek nearly in two, leaving it dangling from his jawline and revealing the man's rotten teeth underneath.

Blood coated Cahir's mouth, and he spat the mouthful of it into his face.

"It was *YOU!*" He punched his nose with all his strength and felt the satisfying crack under his knuckles. He smiled down at him with a sense of satisfaction, watching one of the men who had hurt Seda desperately fighting for his life. The man's life now belonged to him.

The man tried to fight back, but his punches were weak compared to Cahir's fury.

"This is for hurting her, for taking what you could never truly have, you fucking piece of filth." He grinned wickedly, and the blood on his teeth exposed the monster he knew he was.

It felt like a lifetime for him to earn Seda's trust, just enough to get a hug. He recalled all the times her body would tense when he got too close, especially when they were alone, sharing the same space and air. The way her heart would race, and how she would start fumbling over her words and picking at her nails.

She was so different from what he expected when he set out to find her. They sapped her strength, stole her trust, and tried to strip her of the ability to find beauty in life and see the good in people.

They shattered her beautiful soul.

His anger exploded.

He beat his face until blood pooled between his fists, and the man's skull was crushed into the ground. Then he shoved his hands into the man's chest, ripping his ribs apart easily, and tore his heart out. He lifted the organ above his head and crushed it between his fingers as hard as he could, causing it to spurt out his thick blood.

The man's body remained motionless on the ground.

"Cahir!" Seda screamed.

He snapped his head up and saw Seda staring at him with a look of pure panic as the red-haired Rozzer dragged her away through the crowd of panicked people. The Corvids swooped down and clawed at the Rozzer, but he kept his face protected with his wounded arm. Cahir surged to his feet with fierce determination and sprinted toward the stage. He forced himself forward with powerful strides, pushing past the strain in his muscles.

He tried to shift into his Fae form to reach her as fast as possible with his larger size, but his magic refused to accept the change.

The Rozzer roughly threw her into the cell and slammed the door.

Out of nowhere, a dark cloud of smoke erupted, and the people on stage were suddenly gone in a loud explosion. The cell, Lord Mordred, and everyone else on the stage disappeared when the smoke cleared.

Cahir ran onto the stage and frantically felt around, pushing his way through the smoke, wondering if it was an illusion, but no one was there.

Seda was gone.

PART TWO
THE CAMP

CHAPTER 15

<u>Cahir</u>

"It's time to go!" shouted Roya as she landed on the stage next to him, her feathers sleek and blood dripping from her claws. "Now!"

Dozens of Rozzers lay dead around them inside the stadium, their mutilated bodies, riddled with deep cuts and exposed organs, scattered across the rocky ground—the red of their blood blending with their red uniforms. Cahir tripped as he ran down the stairs toward the nearest exit and through the open doors.

His mind was in a frenzy. Where had Seda gone? He had to track her down.

The curfew alarms rang out across the city.

This was planned, he realized.

Outside, people were fighting off Rozzers, and red streaks stained the roads as he sprinted, slipping through the blood. Cells lined the outskirts of the Palatium, already filling with weeping men, women, and children, being collected into their own cells.

Their cries pierced through the air.

Roya flew ahead with two other Corvids as Cahir followed. Their wings flapped in the wind, creating a breeze that brushed around them. With a quick jump, Cahir hurdled over a man on the ground, who was screaming in agony with his leg twisted to the side.

Cahir was like a flame tearing through a dry forest as he ran. He looked over his shoulder and saw the remaining birds dispersing through the sheen of the dome, heading toward their safety in the distance.

They reached the edge of Orience, with farm fields and apartments stretching out before them. A line of Rozzers blocked the road in the dark distance, waiting to stop anyone trying to get through.

"Over here." Roya navigated them to the end of an alley, and the three birds landed gracefully like floating feathers falling from the sky. All three of them shifted into their human forms. Except for their coloring, the women looked identical. Roya had midnight-blue hair, and Ferona had dark hair that transitioned into a baby-blue hue at the ends. Feich had dark green streaks through his hair and was built tall and strong with the same feline eyes and pale skin.

"What's our plan?" Cahir asked as he frantically looked around them toward the end of the alley.

"We need to mask you to get you back to the apartment," Ferona said as she looked around for any movement. The tall bricks of the walls surrounding them echoed her words slightly.

"I don't want to go to the apartment! I need to go after her!" Cahir snarled in response. He was panic-stricken, like a small boat on the sea, charging against monstrous waves. He couldn't think about anything else. He couldn't even come up with a solid plan quickly.

"Shh. We need to *regroup,* Cahir. When you're safely back inside, we can figure out our next step," Roya snipped back quietly. She shifted back into her Corvid form and landed on his shoulder, draping her wing over him and hiding them from view. "We have to be careful."

Roya's claws dug into his shoulder. The other two shifted, and Cahir followed them out of the alley. They flew high into the sky, away from the line of Rozzers, as Cahir slowly walked around them, his footsteps light to avoid making any sound.

"What a mess this is," one of the Rozzers said as Cahir crept past. The hair on his arms prickled, and fear clenched his chest as he sneaked around them, like a kid stealing candy from his father's secret stash. If they found him, it would be harder for him to find Seda.

"What was this even all about?" another asked.

"I don't know," said the first. "Captain told us to collect everyone we could after the curfew rang. Seems unfair to me they held this Wyrd so late."

Cahir stepped on a stick, and the two looked over in his direction, each quickly readying various weapons. Roya dug her claws in firmly, obviously shaken from the loud sound, and Cahir paused his movement.

"Don't question our leaders!" snapped a third, grabbing back the attention of the two, who set their weapons back down. "You know what happens when we do. We can end up in those cells alongside the others. Shut the hell up before you get us all into trouble, and watch for people coming this way. Look, I see some coming now." He pointed at a group of people running toward them. The Rozzers rearmed their weapons.

Cahir carefully stepped over the stick and continued his walk past them. When he was a safe distance away, he picked up his speed, and Roya took off into the air, his illusion now gone. His apartment neared, and he ran up the twisted stairs, unlocked the door, and slammed it closed behind him. He took a deep breath. Sweat was dripping down his back as he paced in the doorway.

I need to find her. I need to find her. I need to find her.

His attention snagged at the portrait of Lord Mordred, and his anger exploded. He dug his fingers into it and dragged them down, ripping the painting into shreds. He grabbed the frame off the wall and threw it as hard as he could, smashing it against the table on the other side of the room. He walked into the bedroom and looked over Seda's things as he paced next to her bed.

Sparkling light caught his eye. He walked closer and picked up Seda's necklace from the dresser. Why wasn't she wearing it? She rarely took it off. He placed the necklace into his pocket. He would find her. Fear raced up his spine when he thought about the dangers she might be in now, that someone could be hurting her.

He walked back out to the living room as the Corvids flew into the apartment from the broken window, landing on the floor. They quickly shifted and looked at Cahir.

"Does anyone know how they teleported?" Ferona asked as she took a step toward the kitchen.

"Mordred must have the stone you're looking for," Roya said, glancing from the shattered portrait to Cahir.

"The stone can do that?" Feich asked.

"I should've protected her from this and just taken her away like I wanted!" Cahir snarled, his body on the edge of shifting as his powers encircled him.

People rarely ever came back from the Camp, and Lord Mordred seemed to have a special interest in her. Twice now, he had singled her out and stared at her. What did he want from her? How did he know her?

Does he know she's special?

The Corvids stood silent and stared at him. Cahir paced around the living room, and the corner of a red piece of paper caught his eye. He bent down and pulled the paper out from under the couch.

"What's that?" asked Roya.

Cahir silently read the paper and stared at the familiar image at the bottom. "Our next step."

CHAPTER 16

Seda

"It's time to wake up," said the familiar voice from her dreams.

Seda jolted awake to darkness, where distant screams and gurgling noises echoed around her. Her breath caught, and she felt a shiver run through her body. Where was she? A slow drip splashed onto her arm as the heavy smell of copper and iron filled the air. Her wrists felt heavy as she slowly stood on unsteady legs, reaching out her trembling hands to explore her surroundings, the sound of rattling chains clinking with her movements.

As the distant screaming grew louder, she backed away as far as she could, her head smashing into the wall behind her, and she slipped on something slick.

She curled her body into a tight ball, the only way she could think to shield herself.

Footsteps echoed as an orange glow lit up the area. Seda peeked out from under her arm and saw that she was trapped, chained in a dungeon deep within a long, dark hall lined with cells. A small, metal bed stained with old, dark blood sat beside her, with a bucket placed near the bars. The walls consisted of large stones stacked haphazardly.

Panic began to seize her throat, and her breathing became labored.

She looked to the right and saw the source of the dripping beside her.

The lifeless body of a naked woman hung from the ceiling with a rope wrapped around her arms. Her body dripped blood from a thick cut across her abdomen.

Seda screamed and scrambled back, hitting the wall again. She looked down, seeing that her hands and clothing were covered with the woman's blood. She cried out, frantically trying to wipe her hands on her shirt, wincing when it only smeared more onto her. Her chest rose and fell rapidly as she struggled to breathe. She couldn't believe what was happening. Where was she? How did she end up here?

"Looks like my albino-freak has finally woken up," a voice drawled from the other side of the bars as the torch grew brighter with their approach. Alexi stood on the other side, his wrist tightly wrapped in cloth. He held a set of keys, jingling them in the air, and Seda saw his arms covered in deep scratches from the birds.

He wickedly smiled at Seda. "Didn't think I'd ever get to see you again. But here we are. So much for those good grades, huh? Welcome to the Camp." He laughed manically and jiggled the keys harder.

Seda choked back a sob.

This isn't happening.

"I cannot *wait* to spend more time with you. But..." He paused and looked at the woman's hanging form beside her. "I have more pressing matters to attend to right now. You see, thanks to your boyfriend back there, I've *finally* been promoted. He was so distracted by that lowlife Michael that he didn't see me escape with you. I captured you for *him*. And now I get the pleasure of being one of your guards."

He jingled the keys in front of the bars again. Then, ever so slowly, he picked a key and watched Seda as he pressed it into the lock. The door creaked as it opened, and he slowly approached her. She pressed her body as far as it could go against the rocks behind her. He bent down to breathe in her hair.

"Mmm, just like I remember. You smell *so fucking good.*" He licked up her cheek, leaving clammy wetness behind, and ran his fingers over the soiled fabric covering her breasts.

Seda cried out and pressed her bloody fist to her mouth. Her arms shook violently, and her lips trembled. Her deepest fears were resurfacing. The metallic taste of blood from her soaked hand covered her lips, and she couldn't stop a strained sob from escaping.

"I'll be back with some food and to give you some... *fun.* I'm really looking forward to this. Maybe I can help you get out of this place. You know, *babies* and all that," Alexi said with a roll of his eyes and stood up, adjusting the bulge in his pants as he looked at her. He gave her a wink and walked over to the hanging woman, pulling out a small knife. He cut the woman down, and her lifeless body fell to the hard ground with a loud thud. He dragged the body out of the cell, locking the doors behind him and leaving a streak of fresh blood behind as he walked. The sound of the woman's body dragged down the hall took away the only source of light she had.

Shrouded in darkness, Seda was left behind, her body tightly curled into itself. She clutched her blood-stained hands to her face and sobbed.

The faint sound of crunching bone echoed through the cell.

SHE WASN'T sure how much time had gone by. She thought she heard a mouse scurrying and listened for it. She began counting quietly as she lay on the hard, sticky floor.

"Five thousand, five hundred, and sixty-three"

"Five thousand, five hundred, and sixty-four"

"Psst..." a whispered voice echoed through the darkness. Seda's head jerked up, and she looked around the dark room. "Are you awake?"

"W-Wh?" Seda hesitantly replied with a raspy voice, forgetting the number she had left off while counting.

"I've been here for..." The voice paused for a few seconds. "Shit, I don't know how long I've been here. I don't remember. I tried counting at first, too."

"You sound..." She thought she recognized the voice, as if it belonged to someone she had spoken to before.

It couldn't be.

"Esper? Is that you?" She jumped onto her knees and quickly shuffled to the bars. Esper. Her old coworker, who was taken to the Camp for misbehavior during a Wyrd over six months ago.

"Seda?" She heard Esper move toward the bars lining her cell, her chains dragging along the floor. "Why are you here?"

"Esper, are you okay?" She firmly held the bars. "There's been unrest in Joro. Our food supply is limited, and the Jotnar have been attacking us more frequently. They held another Wyrd, within six months, due to misbehavior around the city. I was selected."

"It's been six months." Esper paused and then continued, "You must be careful here, Seda. They took..." Esper cried out with a choked sob. "They took Diantha from me. I heard her *screams.*" She struggled to say the last word.

"No... Esper." Hot tears burned behind Seda's eyes. "How's

this even the Camp? I thought we were supposed to be rehabilitated. Where are the doctors? How have you survived this?"

Silence encircled them for a long time. The scurrying mouse squeaked somewhere up the hall.

Seda thought Esper had fallen asleep when a small voice replied so softly she almost didn't hear it, "Because I'm pregnant."

CHAPTER 17

<u>Cahir</u>

The door shook violently as Cahir banged on the wood, the sound rattling against the loose hinges. "Open the *fucking door*, Benny."

He heard shuffling from inside the apartment, and the door quickly swung open. Benny stood in the doorway, his face swollen with bruises and his brown hair a disheveled mess.

"They took her," he said to Cahir and walked back inside, leaving the door open for Cahir to enter. He slumped into a chair, his head sinking into his palms as his leg trembled with nervous energy. "I barely made it out. I had to fight my way through Orience to get back here."

"I need to know what you know, Benny." Cahir held up the red piece of paper. He walked to the window and opened it, letting the warm air and sunlight fill the space.

Benny looked at the paper, and his face paled. "I knew when you saw the tattoo that you would put two and two together eventually."

The Corvids flew into the room, blowing over items on a

table, and Benny jumped up. "Those things were attacking the Rozzers! Why did you just let them in?"

Roya, Ferona, and Feich shifted forms, and Benny fell back into his chair as it skidded across the floor. "What the flying-fuck!"

"*What do you know, Benny?*" Cahir repeated in a dangerous tone. He had no time for introductions. He would cut this information out of this man if he had to.

Roya stepped forward, her lengthy hair swaying in the wind, and circled Benny.

Benny looked over to her and hesitated. "Friend or foe?" He looked to Cahir for reassurance.

"Friend, now *answer*."

Benny paused and sighed as his eyes shifted nervously to the Corvids. "I always knew there was more to you than you let on." He looked down at the healing tattoo on his wrist, its dragon shape a direct replica of the dragon drawn onto the paper.

He inhaled deeply and began, "My father's the founder of The Rising. We've been organized for years. A long time ago, he spoke with what he called an *oracle*. She told him that The Darkened, what he thinks is a flying dragon, would save us from our own. That there would come a time when our food would appear to run low, and chaos would ensue. We needed to stay vigilant and help The Darkened return to save us; otherwise, all could be lost. The Rising has been looking for clues for years."

Jason was always an exemplary figure in Joro. This news was... Interesting. Cahir tried to think back to any clues he had missed in his time knowing Jason that might have led him to believe Jason could be behind any of this, but nothing came to mind. Jason was a model citizen, teaching his children to study hard and obey the laws to avoid any issues within their family.

"What does that mean, *human*?" Roya seethed, annoyed at the mystery. For someone who always scrambled pieces of an already confusing puzzle, she was the worst when the information wasn't readily available to her.

"We don't know exactly. Dad... I mean, Jason... He... He snuck into the library to find more information, but couldn't understand what it meant. Said the library was full of useless data. When he went back looking for the oracle, he could not find her."

"How long have you been a part of this?" Cahir asked.

"I only found out about this within the last year. When Jason was taken to the Camp, The Rising placed me in charge of continuing the search. We meet on Tuesdays and Thursdays after curfew."

"How do you get around at night?" Roya asked as she got closer to Benny. She hovered over him and hissed in his face, "And where do you meet?"

"Whoa. Whoa. *Feisty*. We sneak out. We know the Rozzer's routes through Orience. And we meet in the woods past the Gardvord." Benny pressed his body firmly against the backrest of the chair, away from Roya as much as possible, but Cahir noticed how his eyes glittered in delight at her.

"So you meet tonight," Cahir stated, then looked at the three Corvids. "We'll also go. Have any of The Rising ever been to the Camp?"

"Not inside, but a couple have escaped the dome and traveled down to investigate when Dad was taken. I remained here for Seda and Mom."

"Where's Sara?" Cahir asked, looking around the room. "Did she make it out okay?"

"She's in bed. She hasn't left the house since we got home. First Dad, now Seda." He looked toward the wall and away from everyone in the room. "She's been struggling mentally since he left. Now I fear she might not fully recover."

"These people of yours who went down to the Camp, have you heard from them yet? Do they know a way in?"

"A way in? No… and I expect that after yesterday's events, a way out of Joro is even harder now."

"We need to find and protect Seda before something bad happens to her," Feich spoke for the first time.

"We'll meet you at your location tonight," Ferona chimed in. Roya and Feich nodded their heads in unison.

"I'm staying here until it's time to go," Cahir told the three. "Roya, can I ask you guys to please scout out the area? But be careful. They're on high alert after the Corvids attacked in force yesterday."

The three nodded as they shifted forms and flew out of the open window.

"What the hell are those? Do all of the black birds do that?" Benny asked.

WHEN THE CURFEW'S alarm across the city ended, Benny and Cahir dressed in dark clothing and quietly made their way out of the window, descending toward the road below. They snuck alongside walls and crept low through the fields. Cahir followed Benny. They did not run into any Rozzers as they made their way into the thickness of trees past the Gardvord.

Three men surrounded a small fire as they approached. As soon as they spotted Benny, they stood up and placed their hands over their hearts, revealing dragon tattoos on their wrists that matched Benny's.

"Rising, please meet Cahir. He's Seda's friend. As you know, my sister was taken yesterday, and we want everyone's help to try and get both her and Jason back," Benny said as he entered the circle.

The Corvids flew down from a nearby branch into the circle of men, looking at Benny for approval before shifting.

"And don't be alarmed, but Cahir brought friends." He pointed down to the birds, and the men looked over at them.

"These things went crazy yesterday," said a man in his twenties with blond hair, wearing a Rozzer uniform. "They were cutting Rozzers up left and right, and right now I'm dressed as one. Do they understand us?"

The Corvids shifted forms, and the men jumped back, each reaching for a hidden weapon within their clothing.

"It's okay," offered Benny, holding his hands up and jumping between the men and the Corvids, calming the situation. "They're friends and want to help."

The men all looked at each other.

"How do we know we can trust them?" asked the Rozzer.

"We can trust Cahir, and he trusts them." Benny stepped forward and beckoned Cahir into the circle. "Please meet Askold." He pointed to the uniformed Rozzer and shook his hand. "As you can see, this is how we get inside information. And this is Ruel." He pointed to a tall man in his mid-thirties with broad shoulders. "Ruel's one of three Traversers in The Rising. He knows a lot about what it's like outside the dome. The other two are out there now." Ruel nodded toward Cahir and the three Corvids. "And lastly, this massive fucker is Ojore. Ojore's a butcher and a longtime friend of my father's."

Ojore towered over Cahir in his human form, was built like a house, and had rich, chocolate-colored skin. He reached out to shake Cahir's hand and grasped it firmly instead, pulling him close and looking into his eyes. "You better not fuck this up, *Cahir*. We don't just trust *anyone*."

"Ahem." Roya cleared her throat and walked around the men. "Since you're all introducing yourselves so *politely*, I'm Roya, and this is my murder." She pointed to her siblings before continuing, "My sister Ferona and my brother Feich. Our only goal here is to find and protect Seda. We have the gift of the sky, so whatever you need us to do to help with this, let us know."

The men nodded, and Ojore released Cahir's hand, leaving a cramp behind. Cahir flexed his fingers.

This fucker…

"Leaving Joro is going to be even harder than it was before," said Askold as he sat back down near the fire. "They have increased the guard at the exits."

"There was a crack in the wall," Cahir suggested.

"Not anymore, at least it's not unprotected anymore. There was some sort of fight there recently, and the Rozzers have it blocked. It's now fully guarded."

Cahir and Roya exchanged a glance. Their fight to save Jason might have blocked their only escape. "We need to get out of here. Seda could be hurt right now," Cahir said as anxiety coursed through his body again.

"There's a way out, but no one's going to like it," Ruel suggested as he looked at everyone. "The Murkway. The pipes lead out under the city. No one watches it."

Askold groaned loudly. "No one watches it because no one's stupid enough to go through there. You can't be serious."

"What's the schedule like down there? And can we get a layout?" Benny asked Askold, ignoring his complaints.

He groaned again before replying, "I'll find out."

Ojore sat across from Cahir, watching him intently. "Why do you look so familiar?"

Cahir's eyes remained locked onto Ojore's, not breaking contact once. "No idea."

"Does anyone know how she and the others just disappeared yesterday?" Askold asked. "I've never seen anything like that before."

"Magic, you idiot," Ojore answered, breaking the staring competition with Cahir. "Someone has some fucking magic. This place is so fucked. The oracle was right. We need to get moving and find what we need. But first, let's get Jason and Seda out of that fucking place."

"I say we just go down to the Murkway now and try to get out," Ruel said.

Cahir agreed. He liked Ruel already.

"With no plan?" Benny interjected. "No. We cannot risk getting caught, or no one will be able to save them. We need a plan, a map, and a schedule to navigate our way out so we can reach them safely. Instead of Thursday, let's meet back here tomorrow night. Roya, can you guys get a message to our other two outside the dome?"

Roya stood, her siblings following. "Tell us their names and their appearance. We'll meet you south of the Murkway pipes tomorrow night."

Benny nodded and shared the information with them. Roya, Ferona, and Feich took off through the dark sky, through the glittering dome, and began their search.

"Roya's *stunning*," Benny admitted as he sat back down and ran his hands over his neck.

"She's dangerous and wild," Cahir warned.

The men discussed their next steps into the late hours of the night, until the next shift of Rozzers were due to swap, and then they put out the fire and carefully made their way back home.

The plan will work, Cahir thought. *There's no other option.*

CHAPTER 18

<u>Seda</u>

Silence. Too much silence.

Esper did not respond to Seda when she called out, and no one else appeared to be in the hall with them. Her cell grew colder as the hours went by. She paced back and forth, trying to warm up by rubbing her arms. She walked along the edges, feeling for the grooves in the walls and the bed's placement to find safe spots to step. Ten steps lengthwise. Nine steps across.

She still felt sick from seeing the woman's body and having her blood crusted on her skin. It was hard to avoid the slippery puddle on the ground, but she now knew it was exactly four steps to her right. Seda accidentally walked into the empty bucket and knocked it over; the sound echoed sharply off the walls.

A low, menacing growl echoed out, and Seda's body went rigid. She couldn't see anything, and *something* was with her in this area. Her throat constricted, and she swallowed hard.

Heavy footsteps and the sound of a dragging chain grew

louder, drawing closer. She backed up to the wall, hitting her head again on the stone that jutted out a bit too far. Seda watched in fear, her eyes fixed on the darkness toward the sound.

She gasped and looked up as massive, glowing red eyes appeared, their slitted pupils like a cat's. The eyes were as big as her head. The creature sniffed the air, and heat radiated around Seda's body. She remained frozen as she stared back into them, their glow casting a gentle light in her cell.

It must be an animal, but all the animals in Joro were small —usually cats, dogs, or birds. No, this thing was too big to be just an animal.

It's a monster.

The creature remained deathly still, watching her every movement, every rise and fall of her chest.

"P-Please don't hurt me," she rasped, her voice catching.

The creature squinted its eyes at her, and the room grew darker. A deep voice echoed inside her mind, "Humans are tasty. But you…" It sniffed the air again. "You're *different*. Who are you?" Its deep, hoarse voice rumbled across the ground. Like a furnace spewing hot gas, the voice was heavy and warm, filling her cell with heat.

"I-I'm Seda," she hesitantly offered back.

The creature tilted its head. "Seda," it repeated, as if it were tasting her name in the air.

"W-Why do you have chains?" she asked, attempting to direct the conversation away from herself.

"Because, just like you.. *Seda The Spoken*. I'm a prisoner here. They feed me well, though." The creature chuckled deeply.

"Why don't you fight your way out? Why do they have a monster here as a prisoner?"

The creature huffed and blew heat around her face, blowing her hair off her shoulders. "I'm not one of the *monsters*. I only eat to survive. I once was a protector, a guardian, but that was a very long time ago. I have failed my kin, and I cannot hurt those in uniform, for they hurt me in return. It's now my responsibility to oversee this section of the dungeon—to ensure no one escapes or enters without permission. It's been this way for longer than I can remember."

"W-What goes on here?"

"Some call it a prison, others call it a camp or dungeon. You can call it whatever you like, but the results are the same. Humans come here to be bred or eaten. I'm here because..." He paused and closed his eyes, casting a dark shadow over the room. "I'm here because I don't owe fealty to the stone."

"Stone?" Seda asked.

"Interesting," it huffed. "The *dark stone*. The stone that controls. The stone that wields power. The Monster King stole the stone, and he uses it for his own gain."

"What's your name?" she asked, bravely taking a shaky step away from the wall. It hadn't tried to attack her; maybe it was safe?

The creature watched her approach slowly, its eyes tracking her movements with catlike precision, its pupils dilating.

"I'm named Elco," it said quickly, snapping its giant, sharp teeth against the bars. Seda fell back, landing hard on the rough floor.

"Do not come near me, *human*, for I will eat you and gnaw upon your bones. I'll slurp on your organs with pleasure. I can pull your body out of this cell if I wanted to." It reached a sharp, claw-tipped finger the size of Seda's forearm through her cell bars and scratched the sharpened tip against her foot, causing a line of blood to pool. She pulled it back quickly and scrambled back to the wall.

Elco turned around and slowly sauntered away, taking the soft, crimson light from his eyes with him.

Seda collapsed and started hyperventilating. She curled into another ball, gasping for air and struggling to breathe as her chest heaved violently with each breath.

Hopeless.

Alone.

Benny.

Cahir.

Oh, Cahir… I need you.

"Seda," whispered Esper. "Why were you talking to that creature?"

Seda lifted her head and looked toward Esper's voice. She wiped her tears away and slowly knelt, trying to steady her breathing. "Because it talked to me. Oh, Esper… What're we going to do? We need to find a way out."

"There's no way out, Seda. I've tried. They only come in to throw food at us… Or to… to… *hurt* us. The only time anyone leaves is to be eaten."

Seda curled up, knees to her chest, and rocked back and forth. There had to be a way out. Someone needed to find this stone that Elco said. Lord Mordred had it. How else could he have tricked everyone into believing that the Camp was a place of redemption? Someone needed to steal the stone and put an end to this madness.

"Did you say it spoke to you?" Esper asked.

"Yes," she hiccuped.

"That creature doesn't speak to us, Seda. It only eats and watches. It's a monstrosity."

Silence settled around them once more. She felt the sharp pain in her foot from the scrape he caused. Would she get an infection? How was she going to get out of here? And Esper was pregnant. Whose child was it? What happens to the children born here? There were rarely orphans in Joro. Where was her father?

They promised everyone that the Camp was a place to redeem yourselves, to prove that you loved Joro and could contribute to its survival. That medical doctors would help ensure a pregnancy was achieved. But that was a lie. This place was horrifying, filthy, and oppressive. She contributed to this by conforming to the expectations of being a perfect citizen who performed well and never did anything wrong.

How wrong she was about it all. Lord Mordred had to know that this was the Camp. He was meant to protect them. Everyone looked up to him and prayed, but he failed to intervene.

How did he know her?

The questions kept pounding into her until sleep's stillness swept her away as she lay on the cold, blood-crusted floor.

Her dreams were filled with a sea of black scales, the smell of sandalwood, and the same voice reminding her that she wasn't alone... that she never had been.

CHAPTER 19

<u>Roya</u>

The murder sped through the night with clear instructions to find Seren and Kalon, the last two Rising members. They had flown through the magical dome that was now far behind them, heading south toward the Camp. They kept their eyes peeled for any signs of campfires or movement hidden among the trees. To the west, the Jotnar thundered through, grabbing large rocks and hurling them to shatter into many pieces, searching for precious crystals within. They had several campsites set up around the giant willows, where some sat and cooked animals or humans over the flames. Their heavy footsteps echoed through the night sky.

The murder flew swiftly, carried farther south by the wind past the Willow Grove, where the dome was no longer visible, and the warm desert air began to seep through their feathers. The Camp gradually came into view, with its massive stone walls rising high into the sky, topped with metal blades to prevent escape. Rozzers and Dragors patrolled around the walls and watched the exits. The three birds swooped down and landed on a palm tree to observe.

"Why are we helping these people? Let's go in and get her out ourselves," Feich said to his sisters.

"We can't do this alone, and Seda has to travel north. She'll need more protection than just us for that journey," Roya replied.

The desert was dry and sandy, with dunes rising tall and proud to the east. Beyond the dunes, to the northeast, the massive oak trees of the Heath Forest were barely visible.

"Let's head that way and look for them," Roya said. "We didn't spot them through the Willow Grove. It's also unlikely they're in the willows with the Jotnar, anyway. We should check the Heath Forest."

The three took off into the air and flew past the dunes, the bright moonlight casting their raven shadows on the ground.

As they approached the Heath Forest, they saw several small plumes of smoke rising from within. Roya led the way into the trees, passing ghostly creatures who looked up at them with hostility, transforming into replicas of Seda and hissing toward the sky.

Stupid creatures. Their magic would never lure her.

They landed in a tree near the first smokestack and looked down. The campsite was empty. They took off again and headed toward the second plume of smoke.

Camping below were two men.

"That's got to be Seren," Ferona said, eyeing a tall, slender middle-aged brunette man setting up traps around their campsite, his wrist bearing the same matching tattoo as the other Rising members. "And that looks like how Benny described Kalon." She nodded toward a large man in his late thirties, with a hulking frame and long, dark hair tied back in a braid with a leather tie. Both men were armed with swords.

Kalon looked up at the dark trees where the three Corvids hid, his bright eyes studying the area.

"Let's make ourselves known. Kalon senses us already," Roya said as she took off from the branch, diving deep into the oak forest. Feich and Ferona followed. Roya cawed loudly and swooped into the middle of the men's camp, immediately shifting into her human form.

Kalon and Seren quickly lunged at her with their swords, trying to slice through her. Roya laughed as she danced out of the way, twirling like a wind goddess as she avoided their strikes. Her long hair twirled through the air, flowing like water.

Ferona and Feich landed nearby, shifted into humans, and watched the two men pursue their sister, chuckling.

"You'll not catch her like that, boys," Ferona called out as she played with her long, blue claws.

The men stopped and stared at them, seeing them for the first time.

"What the fuck do you want?" Kalon shouted as he held his sword up, ready for a strike at any moment.

"We're apparently *friends,*" Feich said with a roll of his eyes. "Benny sent us to find you."

"What the hell are you?" Seren asked, his sword held high, distrustful of their words.

"We're Corvids, and we have a message for you and a plan. The Rising needs your help. More has happened in the last couple of days, and they need to escape Joro to find Benny's sister, Seda," Roya answered as she gracefully walked around the men.

"Why're you walking around us like we're food, then?" snarled Seren.

"It's in my nature," Roya said with a small smile and a shrug. "But alas, we're not here to harm you two. The Camp now has Seda, and we must get her out. Benny's requested our help to find you two and bring you back to the south end of the Murkway so they can meet you there."

"When?" asked Kalon. "We're on our way to the Camp now."

"Tomorrow night," Roya answered. "We'll meet Benny and the others. We saw some Hailecs in these woods as we looked for you."

"Crap. We thought we lured them away for the night with some traps and false fires, but there must be more out there," Seren replied.

"We leave now," Roya commanded.

The men packed up their belongings, threw large logs onto the fire, creating a visible plume of smoke for any monsters who might be interested, and headed northwest through the oaks.

The screeching sounds of distant monsters traveled through the cool night air.

CHAPTER 20

<u>Seda</u>

Seda woke up to the sound of Esper screaming. She jumped up and hurried the nine steps she knew to the bars, grasping onto them as she called out, "Esper! Are you okay? Esper!"

Esper's painful moans calmed, but she continued to breathe heavily. "I think something's happening to me. My baby."

It couldn't be true. Esper was taken during the previous Wyrd. She had only been gone a little over six months. How quickly had she become pregnant after being chosen? If this baby were coming, it would be premature. If this baby were coming now, there was something wrong with her friend and the baby.

Esper groaned loudly in pain again. "My baby. My baby. They can't have you. They cannot take you from me."

"Help! Someone, please help!" Seda yelled down the hall, trying to get anyone's attention for medical aid. An orange, flashing light silently flickered on and off in the corridor.

Thundering, heavy footsteps approached her, and she saw Elco's glowing eyes coming closer. She stepped back from the bars, careful not to hit the wall, as the warmth of his breath surrounded her. He peered into Esper's cell, then turned to look at Seda.

"There's no one to help. The women do this alone," Elco said to her as he lay down in front of her bars and looked toward Esper's cell with a huff. She could see a hint of large, spiked scales running down his back from the glow within the room.

"W-What?" Seda asked, as concern and fear spread through her like spiders crawling up her legs. They impregnate women and leave them to give birth alone? If the women die, do they feed them to the monsters?

"Where do the babies go? Where are the men who come to the Camp?" she asked Elco, her voice trembling with the sudden fear that her father was no longer here.

"The men don't last long. They're always food. The women are kept in these cells to produce children, and the cycle continues. I don't know where the children go. I don't think they go to Joro or the monsters."

Seda gasped, her breath coming in shallow, painful gasps. Her father was gone. "But... But... Sometimes people go back to Joro after being here."

Maybe her father was taken back to Joro since he was so important?

Elco waited to respond and calmly said, "That's just for hope, Seda the Spoken. When you plant a little hope in people, you encourage conformity and make it easier to manipulate de masses." He turned to look at her again, and the crimson glow illuminated her cell. "They only send back the most broken."

Seda walked to the bed and sank onto it, her legs feeling heavy as if made of lead. The bed's springs squeaked loudly under her weight. She felt defeated, alone, and scared. She heard the agonizing cries coming from Esper and felt her heart sink to her stomach.

There was nothing she could do to help. She was chained inside a cell, guarded by a massive creature, in a prison built to farm humans. How had Mordred gotten away with this?

Her heart sank even lower as she thought about how her brother and mom would react to the news. She couldn't imagine the horrors her father must have seen before he died, or the pain he must have endured. Then she thought about Cahir—his handsome smile and tender eyes. How he was always so gentle around her, never overstepping, always willing to help in any way he could, but most of all, how he made her laugh and helped her face her fears. Cahir was her home.

She wanted to go home. She wanted Cahir.

She thought about the pain and anger in his eyes as he tore Michael apart, feeling satisfied to see Michael suffer. He made her endure agony all those years ago.

He got what he deserved, she thought.

An eye for an eye. A heart for a heart. He hurt her, and he got to suffer from the trauma he inflicted on her, causing her to live in fear because of his and Alexi's violations.

Alexi. She would not let him touch her. She would not cower in fear when he returned for her. She would never go willingly for him. She would fight, in honor of Cahir, who showed her what it means to stand up for someone you care for, to stand up for yourself.

Esper let out a loud cry, and Seda stood up, rushing toward the bars without hesitation. Elco opened his eyes at her and growled, but made no move to stop her.

"Esper! You got this. I'm right here. I'm with you. You're not alone," Seda encouraged.

"Not alone," Elco repeated, softly humming the words. He looked at Seda and closed his eyes. "Finally... *not alone.*"

The sounds of Esper's pain continued through the night. The

orange, flashing light kept reminding them that something was happening. No one checked on them; no one brought food or water, or even came to bother them.

They were alone, yet not completely; they had each other within these dark walls.

CHAPTER 21

<u>Seda</u>

Warmth radiated against the walls as Elco stayed close to Seda's cell. Esper's screams echoed through the night, and Seda stayed awake, listening intently and offering support to her friend. No one got any rest, not even Elco.

"I've heard this happen thousands of times. Her child will be here soon," Elco told Seda as he studied her.

Seda nervously chewed her nails but stopped when she tasted the dried blood on them. She felt weak from lack of sleep, and dehydration was draining her strength. She stood and slowly moved closer to the bars again, with Elco watching her curiously as she drew nearer.

"Where do you come from?" he asked her, sniffing the air around her again.

Esper's cries faded, and Seda looked at Elco's shadowed form curiously.

"I'm from Joro, Elco," she responded.

Obviously.

"Were you born within Joro?"

"Yes, I was. My parents found me when I was a few years old, wandering the streets in Orience. They tried to find my family, but couldn't locate anyone searching for a daughter who matched my description. I was raised in Joro, Elco. I was found when I was small. I'm from Joro. Maybe I was born *here*." She held her arms in the air, pointing all around her as she considered the idea. It was possible.

Elco watched her in silence.

What a strange creature. Elco threatens, and then he wants to chat?

"Are there any other human cities?" she asked.

"Not that I'm aware of. When the dome was created a thousand years ago, all of the humans were inside," he responded.

"Then I'm from Joro," she stated, crossing her arms over her chest.

Esper cried out again, her labored breathing echoing down the hall. Seda uncrossed her arms and ran to the bars.

"The baby's coming!" Esper yelled through clenched teeth. She screamed into the dark room once more, then silence fell around them.

"Esper?" Seda called out, holding onto the bars firmly. "Esper? Are you okay? Is the baby okay?"

Seda heard the sound of scrambling and patting. "Please... Please... Please..." Esper begged into the darkness, pleading with anyone who would listen.

Seda felt as if her heart had frozen, and she held her breath, praying with her friend for her baby to take its first breath. Minutes passed as they listened to Esper plead for her baby to breathe.

"The child didn't survive," Elco said dimly as he let out a low sound from the back of his throat.

Seda fell onto the hard ground and dry heaved.

Esper's heart-wrenching cries echoed through the room, and Seda's eyes welled up as she sobbed for her fearless friend.

Her friend, who couldn't bear to leave her beloved and had bravely stood up to injustice by joining her at the Wyrd, a friend who suffered assault, a friend who just went through pregnancy and birth alone, and a friend who just lost her only baby in her arms.

My courageous friend.

The flashing orange light stopped.

A sob tore out of Seda, and she cried into her hands, no longer caring for the mess on her palms. How could a world be so cruel, so unjust, so inhumane?

The door opened, flooding the area with bright torchlight and the voices of men. Seda moved back from the bars and pressed against the wall. Elco growled protectively as he stepped in front of her cell. The light illuminated Elco, and she saw him clearly for the first time.

Seda gasped.

Elco was massive, with a back covered in ruby-red, scaled skin and four powerful, black-furred legs with red cuffs tied to chains around his front paws. His long, spiked tail curled around his body, and his black, leathery wings neatly folded against his sides. His mouth had long, jagged teeth, and his head was that of a large cat, with a long, black mane.

Elco was breathtaking.

"She finished giving birth," a Rozzer said as he approached and shone his torch into Esper's cell, drawing Seda's attention back to the men.

"What the fuck is this? It's dead!" Alexi yelled at Esper. "Did you kill it, you stupid cunt?"

"My baby... My baby," Esper whimpered as the creaking of her metal bed rocked back and forth.

Alexi and the other Rozzer hurried to open Esper's cell door and rushed inside. Seda heard the sounds of violence and stood up, running to the bars.

"Stop hurting her! Please!" she begged, her voice cracking. She shook the bars, her chains clattering with every move, desperate to escape and help her friend.

The sound of each punch caused Seda to grip the bars tighter until her knuckles turned white and her hand cramped with tension.

Esper was not resisting. Why was she not resisting?

"My baby," she heard Esper say weakly when the sounds ceased.

The Rozzers dragged Esper out of her cell. Blood stained her clothes from childbirth, and her face was swelling from their violence. She held a very small baby tightly in her arms, pressed against her chest, with the umbilical cord still attached.

Seda gasped and withdrew her hands, her fingers still curled into the shape of the bars, unable to relax her stiff joints.

Esper tenderly kissed the baby's forehead as they pulled her away. But she looked up at Seda, their eyes meeting. Seda felt her stomach drop.

For the first time in months, she saw her friend—beaten, broken, dirty, and severely malnourished.

The sound of the metal door closing blocked out all remaining light. The room was once again bathed in a low, crimson glow from Elco.

Seda's shock and fear were replaced with fury that seeped into the depths of her soul, and a familiar vibration echoed within her chest.

How dare they hurt her friend! How dare they put their hands on a grieving mother! How dare they deprive her of enough food during her pregnancy, force her to carry this child, and make her endure these conditions! How dare they hurt innocent people!

She began breathing heavily through her nose, and her chest rose with each furious breath.

Elco looked at her, and his eyes widened. He slowly backed away from her cell.

"Moon-flutter…" he whispered as he faded into blackness.

She would stand up for her friend, shielding herself and others from the darkness that consumed them, and do everything in her power to avenge those who had hurt them.

As her anger intensified, devouring her submissive obedience like a monster itself, she promised herself that the feeble Seda from before was gone, replaced only by a relentless, wrath-filled drumbeat.

The useless Seda of the past was dead.

CHAPTER 22

Seda

(Some time later)

"I'm baaccckkkk," Alexi called in a sing-song voice to Seda as he twirled the keys around his finger. "Sorry that took me so long. I know you must be thirsty and hungry. And as much as I'd love to spend some special time with you, *you* have an important date ahead and must clean up."

Seda remained sitting on her filthy bed, staring at the opposite wall. She did not give Alexi the attention he so desperately wanted. Let him come in. Alexi clicked the lock open and walked to her, bending down in her face, his red hair falling over his brow.

He stuck his nose onto her throat, right below her ear, and breathed her in. "Fuck, how do you smell this good after being here and covered in his disgusting filth?" He reached down into his pants and grabbed himself, groaning. "I wish I had more time, darling, but Lord Mordred wishes to see you." He removed his hand from his pants and gave her left breast a tender squeeze.

Seda did not shirk away from him and instead remained staring blankly at the wall. The events from earlier replayed vividly across her mind.

"Do you hear me, you fucking weirdo? Lord Mordred's here and wants to see you. Get up. *Now*."

Seda shifted her focus to him, and he gasped, stepping back. "What the *fuck* happened to your eyes? They're glowing!"

She had no idea what he was talking about, but she didn't give two fucks what he thought he saw. She glanced back at the wall and slowly got to her feet, holding out her wrists for Alexi to unlock the chains.

"Do you no longer talk? I asked you what happened to your eyes."

When she didn't answer, he slapped her across the face. Her head jerked to the side, and she gradually turned her eyes back to him, holding out her wrists once more.

"Whatever. I have to get you to Mordred. He can handle your insubordination." He inserted a key into the lock on her wrists, and the chains clanged off. She barely registered the relief on her bloodstained wrists from the removal of the tight cuffs. She followed him out of the cell and past Elco, who was asleep at the end of the long, vast hall. She looked at him as he opened one eye slightly and watched her pass.

Alexi opened the metal door, and the hot, fresh air under the blazing sun assaulted her skin. She squinted and looked at the scene ahead. The central courtyard was large, its sandy floor strewn with pebbles. What caught her attention was not only the number of Rozzers hanging around or the many malnourished people sitting in small circles, but also the serpent-like monsters dressed in the same Rozzer uniforms patrolling alongside them. Of-fucking-course there were monsters here.

They had blue scales and walked upright like humans. Their teeth were sharp, and they carried a variety of weapons. She narrowed her eyes when she saw one of the monsters whip a screaming man tied to a post at the end of the courtyard.

She did not look away.

The courtyard was lined with rows of metal doors, much the same as her own, and at the far end of the yard was a large metal door with a golden handle.

She let out a quiet sigh of relief upon seeing that no children were nearby.

"This way," Alexi said as he roughly pulled her arm to follow him.

He led her to a small door and opened it. A large, shared-style bathroom, with a row of empty showers along the right wall, filled the room. He entered with her, grabbed a torn towel, a worn dress, and a small pair of shorts, like underwear, from a nearby shelf, threw them at her, and ordered, "Shower."

He roughly closed the door behind them, remaining inside.

She walked to the nearest faucet and turned it on. Lukewarm water gushed from squeaky pipes. Alexi stood back and watched her with a wicked grin. She looked at him, refusing to break eye contact as she undressed. His eyes traced along her body when she was bare, and she saw him harden in his pants.

Disgust surged through her, making her stomach churn.

She stepped into the lukewarm water, pumped soap into her hands from the dispenser, and lathered herself. She washed everywhere as Alexi watched.

Let him watch. Let him see what he can never have again. The dried blood washed off Seda's body, revealing her flushed skin underneath.

He unzipped his pants, pulled out his skinny cock, and groaned as he stroked himself. He stepped toward her, staring intently at her breasts, when the door shot open. A Rozzer walked in and looked at both of them, saying, "He's waiting." The Rozzer quickly left without another glance toward Seda.

Alexi stepped back and grumbled, "Hurry up. At least those fucking eyes went back to normal." He zipped himself back up.

Seda turned off the water, dried herself off, then pulled the scratchy dress over her head and put on her underwear. She walked barefoot to the door. Alexi opened it, and he pushed her from behind, directing her where to go as his fingers trailed over her body.

They approached another door and stopped.

Alexi knocked firmly on the door, which looked just like all the others, and then opened it. "She's here, Lord Mordred." He pushed her inside roughly and closed the door, leaving her alone with the lord for the first time.

Seda cautiously stepped into the luxurious room, where rich leather and dark wood created a warm atmosphere. Mordred stood in the corner reading a book, then turned to look at her.

Her heartbeat pounded quickly in her chest, yet she compelled herself to remain upright and kept her gaze steady.

His eyes studied her, and the scars on his face deepened.

"I'm sure you have questions," he said as he placed the book down on a nearby table. "I unfortunately cannot answer all of them."

She narrowed her eyes at him. Oh, she had fucking questions, alright.

"I can't tell you why you were chosen, as it would disrupt plans already in motion, but..." he picked up a crystal glass filled with golden whiskey and took a deep drink, exhaling loudly when he finished. "You will not be harmed while you're here."

What? Had she not already been smacked and subjected to horrors no one should ever witness in their lives? What about the others? What about Esper? What did he want? *Why was she special?*

"Why do you not actually protect our people, Mordred?" She took a step forward and casually strolled around, searching for anything that looked like the dark stone Elco told her about, and running her fingers along the bookshelves.

"What are you looking for?" He asked, ignoring her question, and gently setting his glass on the side table. He stepped closer toward her and paused at his desk. She regarded his mangled ears and grimaced at the deformity. She now saw who he really was, and she hated this man, who was ugly both inside and out.

How could she ever have prayed to him before and looked upon his image with love?

"Are you looking for a dark stone, Seda Arbor?" he asked with an excited grin.

Her stomach lurched. Was she really that obvious?

She calmed her emotions and stared into his eyes, noticing for the first time the color. Not crimson like she saw the other day at the Wyrd, but a soft amber.

He noted how she didn't answer and hummed thoughtfully. "The stone you seek is powerful and used to control. The stone is more than that, though. The dark stone once belonged to the Mother Goddess. Her power's within, as well as in others. Her power was acquired when she *betrayed humanity*." His eyes burned crimson again, and he shook his head, his eyes changing back to amber.

"Why do you hurt the people of Joro and feed them to these monsters? The people you're supposed to protect?!"

Gone was her trepidation over talking with him, replaced with surging anger that radiated through her bones. She felt her chest vibrate.

His eyes flared crimson again as he stared at her menacingly, the scars on his face crinkling. "Humanity's nothing but food, Seda. Humans must be farmed to ensure the monsters survive. Humanity became too confident a thousand years ago, thanks to the help of the gods. Humans and gods alike almost killed off the monsters, *and they almost won*, but when things got too difficult, the gods fled! Life requires balance, yet the gods left us with an unbalanced world. We had to make peace with the monsters. And so the dome was born. The dome, which protected humanity from being slaughtered all at once, continued the cycle of life."

Seda regarded him and his words. If the humans and gods almost won, why would the gods leave?

"Why did you ask to see me?" She was standing still, watching his every move, every flick of his eyebrows, the way his eyes would flash brighter and then dim.

"Because *Seda Arbor,* you have something I want," he grinned at her with his sparse teeth.

"What could I possibly give to *you?*" she sneered, feeling her hatred slip free.

He didn't answer for a long time. He walked around his desk and approached her, brushing his fingers through her hair and gazing down at her softly with his amber eyes.

She fought her flinch.

"Redemption," he whispered as his eyes seared into hers, not saying anything further.

She raised her brow. "Wh— The door flung open, and a serpent creature strode in.

"There's a fight in the courtyard, sir." Mordred looked toward the serpent and back to Seda.

"Take her back," he strode through the door with his long legs and black robe trailing behind him.

"Wait! My friend was taken. She had a stillborn baby yester-day. Is she alive? Where's my father?"

Mordred turned around and looked at her without emotion. "He's dead." He left the room, and her heart sank into the pits of her stomach. Her eyes burned as tears began to form. She was losing her strength. She promised herself she would be strong, but the way he said that... so uncaring. So *evil.*

She followed the serpent creature back toward the door to

her hall. When he opened the door, she pushed through her emotions and bravely commanded, "I want the lights on in here, and I want food and water. I also do *NOT* want to be chained to that wall."

The serpent looked back at her and stuck his tongue out in the air, smelling Seda. "Who do you think you are to talk to me like this?" he replied in a slithering voice, his eyes narrowing on her.

Elco approached from behind, towering over them. He snapped his teeth at them and growled. The serpent turned and fell back toward the door, shrinking away. Seda stood tall and confident as Elco loomed over both of them.

The serpent clicked on a switch that lit lamps down the long hallway. Then he led Seda back to her cell and opened it for her. He locked the bars behind him and left, quickly returning with a fresh bucket of water and a plate of food. He opened the door and set both the pail and the food down, quickly locking the door again. When he left the hall, the lights remained on, and he closed the metal door roughly.

Seda sat on her bed with a plate of food in front of her. She grabbed the piece of bread, which reminded her of her mother, and tears pooled in her eyes as she chewed through the crunchy crust.

Esper was gone. Her father was gone. She was alone in this horrible place. She might never see her family or Cahir again, but she was proud of herself today, and she held onto that small flicker of hope that burned in her chest.

Mordred wanted something from her. She didn't know what yet. She would find out one way or another. Today, she did not cower with Alexi as she usually would have. She spoke to Mordred, not stuttering once, and she advocated for herself with the serpent creature.

If she could do that, *she could do more.*

CHAPTER 23

<u>Cahir</u>

Cahir went to work to maintain appearances, but the office felt different without Seda there. He fucking hated this place, hated pretending as if he cared. Those days were fucking over.

He struggled to finish any work but managed just enough to avoid drawing attention. Most of the day, he found himself staring at her chair. Finally, when he couldn't take it anymore, he moved his things from his desk to hers and sat there, touching her belongings and missing her.

He prayed to the Mother Goddess that this plan was the right choice. He would find a way to get her out of this terrible place, but his time was running out, and she would need others around her if it happened.

If anyone hurt her there…

His eyes locked on a moldy mandarin on the floor. Was it the same one she'd thrown at him the day of the Wyrd? He walked over and bent down to pick it up. As he held it in his hand, he thought about her. She hated him dozing off at work, hated how he always bent the rules, but look what happens when you follow them to the best of your abilities, and something is out of your control. Anger surged through his chest. He shouldn't have been noble; he should've just given her the samples instead of always spitting in the fucking containers.

This was his fault.

He squeezed the mandarin.

AFTER THE CURFEW ALARMS RANG, Cahir and Benny snuck into the grove of trees past the Gardvord again, wearing dark clothing. They met Askold, Ruel, and Ojore, who were waiting for them to arrive and had a pile of short swords with scabbards lying at their feet. The three men stood up and placed their hands on their chests in a gesture of respect for Benny.

Ojore looked over to Cahir and scowled at him. Cahir ignored the insolence of the man and walked into the circle.

"Askold, did you get a map of the Murkway and the schedule of Rozzers down in the Barrio?" Benny asked as he shook the men's hands.

"Yes. We're good to go," Askold answered, who was no longer wearing the Rozzer uniform and was now dressed in dark clothing, matching everyone else. On the dry ground around him were extra swords with holsters. "The shift change happens at midnight, like here. And here's the map." He reached into his pocket, unfolded a folded piece of paper, and handed it to Benny.

Benny opened it and examined it. "This is going to get real shitty, guys."

"Soooooo funny," grumbled Askold with a roll of his eyes, "I just can't wait to traverse through poop. It'll be a first for me."

Ojore looked over at him, "Oh, I highly doubt that."

Askold punched Ojore in the side, and the two began to fight.

"Enough!" Benny snapped. "We've got to stay sharp if we're going to pull this off tonight."

Cahir looked at Benny. "Let me see the map." He held out his hand.

Ojore stepped forward and blocked Cahir. "Benny's the leader here, not *you*."

"Oh, shut the fuck up. We all need to review the map in case something happens to it when we're down there," Cahir sneered.

Ojore punched Cahir directly in his left eye. Cahir flew back but landed gracefully on his feet, feeling his eye beginning to swell.

"I said *ENOUGH!*" Benny shouted, a little too loud considering they were trying to be discreet. "Cahir's right, we all need to review this. We're about to travel through some disgusting waters, and if we lose the map or it gets damaged, we need to know our way around." He stepped around Ojore and handed the map to Cahir.

Cahir looked it over and then handed it to Askold, purposely walking around Ojore, who scowled at him.

Askold chuckled.

When everyone finished reviewing the map, Benny said, "Okay. We'll leave now to make it down to the Barrio in time for the shift change at the Murkway. Then we'll sneak out through here." He pointed to a spot on the map, and everyone nodded in agreement. "Have you all packed weapons, just in case?"

Cahir grabbed one of the extra swords and strapped it to his back. Everyone looked around at each other and nodded, except Ojore, who only glared at Cahir.

"Let's go," Benny said.

They traveled through Orience by sticking against walls, crouching low through fields, and avoiding any Rozzers patrolling. Twice, they split apart to make it through large groups of Rozzers lining narrow passageways with no other way around. They made their way south until the fields began to thin out and the dilapidated homes of Barrio came into view.

The roads were dirt and riddled with potholes. The houses had peeling paint, some with shutters hanging off their hinges, and the sounds of crying babies and drunken yelling came from within their walls.

Benny led the way, looking down at the map multiple times, taking turns, and then circling back. When Askold asked if they were lost, Benny shushed him and kept on his winding path. The smell of the Murkway grew stronger the further south they traveled, and when they approached a short wall that fell deep into a gulch of foul-smelling liquid, Benny pointed down to it.

"We're here," Benny said. "We'll need to get into the tunnels just a ways up." He pointed to the tunnels on the map.

Ruel sighed as he took the first leap into the dark liquid that rose to his stomach. He looked up at the others and gave them a thumbs-up.

"Hey! What are you doing out after curfew?" A Rozzer yelled from a distance, pulling out his gun and running towards the group still above the gulch.

The remaining men exchanged a brief look before quickly sliding into the murky water with Ruel, splashing the foul-smelling liquid around them.

"Quick! Into the tunnels!" Benny shouted, and the men pushed forward as quickly as they could through the water.

"Get back up here!" The Rozzer shouted. He began firing his gun into the darkness at them. The bullets hit the water and splashed around them.

Cahir pushed his legs as hard as he could. A bullet hit him in the back and ricocheted off his skin. The tunnels were getting close, and the Rozzer was yelling curses at them from behind, refusing to dive down into the liquid himself.

Fear gripped Cahir's spine as the Rozzer fired at them, not for himself but for the others. He was okay risking being hit by the bullets, but it wouldn't be the same for them if one made its mark.

The Rozzer was evidently too disgusted by the Murkway to pursue them, as he made no effort to slide down after them. Cahir didn't blame him; this was truly horrible. The stench was so foul it burned his nostrils as he gasped heavily, straining his muscles to reach the tunnel.

When they passed through the large opening of the tunnel, the Rozzer's yelling faded to a quiet echo behind them.

"Was anyone hit?" Benny asked frantically.

Everyone replied with the same answer, "No."

"Do you think he'll call backup, and they will be waiting for us on the other side?" Ruel asked.

"We don't really have a choice now. We have to keep going," Benny replied.

"Well, this is fun." Askold gagged as they followed the flow of liquid, his voice muffled as he held his arm over his nose. "Thanks to that asshole back there, now it's in my hair."

Ruel took the lead and pulled out a flashlight from his shirt pocket. "Glad I put this here and not in my pants." He grimaced and looked around him as he turned on the light.

Light illuminated the tunnel's stone walls as they walked through. Dark green slime grew up the walls where it met with the water, and condensation dripped down the stones.

"Turn right up there." Benny pointed the direction to Ruel as they came up to a split in the tunnel. The men turned right and slowly trudged through, noticing how the liquid deepened with each step.

Benny held the map far above his head and peered up as often as he could. The murky water was up to his throat now, as he was the shortest of the five men. "If this gets into my mouth, I'm going to puke." He gagged loudly and cleared his throat.

Ruel pointed the flashlight at a warning sign plastered on the wall.

"Beware beyond here. Sewer Monster present," Ojore read aloud. "This sounds fucking promising."

"I didn't know monsters were in here! What do we do?" Askold's voice was high-pitched, and he frantically looked around at the brown water surrounding them. He jumped back and shrieked when Ojore walked next to him.

"Boo," Ojore said to him with a bright smile.

Askold shook his head and muttered something like 'fucking asshole' as he pushed himself away.

Ruel continued leading them down the tunnel while holding his flashlight far above his head. Benny swam up to him. "There will be another split ahead. Turn left when you see it." Something suddenly grabbed both Benny and Ruel and pulled them under the water.

The two men, the light, and the map vanished into the darkness simultaneously, leaving Ojore, Askold, and Cahir behind.

Askold panicked again.

"We need to find them," Cahir commanded. "I'll find one. Askold and Ojore, find the flashlight and the other. On the count of three… One, two, three!"

The three men sank into the murky water. Cahir felt around for anyone as he continued forward. This part of the Murkway was deep enough that he could not reach the surface. He swam as hard as he could through the thick water. He felt something brush against his leg and went down. He pulled Benny up to the surface, and Benny let out a breath of air.

"Something pulled me under. Ruel! Who's got Ruel?" Benny shouted.

Ojore turned on the flashlight, holding it as he swam through the water, sweeping it around while everyone searched for Askold and Ruel.

Askold came up for air and yelled, "I cannot find anything! Help!"

Cahir lunged back into the deep, slimy water and reached

around for Ruel. He kicked something soft and went down to grab at it. He yanked, but the object was stuck. He pulled again forcefully, and it dislodged.

Something slid past Cahir's leg as he lifted Ruel's unbreathing body from the water.

"Over here!" Benny shouted from a small landing he found a few paces away. "Bring him here!"

Cahir swam with Ruel to the landing and dragged his body onto it, meeting the others.

"He isn't breathing," Askold observed.

Benny performed chest compressions on Ruel and gave him rescue breaths, gagging between each. Over and over, he repeated the steps.

Finally, Ruel gurgled and choked out brown liquid from his lungs. He looked up at the others. "If *any* of you ever bring this up again, I will kill you all," he said to them, his voice raspy and strained. "What the fuck pulled us under?"

Benny looked around nervously. "I don't know. I didn't see it."

The men watched the dark tunnel as Ojore slowly shone the flashlight on the water, pausing whenever he thought he spotted something, only to find it was just floating feces. The only things they heard were their labored breathing and the dripping of water.

"Look!" Askold said, pointing in the distance. Just a short distance away, the sheer, sparkling dome barrier glistened. "We're close."

"You guys good to keep going? If we swim fast, maybe we can get past whatever the fuck is in here," Benny suggested as he stood.

"Yeah, I think so. Let's get out of this awful place. Why didn't the map say a monster was in here?" Askold's complaints echoed through the tunnel.

"Probably because no one actually tries to traverse through

shit this far down," Ojore grumbled in response. "Explains why the Rozzer didn't come in after us, though."

They looked at Ruel.

"You okay?" Benny asked him. "Think you can swim?"

Ruel, a bit shaken, agreed that he was okay to continue.

They slowly slid back into the dark water and swam toward the glittering dome's barrier, passing through it. The same tingling sensation prickled across Cahir's skin as he pushed through.

Ojore's sudden yell got cut off as something pulled him back under the water.

"What the fuck!" Benny shouted as he quickly turned around, his arms flailing as he tried to stay above water with the sudden shock.

Ojore was flung out of the water, riding the back of a human-sized leech. The black leech had a giant mouth with rows of sharp teeth that tried to curl around itself and snap at him.

Ojore roared and tightly wrapped his arms around the slippery beast, cutting off its airflow.

The leech thrashed in the water, splashing everyone in the process. Liquid got into Cahir's mouth, and he quickly swam away from the fight, spitting what he could back into the murky water.

The monster tried to throw Ojore off like a bull. It attempted to break free from his grip, but Ojore's hold remained firm. He squeezed the beast as tightly as possible.

The beasts thrashing slowly stilled and came to a stop. Ojore pushed himself away from the monster and swam back over to the men.

"How the fuck—" Askold started.

"I don't want to talk about it," Ojore responded before he could finish.

Everyone swam in place, remaining silent, looking between Ojore and the dead monster.

"Welp... Glad you killed it. That was impressive, Ojore. Let's get the fuck out of here. Hopefully that was the only one," Benny finally said, breaking the silence. The men turned away from the leech and continued swimming in the direction they had initially planned.

The murky water gradually became shallower, and the men began to walk through the water that now only reached their calves.

They did it, they escaped the dome! Cahir's mind whirred back to Seda. He was coming for her. The plan worked!

They followed the tunnel to another split, and Benny called out, "Do any of you recall which way to go?"

"To the right," Cahir answered with a smile. He felt so relieved they were so close.

Ojore looked at him but didn't say anything. They turned right, and the end of the tunnel was visible, with the night sky and darkened Heath Forest beyond. At the end of the tunnel, they saw five forms waiting there.

"Fuck, the Rozzer *did* call backup," Ruel whispered.

They all froze, staring at the forms, and Cahir silently scolded himself for thinking they had made it before they were actually out of the Murkway.

Fuck. Fuck. Fuck. I NEED to get to Seda.

The Corvids and the two other Rising members came into view.

"You smell terrible," Ferona said as she approached, not allowing her steps to reach the water. She gagged loudly when she saw them covered in filth.

"How did you know which exit to find us at?" Benny let out a deep breath and glanced at the group in front of him, then jogged over to them.

"Simple, we just followed the sounds of screaming pigs," Roya said to him as she eyed his filthy form.

"Any idea where we can wash up?" Benny asked, clearing his throat and smirking at her.

Roya's eyes narrowed, and she shot him a sneer in response to his flirty grin. Benny quickly looked away.

"Did anyone remember to pack soap?" Askold asked the group. The grimy men shook their heads.

"Ugh, of course you didn't! You're a bunch of stinky men!" Ferona screeched into the chilly air as they exited the tunnel.

"Not me, sister," Feich called back to her as he sniffed himself.

"No, never you, brother," she said back to him soothingly. "Roya's right. These are not men. They're pigs."

Cahir laughed, and the Corvids glanced at him. Then the other filthy men joined in. The Corvids exchanged confused looks, unsure why the disgusting crew was laughing when sewage covered them.

Cahir thought about how filthy they were. He just ventured through sewage. Never in his entire life had he done something so disgusting. He knew without a doubt that he would do it again if it meant saving Seda.

It felt good to laugh. It loosened some of the tension Cahir had built up between his shoulders and his chest. But damn, he could never tell anyone else this happened. No one could know about this, or he would never hear the end of it, *especially* his friend back home, Luelle.

"I think they swallowed too much poop water," Seren observed of the men as he followed Kalon into the oak trees.

They broke into laughter again, and then Ruel doubled over and threw up.

CHAPTER 24

<u>Seda</u>

"Tell me about yourself, Elco," Seda asked him as they lounged near each other at the bars.

"What do you want to know, little moon-flutter?" Elco let out a deep sigh, and the comforting warmth from his breath seeped into her bones.

"You said you were a protector before. What happened?" A mouse darted across the floor between them, and Elco quickly swatted it, smashing the small creature.

"Disgusting things. They defecate where they eat." He lifted his paw and eyed the smashed remains, then wiped it across the floor away from them. He sighed and continued, "I watched over these lands and flew through the sky, reaching for the stars. Oh, how I miss the freedom of the air sweeping through my wings. I've not used them since they captured me. I'm not sure if they would still work. The Mother Goddess was the only being I answered to. Her magic and love protected our people and my friends. I gave up hope on her return many years ago."

Seda sat up, captivated by his story, and cautiously reached out her hand through the bars to touch his scaled back. He tensed and looked at her with suspicion. She pulled her hand back slightly and looked at him with gentle eyes, seeking permission. He nodded and settled back down. She slowly placed her palm on his back again, gliding her hand down and feeling the rough texture of his skin.

Elco let out a deep purring sound.

Elco continued, "When the gods left this place, the Monster King stole her source and left behind a damaged core. He used the dark stone to capture all manner of beasts and has ruled over all since."

"I'm so sorry, Elco," Seda genuinely replied as she slowly ran her hand up and down his scaly skin.

"It's not your fault. You were not around for the downfall. But you do remind me of someone I used to know."

"Who…" Seda started, but the door creaked open, and the sound of footsteps descended upon them.

Alexi came into view, saw Elco with Seda, and paused. "Uhhh…" He looked between them in confusion.

Elco growled at him and flashed his teeth.

Alexi's face flared in anger. "You know you cannot do anything, beast! Back up and let me through the door." He flashed his knife at Elco and then pulled the keys out, holding them up. Elco rose to his feet, retreated to the wall, and hissed.

Seda stood as Alexi placed the key into the lock. The door slowly creaked open as he stood there staring at her. "So now you have made friends with disgusting beasts? You never cease to shock me, you fucking freak. Were you talking to that thing? Have you truly gone insane?" He stepped slowly into the cell, while Seda stayed in her position.

Alexi walked up to her and touched the ends of her bright hair. "What will we do with you?" He grabbed a fistful of it and shoved her face into his, seething. "What did you tell Lord Mordred, you bitch?"

"What're you talking about?" she asked him, calmly staring into his angry eyes.

"He said that no one's allowed to *touch* you. That no one's allowed to impregnate you!" A snarl tore from him as he roughly grabbed the hair in his fist and pressed it to his nose, inhaling it deeply.

Seda did not reply. He reached down and grabbed her butt, squeezing it forcefully. "I may not be allowed to fill you with my seed, Seda. But I'm in charge of this room, and when I'm here, *I am your lord.*" He pushed her down to her knees.

White-hot anger flashed through her. She pushed herself back onto her feet and stared into Alexi's eyes. "No."

"What do you mean, 'no'? You will suck my cock like the good little whore you are." He pushed her down again and quickly unzipped his pants. He struggled to keep her down as she scratched at him, leaving marks on his still-healing arms.

"You fucking bitch!" he yelled as blood dripped down. He backhanded her across the face, and she flew to the side, catching herself on the bed.

Seda's mind flashed back to the day fifteen years ago. The pain and the torment it left on her soul. Then she thought of Cahir, tearing into Michael, and how it made her *satisfied* to see his heart ripped from his chest. Alexi jumped onto her, holding her down. "He won't know if I do it just this once."

Anger exploded within her, and she felt a rush of energy pulsate through her body, starting in her chest and radiating out to her fingertips. She shoved Alexi away, and a burst of purple sparks flew from her hands, sending him crashing against the bars.

His body jolted with an electric shock, shaking as he convulsed across the bars. The smell of fried hair and burning flesh filled the room. Seda watched in horror as his skin turned black. Her eyes went wide with shock, and she continued watching until his body froze, then crumpled to the ground, motionless.

Elco watched from outside the cell before entering through the open door and snagging Alexi's burnt figure between his teeth. His set of keys clattered to the ground as they flew aside.

The sound of crunching bones and flesh echoed within the long hall.

Elco ate him, clothing and all.

Seda stood frozen in horror, looking down at her hands and seeing the glowing purple veins etched into her skin, reaching up her forearms. "W-What was that?"

Elco finished his meal and burped loudly. He looked over to Seda. "I knew you were not fully human. He was a little burnt. Next time, don't toast for so long, please."

SEDA SAT on her disgusting bed and looked at her fading hands.

Where did that come from?

The purple slowly receded with each passing hour. She picked up Alexi's keys and hid them under her mattress, making sure to lock herself back in for when the next Rozzer came in. She had no idea what to say to them when they arrived, which might lead to questions about her. Questions she couldn't answer.

Now that she had the keys, she might be able to plan an escape. She just needed to figure out how and when.

Elco made his way back to the front of the vast hall and sprawled his body out, quickly falling asleep. The sound of his gurgling stomach filled the space.

She killed someone.

She should feel bad about taking a life, but oddly, she didn't.

He deserved his pain for torturing her and who knows how many others in his weak existence of a life, for attempting to hurt her again. She wondered about his mother, how often he visited her, and how she might miss him the next time he was supposed to show up.

My mom says girls like her like to gloat to make us feel inferior.

No, she wouldn't feel bad for his mother, nor anyone else who did not care for the lives of others. She felt slightly better, even happy. Seeing his body writhe on the floor and the smell of his burning skin made her smile.

The hall door opened, and Seda stood up from the bed, hiding her faded purple hands behind her.

"Where's Alexi?" A large, burly Rozzer came into view and stood at her bars, looking at her. His low, slithering voice crawled up her spine.

"Who?" She did not know what to say; playing dumb was in her best interests.

Elco popped his head up and looked over at them, slanting his eyes at the Rozzer. She looked at him and slightly shook her head as the Rozzer looked back at Elco.

"Your guard. He came in here a few hours ago, and I've not seen him since. Why do I smell something burnt?" He looked back at Elco.

"Oh, he left earlier," she tried to make her voice sound weak, pretending to be upset from Alexi's visit. She struggled to hide a smile and pouted instead, catching the eye of the Rozzer.

The Rozzer looked at her with suspicion and then back to Elco. He took out his whip and pointed the butt of it at her. His crimson eyes flashed. "I don't know where he is, but if I find out you're lying to me and that *beast* had something to do with it, I'll be back for you *as well*. I don't care what Mordred said. Punishments here are harsh, and when you misbehave, you get punished."

He walked over to Elco and whipped him across the back.

Elco roared, shaking the rock walls. More lizard creatures piled into the hall, dragging him out and stabbing him with electric sticks. The doors slammed closed, and Seda could hear shouting and the sounds of Elco whimpering outside the walls.

The smoldering embers of her fury began to burn deep within her chest once more.

CHAPTER 25

<u>Benny</u>

They found a stream and washed as best they could with a bar of soap Kalon had luckily packed. Both Seren and Kalon had bags full of supplies that Benny was extremely thankful for, since the Murkway had mostly ruined the items they brought.

Benny's feet ached as they crept through the Heath Forest. They were all taking light steps to avoid any sound that might alert the living creatures in the woods.

The Corvids flew above the trees, swooping down to report any movement ahead. The men avoided the potential conflict and wandered the area, spending hours navigating the forest. As the night sky gave way to the golden glow of dawn, the twinkling stars began to fade.

His gaze kept drifting to Roya, his eyes recognizing her by her distinctive azure-tipped beak, her sleek feathers, and, in her human form, her breathtaking face and flawless body.

The large oak trees thinned, and the ground beneath their feet slowly turned to sand, slowing their steps. Roya, Ferona, and Feich flew down and shifted forms as the trees cleared, revealing a vast expanse of dunes stretching beyond them.

"The Camp's a good distance ahead," Roya told them. Her long, silky hair blew in the wind, and her woodsmoke bourbon scent enveloped Benny. He instinctively stepped closer to her, and she sharply looked over at him, squinting her eyes in his direction. She stepped aside and walked over to Cahir. Making conversation as she kept glancing his way and giving him squinty-eyed looks.

Damnit, he thought.

"Let's rest here for a bit before we make our way through the sand," he huffed in exhaustion. "Did anyone fill their canteens at that last stream we saw?"

Askold and Ruel held theirs up.

"How long do we think it will take to cross?" Cahir asked them as Roya chuckled at something he had said to her.

"About four hours or so," Kalon answered him from behind.

Benny felt the twinge of jealousy. He knew not to be jealous of Cahir. Cahir, although he never admitted it, was obviously head over heels for Seda. But he also wanted to make Roya smile. Her smile was bright and alive, alighting her face with the beauty of a wildfire, fierce and strong. He realized he was staring again. He cleared his throat and looked away.

"I see how you're looking at my sister," Ferona said, sliding in next to him and nodding at Roya and Cahir.

"Is it that obvious?" he asked as he slid his stuff off his shoulder and dropped it to the sand. Ferona sat in the sand next to him and patted the ground for him to sit.

Benny sat next to her, and she handed him a canteen to drink from, likely one she had stolen from Askold. He sipped some water and gazed out over the vast expanse of dunes, rolling out like endless waves.

Benny spent his life following the rules until he learned of his father's secrets. He studied diligently, performed well on his exams, and focused on excelling at work. Sure, he had a few girl-friends here and there, but nothing concrete, nothing wild and careless. No one caught his eye as Roya did. When had he truly ever focused on himself and his own desires? Never. He never had before. He spent the last few years visiting the Medical Wing to give samples to others, hoping that one would be accepted.

"She's gorgeous," he finally admitted to Ferona and looked back over his shoulder at her again. Roya looked back at him and left Cahir's side, walking over to him and sitting on his opposite side.

His heart started racing with nervous excitement.

"So… uh," he began, stealing a glance at her gorgeous hands with their sharp nails, all the while trying to avoid looking her in the face.

"Why do you keep watching me?" Roya asked.

She was so forward, so direct, so *hot*.

"Do I scare you? I hear your heart beating within your chest right now. I'm here for your sister, Benny. I'll not hurt you as long as *you don't get in my way*."

Oh, wowzers, he thought as his heart continued to race rapidly.

"N-No, it's not that," he stuttered in response.

Ferona giggled and stood up. "I'll leave you here to fend for yourself."

Roya looked into Benny's eyes, expectant, waiting for an answer.

He looked over the dunes and blurted out quickly before he thought better of it, "I think you're beautiful, Roya, and I cannot take my eyes off of you." There. He said it. He was open, honest, and truthful. No games like the ones the girls he used to date would play with him. He smiled at himself for being so upfront and honest, and then looked back at Roya.

Roya's face twisted with disgust, and his heart sank. She

sprang to her feet and backed away, transforming into her Corvid form and taking off into the sky.

"Smooth one, Benny," Kalon said as he sat next to him. "You have to ease into these things, you know? See what she likes first before you confess your undying love for a woman. Get to know her a little bit. Also, best not to say these things when you still smell like the Murkway."

His cheeks heated, and he sighed. Roya's face looked so disgusted with his confession. Was it because of his smell? He had scrubbed his body and washed his clothes. They were still damp and smelled like soap when he sniffed himself.

Or maybe he was ugly to her? Not enough of a mystery to her as she was to him?

He got up and looked at the rest of the group. "Let's pack up and head out."

They gathered their gear and started walking through the steep, sandy waves.

CHAPTER 26

<u>Seda</u>

Elco returned to the hall hours later, covered in whip marks and burn scars. He let out a whimper, like an injured animal, and curled up into a ball near her cage. Seda grabbed the hidden keys and tried them all until finally, the last key clicked and unlocked Elco's shiny red cuffs. He looked at her hopelessly but moved the chains beneath him. Seda went back into her cell, making sure to lock the door, then sat next to him, gently running her hand through his mane and stroking his back, being extra careful to avoid his injuries.

A new Rozzer Seda had never seen before brought her food, fresh water, and a new bucket, but was wary as he walked past Elco. He saw her petting him through the bars and did not say anything. He set the items down and quickly left the hall, closing the door behind him. The cool night air from outside rushed in as the door shut.

Slowly, Elco's markings started to fade. He pushed his nose against the bars, and she gently kissed the soft fur above his silky skin.

They slept peacefully, pressed against each other through the bars for hours, until screams woke them.

The violently shaking ground made Seda fall away from him.

"What's going on, Elco? Do you know?" she asked him. His ears were alert and pointed toward the door.

"The Jotnar are here to collect."

Seda's stomach lurched. She heard the horror stories, she felt their attacks upon the dome, but never, not once, had she seen them in person.

Loud sirens blared through the room, and the hall door swung open with a few Rozzers marching in. When they saw Elco, they paused, then kept moving toward Seda's cell and unlocked it.

Seda jumped up, her heart pounding in her chest and her legs seizing.

Not again, not again! She scolded herself for freezing up. She was strong and capable of defending herself. Although she was uncertain how to do it again, maybe she could find that strength within herself once more.

"Seda Arbor, follow us. The Jotnar are here," the Rozzer in front said, holding open the door. She took a tentative step forward and nearly collapsed out of fear, catching herself on the bars. She nervously walked down the hall, each step stabilized by her hand on the wall. She looked back once at Elco, who was watching her intently.

"You'll be okay, moon-flutter, I promise," he said to her. No one else looked at him as he spoke, and no one responded.

The heat pressed against her skin, and the sun blazed into her eyes, making her take a few moments to adjust to the scene. Her cell may now have light, but it was dim compared to the bright blaze outside the walls.

As her eyes adjusted, she saw three massive beings standing at the end of the courtyard.

She looked up twenty feet to the faces of the two males.

Huge, round noses dripping with mucus, wide and flat mouths, and small chins sticking out in a rounded point. Their eyes were too close to their noses, and they had heavy brows. Their bodies were sturdy and weighty, and the large muscles in their arms looked intimidating. One of them wore earth-toned clothing, while the other wore armor.

The lone female Jotnar stood in the center. She was shorter than the other two, but her presence commanded attention. Heavily built, with large breasts covered in minimal clothing and a thick, tree-woven crown atop her head.

The Rozzers pushed Seda into line with a large crowd at the opposite end of the courtyard. The reptilian creatures and the Rozzers surrounded them, their weapons at the ready.

"Where's our dear Monster King?" the female Jotnar asked the crowd, her voice shaking the ground beneath Seda's bare feet.

The burly Rozzer, who had whipped Elco the night before, walked forward into the middle of the courtyard and looked up at the female. "His Highness isn't here today, High Gravemara." He bowed low before her.

High Gravemara looked down at him, like he was a small ant that she hadn't yet decided if she wanted to squish. "How unfortunate. Do you have the collection for us, Captain?"

"It shall be ready soon. Why don't you make yourselves comfortable, and we'll have a cookout for you to snack on while you wait." He waved his hands to a few Rozzers, and they stepped forward, grabbing men at random. They ran their swords across the throats of all of them quickly, dropping them into the sand.

Everyone in the crowd collectively gasped. Seda's eyes widened, and her heart rate spiked as she watched the men's bodies crumple on the ground.

She heard panting and looked to her left, seeing a young man, about twenty or so, who was urinating in his pants. She quickly looked back at the Jotnar, unable to keep her attention on anything else.

High Gravemara stood tall and proud, with her thick knees, bowed legs, and her plump rolls spilling over her shorts. Her snot was brightly colored as it slid down her nose toward her wide, crooked smile, overlined with blood as lipstick. Her long, thick, wet tongue came out and licked at the discharge, causing Seda to hold back a gag, her mouth watering with disgust.

She couldn't make herself look away, despite wanting to.

High Gravemara looked at the crowd of humans, licked her lips, smudging her lipstick, and smiled brightly, revealing her rotten, crooked teeth.

"Oh, why isn't he here today? I thought he loved to visit us when we came to collect," she whined sweetly at the Captain.

"He had business to take care of," he said, directing the dead bodies onto a large barbecue pit as the smoke stung Seda's eyes.

Seda wasn't sure how she felt. Was it fear? Disgust? Hatred? These monsters made her and thousands more of Joro citizens' lives hell. Seda lived her life in fear over these... Gross beings before her.

As the slain people cooked over the fire, with the choking smell of burning clothing and hair, the rest of the Camp inmates were expected to stand still and not move. A few Rozzers and serpents slashed their whips at the people who moved around too much. Seda's legs cramped, but she remained upright and still, watching the sun slowly move across the sky.

The young man, who previously urinated in his pants, grew increasingly fidgety alongside her. "Th-They're going to eat us next," he shouted, and the other prisoners looked at him. "We have to run. We have to escape!"

Without delay, he ran toward the guarded, narrow exit past the barbecue.

The unarmored male Jotnar laughed loudly, like a small child, a long string of drool trailing from his lips. He swiped his hand through the air and grabbed the young man running for his escape. His screams quickly silenced as the Jotnar bit off his head and began to chew loudly.

"Mogthud! Quit playing with your food, son!" High Gravemara yelled at him, the ground shaking with her anger. "How many times have I told you that *royalty* never eats them raw!"

Mogthud pouted, peering at the remains of the small man in his palm. "Bring the rest of him over here. We will cook this one special for you, since you caught him like a big boy," she called to him. He walked the remainder of the man over to the barbecue and threw his body onto the fire.

Mogthud watched with an excited grin.

Her eyes were wide with horror, but Seda remained frozen in place, even though she really had to go to the bathroom. The pressure of holding it was hurting. What was stopping her from just going down her bare legs the same as that man? He likely wasn't the only one who had.

She decided against it, unsure when she'd get another chance to shower.

The Jotnars poked into the bodies with large sticks, pulling them off the flames. They munched on stomachs first, slurping through intestines as Rozzers lined up mobile cells near the exit.

"Captain, how many have you allotted for us today?" High Gravemara asked as she nibbled on a foot and picked her teeth with a stick, flicking out something that had gotten stuck between them.

"The Monster King has allotted one hundred for you today," replied the Captain.

High Gravemara set down her toothpick and looked at him with furrowed, heavy eyebrows. "And what of the other hundred due soon? My people will starve if we do not have enough to eat. It's been difficult for them to hunt with less and less allowed outside of the dome."

"He's aware and wishes for the dome to fall soon."

"We have a *deal*, Captain. Please remind him of this the next time you see him. Or our deal expires soon."

The Captain nodded and turned to look at everyone watching the Jotnars eat. "All males line up to my left! I need a count of how many there are of you."

The hesitant men lined up, and the Captain counted them. He looked over to High Gravemara and said, "We're short ten. We will allow you to choose from the women who are not pregnant."

What the hell?

As the men lined up, they started exchanging confused glances. One of them yelled, "Where's my chance to prove myself? I scored in the ninetieth percentile! I'm part of Cascade!" A serpent walked behind him and hit him over the head with the butt of his gun, causing the man to fall.

"High Gravemara, you can now pick eleven from the remaining prisoners."

High Gravemara stood and thundered quickly, too quickly, for someone her size, over toward the women. Everyone gasped and stepped back. Some women cried loudly, begging for themselves and praying to anything that would hear. High Gravemara eyed pregnant bellies and thin women who had been malnourished for too long.

"What a fun choice! They all look so appetizing," she licked her lips as she observed them.

Mogthud clapped his hands in excitement.

Fights broke out amongst the men as they rounded into the cells, but the power of the Rozzers and the serpent creatures was no match against their defense.

"You!" She picked a short, stout woman who looked to be in her thirties. The woman turned to run, but a serpent snagged her from behind and dragged her off. Seda listened to her screams as they threw her into the cell.

Seda's chest vibrated.

"Oh, this is so fun, let me pick always, Captain." She drooled as she loudly spoke to the Captain. She continued pointing to women, and the Rozzers collected them.

"How many was that?" she asked as she looked at the remaining women.

"Ten, High Gravemara," the Captain answered.

Her eyes rolled over the crowd and landed on Seda.

"Oh! Look how beautiful this one is. She would make a special dinner, wouldn't she? I will take her for myself."

Everything fell silent for Seda, and her vision went blurry.

"You cannot take that one, High Gravemara," replied the Captain.

"Why not?!" she roared. "You said I could pick! I picked that one! She's pretty, and I bet she tastes divine!" She pounded her foot into the ground, and the earth shook, causing people to stumble, including Seda.

"We have orders, High Gravemara."

"I *don't* care. I want that one! Load her up… right now!" she screeched.

Everyone paused and looked between Seda and High Gravemara. The other prisoners whispered in confusion.

"Why is she so special?"

"Why can she not be taken?"

"If you don't load her up right now, I'll take her myself, Captain. This one's for me. The Monster King may come and talk to me after, if he likes. He's not here to tell me no, and I don't trust you in this! I think you want her for yourself, and I refuse! I must have the best! I'm a *queen,* and I demand the best!"

"She's not to be touched, High Gravemara. We deeply apologize," the Captain said calmly.

High Gravemara stomped her foot forcefully, causing the ground to shake. She let out a bloodcurdling scream and tugged at her long, dread-filled orange hair. She looked back at Seda and quickly snagged her from the ground, lifting her high into the air within her palm, and licked her lips excitedly. The sudden adjustment caused Seda to black out briefly.

The Rozzers and the serpents looked at each other, not sure what to do in this situation. The Captain pulled out his gun and fired it at High Gravemara. She shrieked and stomped the ground. The other guards followed and did the same. High Gravemara circled, making Seda dizzy, and tried to smash the people below her. The other two Jotnar yelled and did the same.

The remaining prisoners let out screams and took off, desperate to escape.

High Gravemara was holding her too tightly, and it was making it hard for Seda to breathe. Her mind whirred as she flung around within her palm. She was never going to get out of here. She would never see her family again. She would never get to say goodbye to Cahir.

No. Fuck this spoiled rotten monstrosity.

An inferno built within her chest, and her hands began to glow purple. She slammed them into High Gravemara's fingers, and purple electricity fired through Seda's palms. An explosion of purple filled the air.

High Gravemara wailed loudly as she crashed to the ground, convulsing while still holding onto Seda.

The Rozzers saw her struggling and ran over to her, stabbing her with too small swords. High Gravemara's hand opened up, and Seda fell to the ground, high enough to twist her ankle.

She hobbled as far away from the giants as she could, struggling to catch her breath. Guards kept firing at the Jotnar, but the Jotnar were swatting them away like flies.

With a sudden burst, a door swung open, and Elco rushed out, like a vision of a flame tearing through the night. He opened his black wings, and they expanded twenty wide feet as he flew into the air. He looked down and saw Seda pulling herself to the side of the courtyard and roared.

The guards, the Jotnar, and the remaining prisoners screamed.

The Captain looked up and seethed, "Forget the fucking Jotnar, get the Lionne!"

Elco tucked his wings in and dove into the chaos. He grabbed Seda with his front paw and flew back into the air. Bullets flew past them as they went higher into the sky. She pointed her hands back down at the Jotnar and fired her power again.

Seda saw the courtyard turn purple and shrink in size as she faded into darkness.

CHAPTER 27

<u>Cahir</u>

The team trudged through the sandy dunes for hours until they caught a glimpse of the Camp in the distance. They hid behind a tall dune and looked over. The Camp was unlike anything he expected. Tall, stone walls formed a large square with spikes along the top, and a big plume of smoke rose from the center. Guards were posted all around the Camp, and he could hear the distant screams.

Roya swooped down from high above and told Cahir, "The walls are heavily guarded, and that isn't all…"

"What do you mean?" Kalon asked nervously, his eyes flicking between the Camp and Roya. "What else is going on in there?"

Roya shifted her form and looked at the men. "There are three Jotnar in the middle of the Camp. They appear to be cooking… people."

"Fucking a," Askold said. "How do we get past three Jotnar?"

A bright purple flash exploded through the center of the Camp, and the group watched in horror.

Loud screaming wailed through the air, and the sand shifted beneath their palms with the pulsating beats of the earth shaking. The sound of gunshots echoed across the distance.

Ferona flew down and quickly shifted into a human. "They're shooting the Jotnar."

"What the fuck..." Benny said, looking back at the Camp in horror.

"I have to get Seda out. Now!" screamed Cahir. He had no idea what truly went on within those walls, but this wasn't what he expected.

This was *really* fucking bad.

"Look!" Benny pointed at the Camp. A giant, winged creature flew from the center, holding a pulsating, purple form.

"Get back up there, Roya! See if you can see Seda in all of this!" Cahir commanded. Roya and Ferona shifted forms and flew back into the sky.

Seda, his *best* friend and the woman who was his entire world, the thread that bound his broken seams, was alone in all of this chaos. He couldn't imagine what she was seeing or feeling.

If she got injured in this, or *worse*... Cahir's breathing became labored.

He quickly stood from his crouched position and marched toward the Camp.

Ojore tackled him from behind, throwing him back down onto the sand. "Do you want to get us all killed, you fucking idiot?"

Cahir didn't care. He just wanted to reach her. Fuck these other people's lives. What mattered was Seda, and right now she was caught up in all of this. He would let everyone die if it meant saving her. He shoved Ojore off him and began to shift, not caring if his secret was revealed, but Roya flew down again and yelled, "She's there!" She shifted forms and pointed to the winged creature flying in the distance over the dunes. The beast struggled to stay airborne, its wings giving out. It crashed into the sand about a mile away.

Cahir ran as fast as his legs would take him, not allowing his weakening breath or the blazing sun to slow him. He heard the others following behind and saw the Corvids approach the winged beast. They flew down and shifted forms, circling the creature and bracing for battle. Cahir pushed his legs harder.

When he neared, he took in the size of the beast before him. Massive wings lay splayed out around it, with both fur lining its legs and head, and the scaled skin of a reptile. He ran up to the beast, and it snarled, snapping at his face. He looked for Seda and saw the beast holding her in its paws, protectively drawing her closer to its chest. The others approached and pulled out their swords.

"Stop!" Cahir yelled. "It's not trying to hurt her."

The beast narrowed its eyes and growled at everyone around it, slowly tilting its head and watching them, its crimson gaze glowing brightly against the sun. Cahir noticed the dark, blood-drenched wounds on its scaled skin and torn wings. "It's injured. Backup!"

Cahir held his hands up and slowly approached, staring the beast in the eyes. "You have someone I care for. I need to make sure she's okay. May I please come close and check on her?"

The beast growled menacingly, untrusting of Cahir. "I know Seda, she's my best friend. I came here from Joro to rescue her."

The beast studied him with untrusting, crimson eyes and hesitantly released Seda from its grasp, giving a warning snap of its teeth in Cahir's direction.

Cahir looked down at Seda, keeping his hands in the air to show the beast he meant no harm, and slowly walked up to Seda's side. He crouched into the sand and placed his hand on her throat, checking for a pulse.

"She's alive," he said as he sighed in relief and ran his fingers over her flushed cheek. He looked at her arms and saw the purple streaks trailing up from her hands to her biceps.

"She's found her power," Ferona said.

"What do you mean by 'power'?" Benny asked. The three Corvids looked at each other, not answering.

Seda stirred, and Cahir gently picked her up. The beast loudly growled but did not move from his spot. Cahir cradled her in his arms, and she slowly opened her eyes.

"Cahir?" she wheezed. Cahir gasped when he saw her glowing eyes, but they fluttered back closed.

"She's hurt," he said, looking over his shoulder to the others. "Does anyone have medical supplies?"

Seren stepped forward, hands in the air, to show the beast he meant no harm. "I have some in my bag." He pulled out a medical kit from his backpack and handed it to Cahir.

"I'm here, Seda. I'm here." Cahir rocked her gently in his arms

Seda drifted back to sleep as Cahir carefully bandaged the scrapes he had found, using a gentle touch. He saw her swollen ankle, so he wrapped it up tightly. When he finished, he picked her back up and turned to the rest of them and announced, "I'm taking her to Umbrea."

"You cannot do that!" Roya yelled at him and took a step forward.

"Yes, the *fuck* I can!" Fuck these people, and also fuck the Corvids and what they thought the Wisps wanted. *Fuck the Wisps.*

"Whoa, whoa... We're not leaving here without my father," Benny interjected. Both the Corvids and Cahir looked at him.

"Your father's no longer with us, Benny," Ferona said to him.

"He might still be in there! We can't give up. Seda got out, maybe he did, too!" he shouted as he pointed toward the Camp, where some prisoners were escaping in the opposite direction.

"They don't keep the men alive long, Benny," Roya said to him as she took a step closer and placed her hand on his shoulder. "The men usually die within a few days at most."

Benny crashed into his knees and cried into his sandy palms. Roya bent down and hesitantly patted his back, offering what she could to console him.

"What's Umbrea?" Askold asked, wiping his eyes.

"It's the kingdom of whiners and losers. She'd be better in Tuath," snarled Ojore.

Cahir looked at him sharply, but did not fall for the bait. He knew something was off about this man, and that statement made it obvious. He was holding onto Seda, and nothing was going to get him away from her now. Well, he hoped. How many days were left?

"Umbrea's the Fae realm. Seda will be safe there. We will *all* be safe there," he said instead.

"Yeah, right. You really think once the Jotnars bust down that dome and consume everyone within that, they won't try to travel north to Umbrea?" Ojore snarled at him.

"And how exactly do you know about Umbrea?" questioned Cahir.

Ojore snarled, "The same as you do about Umbrea."

"How far is it from here?" Seren interjected.

"A couple of weeks on foot," Kalon answered. "And it's a dangerous trip." He was looking down at Seda with a peculiar glint in his eye. Cahir sensed that he was looking at more than just her injuries and pulled her tighter to himself.

"Oh great, so almost everyone knows of this Umbrea realm besides Benny and me?" Askold asked in a huff.

Roya stood up from Benny's side and marched over to Cahir. "She cannot go to Umbrea without visiting the Wisps, Cahir. If they allow her to go further, then we'll support that decision." The Corvids stood together, with their arms crossed across their chests, unbudging.

He sighed. "We wait for Seda to wake and for her new friend over there to heal some. And the decision's *hers* to make on which location."

He pointed his head to the beast, who just silently watched them. "I just hope his healing is quick because we're not far enough away from the Camp to be in a safe place for the night."

Everyone gazed out into the distance. The Camp had grown much quieter since they discovered Seda and the beast.

"So are there pretty ladies in Umbrea?" Askold asked them with a wink and a bright smile.

PART THREE
THE JOURNEY TO THE WISPS

CHAPTER 28

<u>Seda</u>

Seda woke to the softness of arms holding her, cracked her eyes open to the blinding sunlight, and felt the heat on her cheeks. She let out a gasp as memories of the Camp flooded back, causing her eyes to widen as she saw Cahir holding onto her. He tightened his grip, and she coughed as a result, looking up at him in confusion. Her stiff ankle throbbed, and she could feel sand wedged between her toes.

"Cahir? Is it really you?" she rasped, gazing up into his gentle, emerald eyes.

"I'm here, Seda," he whispered and kissed her forehead. She held back tears, overwhelmed with relief at being finally reunited with him. She had missed him deeply, and now she was in his arms, his embrace comforting her. Her sob tore loose as she cried into his shoulder.

She wondered if this was just a wicked dream.

"What happened? How are you here?" she choked out, glancing around for the first time at the other people watching her and noticing Benny in the group.

She had to inform him about their father.

"Benny!" She tore herself out of Cahir's arms and tried to run to him, but collapsed into the sand and winced in pain from her throbbing ankle.

Everyone seemed to rush toward her at once, and she shrieked in response, shielding her head, accidentally throwing sand into her face.

"Stop! Everyone give her some space!" Cahir yelled.

Benny slowly approached and knelt beside her, gently touching her shoulder. She pulled away at the gesture, recalling Alexi's touch, but then took a deep breath and looked up at her brother. "How are you here? Who are all of these people?"

Benny helped her to her feet and hugged her tightly; the sand's heat seared her bare soles. "We came for you and Dad, Seda. We escaped the dome. What happened there? Did you see Dad at all?"

Tears slipped down her cheeks, and she wiped them away, the rough sand scratching against her skin. She shook her head and looked away from him. "I didn't see him when I was there, and they had collected all of the men when the Jotnar arrived." She let out a whimper, missing her father and worrying he'd suffered a painful death like so many others. "I don't know where he is."

Benny looked at her with glassy eyes and slumped shoulders. "I was worried about that."

They stared at each other for a long moment before Benny reached out and hugged her tightly, "I love you, sis."

She hugged him back, as swirling images of her escape, being in the hands of the Jotnar, and how Elco had rescued her flashed through her mind. She released herself and frantically looked around for him.

She saw Elco lying down and limped across the hot sand to him, running her hands through his mane. "Oh, Elco. You saved me. You saved me, Elco." She hugged him, and he nuzzled into her embrace, emitting a rumbling purr.

"No, Seda. You saved me. I had lost hope that I would ever escape that place."

Cahir stepped forward, and Elco growled at him. Cahir stopped and asked from a safe distance, "You called that thing Elco?"

"Yes, this is Elco. He's my friend. He saved me. The Jotnar had me, and he *saved me*." She let out a gasp through her tears, her final words stuck in her throat, and wrapped him in another hug.

"That escape was absolutely magnificent, Seda." Seda looked over at a handsome man with a black moth tattoo on his neck. He walked over and stood next to Cahir, his smooth, deep voice tickling her memory. "I'm Kalon. It's great to finally meet you. I've heard a lot about you from Benny here." He pointed his thumb over to Benny, and Seda looked at her brother in confusion.

"Seda, there's a lot we need to catch up on," Benny started, wiping his eyes and taking a deep breath. "Please meet everyone. You just met Kalon; he's a Traverser, and so is Seren over there." He pointed to a tall, thin man in the distance, and the man waved at her.

He gestured toward a large, muscular man with a thick brown beard and curly hair. "This is Ojore, a butcher and long-time friend of Dad's." Ojore stepped forward and nodded his head.

"This is Askold, he's an undercover Rozzer." Benny patted Askold on the shoulder, and Askold winked at her, smiling brightly and showing off perfect, straight teeth.

Cahir growled at him, and Askold raised his hands in surrender, chuckling.

Benny let out a strained laugh and then pointed to a tall man in his mid-thirties. "This is Ruel. He's another Traverser. These men were under Dad as part of The Rising. I'm sure you have a lot of questions, and we'll answer them."

Seda's eyes widened, covering her mouth with her hand. Was her father the leader of that rebellious group?

She got up slowly, her mind hazy and dizzy, but trying her best to be polite. "Um… It's nice to meet you. I've heard of The Rising but didn't know who was behind it. It's fascinating to find out my dad and brother were involved in that, *especially since they're such good rule followers.*" She looked at him again and raised her brows.

Benny shook his head. "Lots to catch up on, Seda. I'm just so glad to see you safe from that place. Mom's safe, too. She's home, focusing on her work. The neighbors have been checking up on her. When you and Dad left, she broke down even more. But she was doing okay when we left. She's keeping focused on the orchard."

Seda let out a sigh of relief for her mother. Her sorrow must be eating her alive, but she was a strong woman, and she was safe. She had the registration stating that she had a child, and she also had a good job. She would be okay with them all being away from Joro for a while.

She caught sight of three people with unique coloring, their hair in shades of blue and green, standing near Cahir.

A woman with azure black hair and slanted eyes stepped forward and introduced herself, "I'm Roya, and this is my murder." She pointed to a mirror image of herself, except for the baby blue ends in her hair. "This is Ferona." And then to the man who matched the woman, except that he was taller and broader. "And this is Feich. We have been watching over you for a long time, Seda, but you did not know we were here."

The three of them shifted into ravens and then back into humans before her eyes.

Seda gasped and fell into the sand.

She was utterly exhausted, and she didn't know how much more she could take in. She looked down at her fading fingertips. "There's been a lot I've seen in the last few days." She shook her head in confusion and bit her lip. Then she said, "I fear I'm having a hard time taking it all in. Were you the ones following me around? I take it that you know about this, too?" She held her hands up for them to see.

Roya stepped forward and lightly took her hands into hers. "Yes. We didn't know when this would show. But, we knew you would someday show signs of magic, and we're here to help guide and protect you along your path."

"The purple explosion came from you?" Askold asked from where he was standing.

"It exploded?" Seda asked back, looking up at him in confusion.

Kalon added, "Yeah, we saw it as we were nearing the Camp. A huge eruption, and then all of a sudden, your friend, Elco, came flying out of there, holding you. You were pulsating in the sky. It was truly amazing."

She looked at Kalon and then back down at her injured friend. "He needs more time to heal. They shot at us, at *him*, when we were escaping."

A loud alarm sounded from the Camp, and everyone looked over toward it in the far distance.

"We need to move," Cahir said as he stepped forward and held onto Seda's shoulder with a single hand. "I can help you walk if you want? The sand's hot."

"I'll not go until Elco can travel," she said adamantly as she pulled away from him, concerned that her friend would not be able to walk or fly.

Elco's voice rumbled across the sand, "I'll be okay. I'll lie here a bit longer and catch up to you guys. Can you ask them where they're headed? They cannot hear me… only you. If you go back to Joro, I won't be able to come. Please ask them for me."

She looked up at the group, and she finally realized that only she could hear this magnificent creature before her. "Elco wants to know where we're going," she said to the others.

The group looked at each other, confused. "He talks to you?" Cahir asked.

"Yes. And he's still injured. He cannot go to Joro. He wants to know where we're going so he can catch up to us. Please don't say we're going back there. Everything we have known has been a lie, Cahir," she looked over to him, and tears pooled in her eyes. "Terrible things happen there. Women are *hurt* to produce children, people are being eaten alive, and Lord Mordred's aware of it! We cannot return to Joro."

"We're going to the Wisps," Ferona said. "They wish to talk to you."

"She has a choice, remember? I want her to go to Umbrea," Cahir urged firmly.

"I don't care where we go, I just want to go far away from here."

"We need to visit the Wisps, Seda. Everything depends on their information," Roya said, glancing at Cahir.

Benny walked over to Roya, and she quickly glared at him, taking a small step back.

Elco huffed from her side, "If the Wisps want to talk to you, you must go. They're the divine servants of the Mother Goddess. I'll catch up. They cannot see me hidden behind this dune."

Seda looked across the distance toward the Camp. She wasn't sure if leaving Elco here was a good idea. If the Jotnar left that place and ventured this direction, they would see him. Who were the Wisps? How did Cahir know about a place called Umbrea?

She was so tired. She felt like she could sleep for days. She never heard about any of these things, but she would risk a new place to avoid returning to Joro.

But what if these new places are worse? What if Elco gets caught?

"I cannot leave him," she said, choking back a sob. *"He's my friend."*

The sand shifted beneath their feet, indicating that the Jotnar were moving.

"Please, go. I promise I'll find you. I can't leave now. You need time to get as far away from here as you can."

"But what if they find *you*, Elco!?"

"I have enough in me to fight back if they do. I've not fought back in a thousand years. You gave that to me, Seda. You gave me a reason to fight back. I'll find you."

Seda crashed down onto the ground next to him again and cried into his inky mane. "Do you promise?"

"I promise."

"We're going to the Wisps," she stated as she stood on her injured ankle and wiped away her tears. She took a limping step toward the unknown and away from the Camp.

Cahir ran up to her.

"May I?" he asked as he held out his arms.

Seda gazed into his beautiful, kind eyes, feeling the calm after a storm. As she looked into them, a wave of happy, safe memories from years past washed over her. She finally felt like she had come home.

She nodded her head, and he pulled her up into his arms, cradling her against his strong, warm chest, and took another step forward. The group followed them from behind.

"What happened to your eye?" Seda asked him as he walked through the hot sand.

"That guy, Ojore, has it out for me," he chuckled. "I kind of deserved it."

She laughed, nuzzling her nose into his shirt and breathing in his familiar cedar scent. As he walked away, she glanced over his arm toward a fading Elco in the distance on the sand, hoping she'd made the right decision.

CHAPTER 29

<u>The Monster King</u>

"You guys did what?!" The Monster King snarled at his Captain.

"The Jotnar got hostile with us, Your Highness," the Captain replied. He returned to the outskirts of Joro with a few guards and a disoriented woman they had decided to bring back to the city. The woman was bound but did not resist in the cell on the way home. She had recently given birth, and her baby did not survive. The woman sat in the cell, rocking back and forth, mumbling incoherently.

The Monster King growled and moved toward his Captain, striking him on the side with a baton. The Captain dropped to his knees and hissed in pain.

"Do you realize what you just did? I'm gone from their collection once, and now hell has broken loose! You let that disgusting winged creature escape, and you lost Seda Arbor! She was the key to all of this! I need her! I need *both* of them!" the Monster King seethed.

This deal with the Jotnar, exchanging bloodstone for people, was wearing him down. He needed them now more than ever if the Fae were returning. They had been collecting the bloodstone for years, tearing apart the rocks within the Willow Grove to extract it. Bloodstone was the only material that could stop the Fae and other magical creatures—not all, but most. He didn't know if it would work against his number-one target, but it was worth a try.

The Captain stood back up on his legs and stared stoically at the Monster King, hesitant that he might get struck again with his stick, but smart enough to show respect. The Monster King pulled out his dark stone and held it up to the light, letting the dark sparkle reflect across the area. The Captain shrank back when he saw it and hissed again. He squeezed it and watched as the Captain shrank into himself in pain, his body convulsing in and out of his magicked Dragor and human forms.

A man stepped beside the Monster King and observed as the Captain convulsed. The Monster King put the stone back into his pocket and snarled down at the Captain, "You've been demoted." He grinned wickedly. "If you ever want to rise again in my ranks, you'll follow all of *my* orders." The Dragor curled his tail around his face, lowering himself close to the floor.

The Monster King looked at the man. "Thank you for joining me today. We have a mess to clean up here, and I expect great things from you. I'm promoting you within my rank as a mark of honor. But first, I want to know *everything* you know about Seda."

The man bowed respectfully and looked up, his long beard and graying hair gently blowing in the warm breeze. "I, Jason Arbor, accept your offer, and I will not fail."

The Monster King smiled and extended his arm toward the woman in the cell, signaling Jason to give the command. Jason turned to the demoted Dragor. "Arrange for this woman to be taken to the medical wing. Make sure they give her enough drugs to keep her from speaking about the Camp again, and ensure they throw a small celebration for her successful rehabilitation."

The Monster King nodded in approval.

The Dragor rose to his unsteady hind legs and gave the Rozzers instructions on what to do once they passed through the dome.

CHAPTER 30

<u>Cahir</u>

The night sky was waking with the first set of twinkling stars, and the sand slipped beneath their feet as they entered the mist of the Heath Forest, where the thick fog smelled like a blanket of damp moss. He could hear the soft song of crickets and see the partial moon illuminating the giant oak trees. Their tops clamoring for the freshness of the sky two hundred feet above. Deep red sap oozed down their trunks and gathered on the forest floor, where claw marks had torn into them, leaving scars that bore the weight of sorrow in the darkness.

Seda slept all the way through the dunes and had just woken up. He had spent hours watching her peacefully sleep as he held her, taking in the small details of her perfect face, like the freckle on her chin, the pink tint on the tip of her nose, and her pale eyelashes. She had one eyelash that stuck out to the left of her right eye. He wanted her to sleep longer, to heal and rest. He felt a profound sense of relief as he held her, and he was happy that she felt safe enough to sleep.

Cahir approached a large rock covered in moss and gently lowered Seda onto it. She moved her injured ankle and curled her toes. He watched her hand go to her lips to bite her nails nervously, then she lowered it before they connected.

"Thank you for carrying me. I'm sorry to be a burden," she said to him.

He almost wanted to laugh. If only she knew how he felt, having her back with him. She would never become a burden—ever. "I'd carry you all the way to the Wisps and beyond if you'd let me," he smirked sideways at her. Cahir observed her cheeks flush pink despite the darkness, and she averted her gaze, concentrating on the bleeding tree.

"What is this place?" she asked.

"This is the Heath Forest. We need to be careful here. Hailecs roam these woods," Ruel said as he walked up to the rock, panting from the long hike.

"What are Hailecs?" Seda asked, her eyes becoming wide with fear as she scanned the dark woods. Cahir placed his hand on her shoulder to comfort her, and she glanced up at him before quickly looking back at the haunted trees.

"Evil forest spirits that camouflage themselves as your desires to lure you away. If you see one, they could use their magic to enchant you. We need to be careful here," Kalon said as he approached the rock and set down his bag. He sat beside Seda on the rock, their legs touching, and Cahir felt a flash of annoyance. He shot him a warning glance, but Kalon winked at Cahir and left his leg where it was. "Are you thirsty?" Kalon offered Seda a flask of water.

"Thank you," she said as she took the flask from his hand and took a sip. Cahir watched her drink from the flask and ground his teeth together. He should have offered her water.

"Let's set up camp here," Benny said as he stepped out of the gloomy darkness, walking with Roya, Ferona, and Feich.

The group set up a small campsite and lit a fire. Ruel, Ojore, and Seren went to find something to cook, while Roya, Ferona, and Feich took to the skies, watching for any danger. Cahir had no desire to leave Seda's side. He, Kalon, and Benny found ways to stay focused where she could see them. He constantly found himself gazing at her, checking to make sure she was all right, and scolding himself whenever he had trouble keeping his eyes off her exposed legs. He really wanted the chance to talk with her privately, away from prying eyes.

As the night wore on and they settled down to rest, Cahir got up to find a place to relieve himself. Roya remained in the sky, taking turns with her siblings to guard from the skies, while Seren took turns with Kalon, guarding the ground.

He made his way around a large, bloody tree and unzipped his pants. The cool, misty air stung his exposed skin as the fog wrapped around his thighs.

"Cahir?" He looked around and saw Seda taking steps toward him, her leg limping painfully.

"What are you doing out here?" he asked, quickly zipping his pants back up. It was too dangerous for Seda to be alone out here at night.

"I had to find you." Her long, silky hair sparkled like starlight in the darkness, and his eyes locked onto her full, rosy lips.

"Do you want to talk? I'm so sorry I could not protect you at the Wyrd. I'm so, so sorry. I will never live that down."

She looked at him quizzically. "I missed you so much. I thought about you the entire time." She walked a distance away from him and sat down on a large, decaying log, patting her seat, inviting him to join her. He stepped toward her, grateful for the chance at privacy.

She gazed at him with heavy-lidded eyes, and Cahir drowned in her beauty.

Her lips. Her breathtaking amethyst eyes.

He began to move toward her, the only thing in his line of sight.

"I want you, Cahir," she whispered, her mouth moving in slow motion as she spoke. He watched her tongue slide across her lips, and his body responded instantly, his pants growing tight with desire.

Feeling drunk, he stumbled on a root and fell to the mossy ground. "I fucking want you, too, Sed. For so fucking long," he slurred. He got up, his mind still reeling. The world started to spin around him, blurring out of focus.

"Come to me. Come *with* me, Cahir. I need you," he thought he heard her say as she giggled. He didn't know which way she was, but he kept walking toward her voice. Desire consumed him whole, and he felt himself throb.

He saw her from a distance and turned her way, but he kept losing sight of her in the thick fog.

"Where are you?" he lazily called out, his hand instinctively reaching over his hardened length and squeezing it through his pants. A low growl rumbled from his throat.

He craved more; he *needed* her.

Sharp teeth sank into his shoulder as a powerful force slammed into him.

The pain jolted him awake, snapping him out of his haze. The ugliest creature he had ever seen pinned him to the ground. He held the monster away from his face, preventing the elongated, sharpened teeth from sinking into him again. The smell of death surrounded him as a Hailec snapped in his face, its transparent body flickering in and out of view.

Its skin was wrinkled and rotting, its eyes sunken and hollowed in the darkness, and its limbs long and skinny, with swollen joints.

He threw the Hailec off of him, causing it to flip over on the ground, and stood up, quickly grabbing the sword strapped to his back.

It quickly straightened itself and lunged again, coming for his throat.

He raised his sword into the air, readying for the satisfying kill.

Roya flew down, shifted, and sliced through its too-thin neck with a single long, extending claw. Its head dropped to the floor, its snarled expression illuminated by moonlight.

"I thought you were smarter than that!" She turned to him and seethed, flashing her teeth at him in an angry snarl.

"I had that thing!" he yelled back, setting his sword back down.

"No, you were too drunk in love, you fucking fool." She glared at his tented pants and then at the blood trickling down his arm. "Look at your shoulder." She nodded to his injury, and he looked down at it.

Fae blood trickled down and dripped from his fingertips.

"Shit. I have to hide this. Is there water around here somewhere?"

"Why don't you just show her who you really are?" she questioned in an exasperated huff.

"She'd never trust me again. I cannot do as you did and show her. She would ask me more questions than she did of you, and I can't answer them. Not yet. Once this fucking deal is over with the Wisps, I can do that."

Roya stared at him for a bit and then said, "As you wish. However, I know that it will happen eventually. It's best to be as honest as possible *now* before this whole thing gets any worse. Follow me."

He followed her to a stream and then rinsed the blood from his shoulder and arm. The cuts were quickly closing up, thankfully.

The chilling sound of a man's scream echoed through the night. Roya and Cahir turned sharply to the left, where the sound had come from.

"More Hailecs," Roya whispered. She quickly shifted into a Corvid and flew off in the direction of the scream.

Cahir ran after her. He jumped over large roots and rocks, cut around tree trunks, and stepped through vast patches of ferns. Roya came into view, holding onto a bloody body, a dead Hailec by her side.

Ruel was injured and coughing up blood, with bite marks all over his neck and deep scratches running down his body. His clothing had torn across his chest, and his blood coated the front of his shirt, where only scraps of it remained.

"Let's get him back to the Camp. There could be more out there hunting us right now." Cahir picked up Ruel's body, who groaned in pain, and quickly carried him back to the others.

When he entered the area, everyone was alert. Kalon had his sword out, standing near Seda.

Thank the gods, he thought.

Seda saw Cahir and stepped forward from her spot. "What happened?" She looked down at Ruel, and her eyes widened.

"A Hailec attacked Ruel," he answered.

Seda gasped and attempted to get closer to them.

"Stay here, Seda. Let them tend to him," Kalon said to her. She took a step back, standing next to Kalon, who placed a gentle hand on her shoulder. She did not shirk away from him. She nervously bit her nails and looked at the bloody body of Ruel in Cahir's arms.

Cahir growled low in his chest but focused his attention back to Ruel.

Benny ran up and looked at him. "Fuck," his face paled. "Put him here." He grabbed a small blanket and laid it out on the ground. Cahir placed Ruel down, and he groaned loudly in pain.

"My daughter. I saw my baby," Ruel panted as pain ripped through his body. Cahir and Benny looked at each other.

"Seren! We need that medic bag!" Benny shouted. Seren ran over and handed it to him. Benny pulled out some gauze and placed it against Ruel's open wounds.

"It's no use, Benny," Cahir said as his blood continued to

soak the cloth. Benny kept trying to mop up the blood, refusing to give up. Ruel groaned in pain and coughed.

"No more, please," he begged Benny. "It's my time. I will see her again, this time. I'm coming for you, sweetie."

Seren, Kalon, Ojore, and Askold walked up and circled them as Roya remained near Seda. They held their hands over their hearts and hung their heads solemnly.

Ruel slowly stopped breathing.

"Mother Goddess, guide Ruel into the afterlife. Watch over him and grant him safe passage. Forgive his sins, for he has loved and lost but has had you and Solios in his heart. May he rest in peace and get to share his love with his daughter once more," Ojore prayed.

Cahir looked over at him. Praying to the Mother Goddess and Solios was not a common practice among humans. They prayed to Lord Mordred for their protection, further proving he wasn't who he was pretending to be. Cahir held his hand over his heart and said "amen" with the others. He did not know Ruel long, but they shared laughter and triumphs. He prayed that Ruel would find his peace and that the Mother Goddess would bless his soul, for this life is hard and good people deserve solace.

While they all said their goodbyes, Roya flew into the sky and searched for more Hailecs, while Ferona and Feich stood back with Seda, protecting her in case any appeared.

THEY TOOK turns sleeping after they laid Ruel to rest in a dark patch of soft ferns. No more Hailecs attacked the group for the remainder of the evening. As the sunrise cast its coral-colored glow across the sky and through the scattered trees, and the mist dispersed, Cahir looked down at Seda. Her face was so peaceful as she slept.

What magic was purple? The Fae were green, and monsters generally favored the color red. He never heard of purple before in his long, magic-filled life.

He watched Seda as she slept, her chest rising and falling with gentle breaths. His hand lingered in his pocket, where he still had the necklace he needed to return to her. Never before in his life had he felt such emotion for another being, and the way he was starting to think and act was concerning. His desire to care about this whole ordeal was decreasing day by day.

He no longer cared if the monsters continued their rule, if the dome fell, or even if he had to burn down villages or kill people to keep her safe. More than anything, though, he was starting to worry that he wasn't going to be around to get her *home*. He had less than ten days. Actually, he didn't even know how many days remained; the last few were a blur.

She stirred, and he quickly glanced away, not wanting to get caught staring at her while she slept.

He almost died last night because he couldn't think straight. When had Seda ever said things like that to him? *Never*. She only saw him as a friend. He felt a twinge of sadness pierce his heart at the thought.

Would she only ever see him as a friend?

Sure, they were close. But not in that way. Roya was right; he was a fool for falling for the Hailec's tricks. He needed to distance himself from his own heart and to keep his head straight. He would still be her friend, but he could not allow his foolish emotions to get in the way of the one thing he had to do most.

He had to protect her.

He needed to *care* about the lives of others, the murderous rule of the monsters, and the farmed humans living in Joro for the monsters' consumption. It's what Seda would want.

She had compassion and kindness. She couldn't even witness

an injured person at the hands of another without needing to look away.

Seda opened her eyes and looked at Cahir. "Morning," she said to him with a yawn and sleepy eyes. He gazed back at her, his eyes lingering on her soft lips before quickly looking away.

Stupid, unlearning fool.

"How'd you sleep?" she asked him.

"Fine," he replied. "How's your ankle this morning? You think you can walk today?"

She looked down and rolled her ankle around. "It feels much better." She smiled over at him, and he quickly looked away, feeling his gaze drawn to her perfect, full lips once again.

"Is everything okay?" she asked.

He nodded and pulled the necklace out of his pocket, letting it catch the morning sunshine and glitter in the light.

"My necklace!" she exclaimed. "Oh, Cahir, thank you so much." He reached out, and she excitedly took it, placing it over her head and tucking it into her dress.

She looked back at him, her brows knitting together. "How do you know of this place called Umbrea, Cahir?" she asked him.

He looked at her with softened eyes and said, "Seda, there are things I wish to tell you. When the time comes, I need you to promise me you'll keep an open mind. I'm, and have always been, here for you."

Her gaze remained on him, threaded with quiet confusion. "Why can't you just tell me now?"

"I—" he tried, but his lips froze. *The fucking Wisps!*

Askold stirred from his sleep and farted loudly. Seda and Cahir exchanged a glance before bursting into laughter.

Askold jumped up and looked around in confusion. "Hailecs?" he asked as his eyes darted around in his sleep haze.

Both Seda and Cahir erupted into laughter again. Cahir

quickly rubbed away the tears welling up in his eyes. He missed her while she was gone, and he was happy to have her back.

She was his best friend... and more.

CHAPTER 31

<u>Seda</u>

"Does anyone have toothpaste?" Benny grumbled as they packed up their campsite. Seda's tongue automatically grazed her teeth. She definitely needed to brush; it had been way too long.

"Just chew on a few mint leaves. That always works for me," replied Askold as he was folding up a small blanket to fit inside one of the backpacks.

"Where can I find those?" Benny asked. Seda was listening. She desperately wanted to chew on some, too. How embarrassing. She was usually so clean. This was the first time in her life that she had gone so long without regular showers and clean teeth.

"I don't know. Just don't breathe on me," Askold replied.

Seda smiled. Cahir was right; not all of the Rozzers were bad. Askold was pretty funny sometimes.

"Har-har-har," Benny said, letting out a loud huff. "Come over here so I can *har* in your damn face."

"Really mature, boys," Roya said as she walked around,

waiting for them to finish bickering. "Here, Benny." She reached into her pocket and pulled out a stick. "Chew this. It cleans your teeth and freshens your breath."

Everyone turned to look at the stick she was handing him.

"What's that?" Askold walked over to Benny and examined the stick closely.

"Datun," she replied nonchalantly.

"Do you have more? Where can I find it?" Askold asked.

Seda was very interested in this plant.

Roya looked at her nails and picked something out of one of them. "It's over there." She glanced at a small leafy bush.

He hurried over, broke off a branch, took a sniff, and then looked back at her. "You promise you're not just trying to poison me?"

"If I wanted to kill you, you'd be dead. And right now, with all of this bickering and these stupid questions, I'm starting to feel like that might be a good idea."

Askold put the stick in his mouth and started chewing, first grimacing in disgust, then raising his eyebrows and humming in approval.

Benny chewed his piece and spit it out. "Wow, that really works. Thank you, Roya." He smiled at her with a chunk of the stick stuck in his tooth.

She examined his tooth, nodded in acknowledgment, and then walked away. Benny observed her graceful figure as she left.

Did he just look at her butt?!

Seda walked over to the bush and picked a stick. She put it in her mouth and chewed. It was tough to start, and not anything like a toothbrush and toothpaste, but the natural taste was interesting. She spit it out, her mouth now fresh, and broke off ten more, just in case, and placed them into her threadbare dress pocket. Now she just needed a shower and better clothes, and shoes would also be nice.

How was she going to walk these woods without shoes? She would step on sticks and worse... her feet would get even *dirtier*.

"Camp's packed," Ojore said as he walked up to Benny.

Benny nodded and looked at the others. "Time to move."

Feich and Ferona shifted and took the lead, flying high and keeping a watchful eye on their surroundings. Cahir was at the front of the group, and Seda kept looking around to see him. Did she do something wrong? He was acting so differently toward her than he had just the day before.

She fought the urge to go to him. Maybe he just needed a moment to breathe and think about everything happening around them.

Roya walked back to Seda. "Did you like the datun?" she asked.

Seda's distracted thoughts were immediately pulled away from Cahir. "Oh my goodness, yes! Thank you so much. I didn't get to have things like a toothbrush while in the Camp." She smiled at the woman and really took her in. She was beautiful. Her features were unique and magical. She could see why Benny would be attracted to her.

Cahir was the first to follow up the path, followed by Benny and then Ojore. Askold came fourth, and then Roya and Seda, the two of them walking side by side. Kalon went last, looking around for movement from behind.

"The Hailecs don't typically hunt much during the day," Roya said to her. "We should be okay, but if not, Feich and Ferona are watching from above."

Seda looked up at Roya's siblings, "You called them your murder. What's that about?"

"A murder is a term for a small group of Corvids. Those two are my closest in command. There are more of us, as you know, based on what happened during the Wyrd when you were selected."

"You guys got the Rozzers and Lord Mordred really good.

You should have seen him after he transported us." Her smile vanished, and she gazed up at the trees, seeing blood trickle down their trunks and their tall branches reach for the clouds.

She changed the subject. "A murder. Interesting word to use." Seda smiled at her. "Does seem rather fitting."

Roya chuckled, then looked at Seda, her expression turning serious. "Seda, we've been keeping an eye on you since you arrived here. We made a point not to interfere much, but we've always had you in our protection."

Seda thought back to the day that Alexi and Michael hurt her. Distant memories of birds flitted through her mind, but they were fuzzy. Then she thought about the black bird leading her into the grove of trees past the Gardvord. "Was that you who led me to that strange wall through the trees back in Joro?"

Roya nodded.

"Why did you show me that? I thought I saw a door, but when I looked away, it disappeared."

"I can lead you and show you things. But you must piece it together on your own. There are others in the same position as us."

"Ferona and Feich," Seda replied.

"…Yes," Roya answered hesitantly.

As Seda leaped over a puddle of the blood-sap draining slowly from the oak tree, she landed on a sharp stick and felt the pain shoot up through her leg. She was about to fall, but strong, warm arms surrounded her. She looked up, expecting to see Cahir, but she saw Kalon's handsome face staring down at her with a smile. His seafoam-colored eyes looked into hers, and her heart skipped a beat.

"Careful there," he said, gently placing her down.

She took a step back, a little embarrassed at her clumsiness. "Thank you," she said as her cheeks heated.

Roya glanced at both of them, shook her head, and then walked away, muttering, "Damn men."

His eyes sparkled as he looked at her. "Why don't you hold onto my arm for balance? These woods are full of sharp sticks like that one. Well find you some shoes soon."

She accepted his offered arm, and he guided her through the woods, occasionally pointing out things to avoid. His arm was solid and strong. She could feel his muscles tense whenever she shifted, and she kept glancing up at him. He was exceptionally tall, surpassing Cahir's height, with a strong jawline dusted with stubble and captivating dark features that contrasted with his olive skin.

He looked down at her and saw her staring at him.

She quickly looked away.

"You were so brave back there," he said to her as he smiled down.

"Uh, me?" she asked, hesitantly looking back up.

"Yes, *you.*" He chuckled. "I haven't seen someone ride a Lionne in a very long time."

"Oh, I wasn't riding him. He picked me up," Seda said, blushing again, a little embarrassed by his compliment.

"It looked the same to me. Those creatures are ferocious. They don't like just anyone. I've only ever known them to like one person, actually." Kalon helped her over a large log, and his fingers grazed against her arm, sending a shiver of goosebumps along her skin.

"When did you see more of them? I didn't even know he was called a Lionne," she asked excitedly, hopeful for Elco that he could find his friends again soon.

"Not in a very long time," he replied.

"Oh." Seda frowned. "You must have seen a lot of things being a Traverser."

Her cheeks warmed again as she gazed at his handsome face, and Kalon smiled. She had to look away.

"The Jotnar are the worst lately; they're spoiled, nasty creatures. But the Lionne? He's truly the most terrifying. He can breathe fire and pounce like a large cat. You'd never see him coming if he were hunting you," he said.

She remembered the first time she met Elco and how intimidating he had been, but now she saw him in a new light. He was her friend, and she was secretly thankful she had a friend like him on her side.

"I hope Elco's okay," she said to him. "When we were in the Camp, he was injured by the guards. They beat him badly. It took him hours to heal. I really hope he finds us soon. I keep thinking about him."

"He's likely hunting us now."

Glancing back into the overgrown forest behind her, Seda caught sight of a Hailec watching her from a distance, its knees pressed into the damp ground. She let out a gasp, and Kalon spun around.

She froze, and Kalon slowly drew his sword, but the Hailec made no move toward them. It simply knelt there, watching Seda with its dark, unblinking eyes. Then, it lowered its head to the ground and disappeared into the eerie darkness. Images of Ruel's torn body raced through her mind. This Hailec had been following them, and they hadn't realized. Why didn't it try to attack?

"Elco will find you, Seda," Kalon said, lowering his sword. "I just hope he doesn't eat all of us when he does."

CHAPTER 32

<u>Cahir</u>

As they traveled through the Heath Forest, Cahir struggled to resist glancing back at Seda, reminding himself to maintain a safe distance and let others alert him if needed.

His mind was racing, and she was at the center of all his thoughts. She must be horrified after witnessing Ruel pass away right in front of them. Twice, he stopped in his tracks, causing Benny to run into him, and he fought the urge to turn around and go to her.

They wandered among the large trees for hours, with no sign of danger. A large clearing appeared, and he paused.

"A good place to stop for lunch?" asked Benny beside him.

"Looks like it, let me ask Roya and the Corvids to circle the area to check for anything dangerous first."

He turned around and began to walk back when he saw Kalon and Seda's arms intertwined. She was smiling and blushing up at him, and he was laughing in response.

An intense surge of emotion, like a wildfire fueled by the

wind, swept through him. He let out a fierce growl, mimicking a beast, and lunged at Kalon, pushing him to the ground. He swung to punch his face, but Ojore, Askold, and Seren pulled him back.

Kalon, as quick as a serpent's strike, jumped back up.

"Keep your hands off of her!" Cahir seethed as he struggled to break free from the hands holding him down.

Benny came running back. "What the fuck happened?"

Kalon smiled at him as he dusted off the sticks from his shirt, and Cahir fumed. Seda ran up to him. "I'm okay, Cahir! I'm okay! He was not trying to hurt me."

He looked at Seda with her pleading eyes. "Please, Cahir. He wasn't trying to hurt me. He was helping me."

"I don't think he's worried about me *hurting* you," Kalon said loud enough for everyone to hear.

Cahir flew into a rage again. He pushed Seren off and lunged for the annoying prick, but the giant brute, Ojore, punched him across the face, hard. He fell back onto the ground with a loud grunt.

"Cahir!" Seda ran up to him and held onto his chest. "Why did you punch him like that?" She turned around and looked at Ojore with anger written across her face.

"He's acting like a jealous fool," Ojore said with a shrug.

Cahir pushed himself up and marched over to Ojore. "I swear to the fucking gods if you punch me one more time..."

"You'll what? Strangle me with magic?" Ojore provoked.

Cahir went deathly silent, his magic now simmering beneath his skin, attempting to break free and kill these fucking assholes. No one said anything for a long breath, as they all stared at Cahir and Ojore.

"What does that mean?" Seda broke the silence as she grasped Cahir's arm and reached for his bruising face.

He looked down at her and said, "He's an asshole."

He broke away from Seda and marched up to Roya, seething

in frustration. "Have the Corvids check the area around here. We want to have lunch." He walked away, needing to distance himself from the group.

THE TEN OF them ate their meager lunch in awkward silence. Cahir and Kalon were at opposite sides of a long, shared log. Seda was not sitting next to either of them.

"So, uhhh... the weather's nicer here than in the dunes," Askold stated, trying to start a conversation.

"Shut up, idiot," Ojore said to him.

Everyone went back to eating silently, slowly munching on dried meats, and the nuts and berries Ojore gathered along the way. The sounds of their chewing and the soft chirping of finches nearby filled the quiet.

Roya slowly began to laugh. As everyone turned to look at her, her laughter grew louder. She wiped her eyes and said, "Pathetic men."

Ferona chuckled, and they both looked over at Feich, who just shrugged.

"I'm so glad that my bruised face is of humor to you, Roya," Cahir sneered from next to her.

Benny chuckled and then cleared his throat when Cahir glared at him. "Uhhh... that does look pretty gnarly. The last one just healed."

Roya laughed again, slapping her knee, and Benny quickly hid his smile with his hand.

"Whatever." Cahir stood up and stretched his legs, locking eyes with Kalon.

Kalon flipped him off and then licked his finger, sucking it into his mouth. Red-hot anger flooded Cahir's face. He knew exactly what that meant, and he wasn't about to let him get that close to her again. He wanted to rip his fucking finger off and repeatedly shove it into his eye sockets so he could never look at Seda again.

"Do you have a death wish?" Ferona asked Kalon from her position, chewing on a cricket she had found on the log.

Kalon responded with a wiggle of his brows.

Seda didn't say anything, silently staring down at her hands. He needed to talk to her, to explain, to tell her how he felt. She must be confused.

No, he couldn't do that. He couldn't risk their friendship by confessing his feelings. He would control himself.

His warring emotions were causing a rift, and he wasn't in a place to tell her anything, not yet. He needed to remain her friend, her *gods-damned-friend,* and he needed to remember that Seda always had a choice. If Seda chose to be with another man, that decision was hers and hers alone. He knew that. What had been going on with him lately? He sighed and looked at Kalon. "Truce?"

"Depends."

"On?" His patience was already thin. If this bastard kept pushing it...

"On *you.* I was just being friendly and helping Seda. There was no need to attack me. She's barefoot and walking through these woods. Maybe if you weren't trying to lead from the front today, like a commandeering asshole, you could've seen that. I promise you I had no intentions of hurting her."

Cahir felt the burning sensation of shame. He had forgotten about her lack of shoes. He was so focused on trying to control his own emotions and lust that he asked her to walk today.

Seda looked up at Cahir with pleading eyes.

He took a deep breath and sincerely said, "I'm sorry, Seda." He looked her in her eyes and then looked over Kalon's shoulder, not meeting his. "And I'm... I'm sorry, *Kalon.*" He sighed. "I'm protective of her. She's been through a lot, and I don't want to see her hurt."

Seda walked over to him and hugged him, her lilac scent teasing his nose. He placed his palm on her shoulder and lightly pushed her back so he could look into her beautiful eyes. "Whatever you want, for *you*, Sed. *Always.*" Then he pulled her back into a hug and kissed the top of her head.

CHAPTER 33

<u>Cahir</u>

The group continued through the Heath Forest until twilight, discovering a small, lush grove with waterfalls of fading light filtering through a mix of giant ferns, oaks, and pines. The bloody oaks thinned as they moved further north, giving way to vibrant, verdant landscapes. Seda refused any more help from anyone as she traveled throughout the day, leaving Cahir angry with himself. He repeatedly offered to help her, but she rejected his help each time.

A large, glittering pond sat at the center of the grove, with fireflies dancing above it, their glowing rays of light reflecting off the water. Their peaceful radiance reminded him of the home he wished to share with Seda someday.

"What a great spot," Seren said, setting his pack against the trunk of a giant pine tree. "Plus, we can all bathe." He pulled a bar of soap from his pack and showed it to everyone. "I'd say ladies first," he said, as he looked toward Seda. "But I'm selfish. If no one wants to see, you'd better look away now."

Kalon, Seren, Askold, and Benny all walked to the shoreline

and removed their clothing. Cahir stayed behind with Seda as Roya, Ferona, and Feich took to the sky. Seda sat behind a large oak, and Cahir sat next to her.

"No bath for you?" she asked him as she played with a bit of moss in her palm that she picked off the tree.

"I will later," he shrugged.

They both gazed down at the moss, unsure of what to say next. Cahir felt ashamed about what he'd done earlier. Not because he'd wanted to kill Kalon, but because he'd missed the opportunity to help her and had only added to her confusion instead.

Fuck Kalon.

"I'm sorry I couldn't protect you from the Wyrd," he admitted. "I came for you as quickly as I could. I couldn't even think straight. I just had to get to you."

"I know, and it isn't your fault." She dropped the moss from her hand and watched it fall softly to the ground, then looked back at him. "It's horrible there, Cahir, truly horrible."

"Were you hurt?" He felt his heart start racing as he waited anxiously for her response.

She drew a deep breath and glanced down at her nails, dirty from her time in the Camp and the journey north. "Not in the way you'd expect. I was locked up in a dark cell and..." She fought back a sob. "Esper was locked up right next to me."

Cahir looked at her in shock. "Esper? Was Diantha there?"

She shook her head. "Diantha had been killed before I arrived. But Esper *was pregnant*, Cahir. And the cell was so dark and so lonely and so cold, I couldn't see her. She gave birth while I was there. Her baby was stillborn. I'll forever be haunted by her screams and the sound of her praying and rocking her baby. The guards came in and saw that she had given birth, and that the baby had died." Tears streamed down her face, and she wiped her nose with the back of her hand. "They beat her, Cahir.

They beat her after she went through that. And then they dragged her out of the cell and killed her."

She gazed up at him with a fury that Cahir had never seen in her before, and her palms and eyes started to glow. "The Rozzers *raped* her into pregnancy, did not feed her well, kept her in that cold, dark cell, and when she finally gave birth, they hurt her again. That's what Joro's society is about. I'm so upset that I was an unknowing supporter of it!"

A wave of disgust and horror roiled through him. The thought of what went on at the Camp, with Seda there to see it, and the fate of Esper and Diantha, made his stomach churn and his head spin.

Her eyes were flaring the brightest amethyst he had ever seen. He hesitantly asked, "How did you?" He paused, unsure how to ask. "How did you not receive the same treatment?"

She laughed angrily and fixed her gaze on her glowing palms. "Lord Mordred wanted to see me. He had me meet with him. I tried to ask him about this 'dark stone' Elco told me about, but he didn't answer. He told me that I was there for a reason. And you want to know what he said?" She looked over at him, her eyes burning and her nose running. "He said I was there for 'redemption'. Whatever that means. He gave an order that no one was allowed to touch or hurt me. That didn't stop Alexi, the Rozzer who dragged me away from you at the Wyrd, from trying, though."

Cahir's growl rumbled low in his throat, and Seda looked up to him and whispered with a devious smile, "I *killed* him, Cahir. I killed him with these." She held up her purple palms for him to see. "It came out of nowhere. I was so mad, *SO MAD!*" She shouted the last two words as she slammed her palms on her knees, releasing a small spark that did not affect her. "He wanted to hurt me again, *so mad* at that place and hearing and seeing the pain of those innocent people, all I could think about was hurting him like how you killed Michael at the Wyrd, and how *good* it felt to see you rip his heart out, and then all of a sudden he was lying on the opposite side of my cell convulsing."

She did not show any signs of remorse for killing Alexi. That confused him, not in the sense that this change of character was bad, but rather that it was so vastly different from how she had been in Joro. He was glad that she got her revenge, *thrilled* even, but she didn't seem to mind taking the life of another, even if they deserved it.

What does she know about the dark stone?

"An eye for an eye," she said with a malevolent grin.

The purple in her arms and hands began to fade, and her eyes returned to their regular shade. "Does this scare you?" she asked about her magic.

He responded immediately, not needing to consider his answer. "Not at all. I'm not sure what kind of magic it is, but the fact that you could protect yourself, Seda... that you *DID*? I'm so impressed and so *proud* of you. You have no idea." He smiled, and he knew it showed in his eyes. "So fucking proud, Sed."

"Ladies are up," Askold announced as he circled the tree, his blond, damp hair plastered to his scalp. He stared down at them. "Where are Roya and Ferona?"

They both shrugged, and Cahir replied, "Maybe hunting for mice or something."

Askold laughed. "Between us, I think Benny wants to kiss the mouse breath."

Seda laughed. "I saw him watching her. He really does have the hots." She stood up and stretched her legs. "How will I know no one's watching?"

Cahir stood with her.

Askold raised his palm over his heart. "I, Askold Gardner, solemnly swear not to piss off Cahir." Cahir looked at him impatiently. "Now we just need to get Kalon to swear the same thing."

"I make no guarantees," Kalon said as he walked around the tree, shaking out his long hair and sporting a serpentine smile. He looked at Seda and winked.

This fucking man.

"Dude, stop trying to start fucking fights," Askold scolded.

"Nah, I won't look, Seda," he responded. "I'm not a desperate puppy dog." He fixed his gaze on Cahir, and Cahir's nostrils flared.

He was going to take this man's fucking life slowly and savor every gods-damned moment.

"I'm going to find Roya and Ferona first," Seda ignored them and walked around the tree, leaving the men alone.

Seren and Benny approached them.

"How long do we give them?" Benny asked.

"Until they say they're done," Cahir said as he sat back down on the ground. The others sat down next to him.

"What about Feich?" Benny asked as he played with the same piece of moss Seda had earlier.

"That guy's more bird than man," Seren said with a laugh.

Cahir waited with the others while the women bathed in the pond. He half listened as the other men bickered and joked with each other. He thought about what Seda had been through, what she had discovered, and Lord Mordred's meeting with her.

He knew she was special, but how did Mordred?

He had the stone.

He thought about the lack of desire to finish his journey to find the stone. He thought about how he failed at retrieving it for Umbrea, despite all of the 'meetings' he had spent looking. It was something he had been after for the last few years, but instead of spending time finding the stone, he spent his time with her.

He didn't care anymore. Let Mordred and the monsters keep the fucking thing.

He thought about Seda's anger toward those who hurt her

and others, and how her magic flared to life when she spoke of it. She was absolutely stunning.

She would want the stone, but would it also benefit Umbrea's cause? All of this was intertwined, and he didn't know how the pieces fit together. His emotions for Seda kept getting in the way, and now, as a result, he gave no fucks about finishing his tasks.

He just wanted to get her to Umbrea, where she could live her life safely... with *him*.

"All done, boys," Ferona said as she walked around the tree, chewing on a crunchy bug.

"How do you keep finding those?" Askold asked her with a shiver. "So gross."

"This is the forest, Askold," Ferona said as she rolled her eyes. "What's gross is the sludgy part of the pond you left behind when you bathed," she retorted and threw the last of the bug in her mouth, purposely crunching it louder.

He raised his arm, sniffed his armpit, made a face, and then shrugged. "I personally think the pond appreciated my manly musk."

Ferona rolled her eyes again and walked back down to the pond. Cahir got up and followed the others. They finished setting up their campsite for the night and stayed up chatting until the stars reflected across the water and the fireflies had vanished.

Once the others fell asleep, except for Ferona and Roya, who kept watch, Cahir got up and walked to the pond, where the soft waters reflected the glow of the campfire.

He looked around to make sure no one was watching, undressed, and stepped into the cool water, grabbing the bar of soap from the shore. He washed himself and went in deeper, diving in and swimming around. The water lifted his anxiety away, like plumes of smoke escaping a volcano. He floated on his back and stared up at the sparkling stars.

Seda was his best friend, but his heart longed for more. How long could he truly avoid these feelings?

He heard Seda's voice and turned to see her sleeping form. Seda called his name again from another direction, and he let out a groan.

Not again.

He swam toward the shore and carefully grabbed his sword.

"Cahir…" the voice called.

As Roya descended, he nodded toward the dark woods ahead and slowly walked into the trees with his sword drawn. Through the trees, he spotted Seda standing naked; his eyes flicked off guard for a moment, but he resisted the urge to be entranced.

Roya and Ferona let out loud caws, rousing the others.

"What are you doing out here?" he asked, pretending to believe the creature while holding the sword.

"I missed you so much," it said in a voice that was a direct replica of Seda's.

"I'm sure you have," he replied.

The Hailec's enchantment wasn't working on him, and its illusion flickered, showcasing its wretched form for a split moment.

It lunged for him, dropping the illusion. Cahir brought down the sword and sliced off its head. He bent down and picked it up from its scraggly hair, noting its sharp teeth and melting skin on its face. He carried it back through the trees.

Everyone was up, looking in his direction.

He hurled the Hailec's head to the ground and drove the sword through the top, impaling it into the dirt. The sword shook back and forth as Cahir released it.

"Someone's got a horse," Askold said, and the others chuckled.

Cahir looked down and remembered he was naked.

CHAPTER 34

<u>Seda</u>

It took a few more days, but the scenery eventually changed. They didn't run into any more Hailecs since Cahir had taken out the last one at the pond. She noticed how he had been with her since the Camp. He appeared even more unwavering in his protection and affection for her than before, almost as if, perhaps, he saw her as more.

A faint glimmer of hope began to melt the hardened ice surrounding her heart.

She couldn't shake the memory of how his stomach muscles tensed as he drove the sword into the creature's head with a powerful thrust, and she also couldn't stop thinking about the way his penis, the same one she'd seen the other night, had pressed into her when they woke up together in their apartment. She had no idea it looked like that. No wonder the bulge in his towel looked the way it did.

She wanted to see it again.

She felt her cheeks and ears immediately start to flush and turn red.

His muscular form reminded her of a character from her favorite book from her teenage years. Not that the book got into those kinds of details... at least not that her parents were aware of.

"What's the name of this place?" she asked, trying to distract herself from her racing thoughts as they drifted up to the tallest trees she had ever seen. Pines and redwoods towered overhead, filtering the sun in waterfalls of light. The forest floor was dim, faintly shimmering with a misty haze that shifted as they walked. Even in the morning light, the mist seemed to draw them further into the woods. The soft ground was a relief to her sore feet, with patches of ferns and moss that were oddly more slippery than in the Heath Forest. She stepped over a fallen pinecone and was glad she could see it through the haze.

"Don't know if this place has a name. I've always just called it the redwoods," Seren said from her side.

"Are there Hailec's here?" she asked him, now and then looking around, in case she spotted something.

"Not this far north, thankfully. But there are other things we need to watch for," he replied. She shivered and glanced around nervously in the dim light. Fearing that she was sensing someone watching, whispering, and tracking her every move.

They wove their way through the trees as the wind picked up, billowing her dress around her knees, and the mist thinned out like a stream flowing away. Something wet and prickly wrapped around her leg, and she tried to jump back, but the thing tightened its grip, pulling her onto her back and dragging her across the ground.

She screamed.

Roya swiftly jumped down and caught her hand, attempting to pull her back. "The Gnashing Flora has her!"

Seda looked down at her leg and saw a thick vine wrapped around it. It yanked her again, violently dragging her and Roya along the forest floor, Seda's dress riding up her back to reveal her bare legs.

Fear shot through her spine like shards of glass. Her body rushed through ferns and random pinecones that scraped against her back. Plants the size of her snapped at her, trying to bite as she blew past.

"I have you!" Roya shouted as she firmly held onto Seda's hand.

The vine pulled them faster than the others could keep up, and they lost them in the distance.

A loud screech pierced through the thicket, and Seda looked in the direction the plant pulled her. A massive yellow flower emerged, its menacing thorns dripping clear liquid as it opened its mouth.

A bloodcurdling scream tore from her lips.

She survived the Camp, experienced horrible creatures, and survived the palm of a Jotnar throwing a tantrum. How had it all come to this? She didn't want to die by a plant.

Another vine lashed out and wrapped around Roya, yanking them apart. They were both lifted off the ground and into the air. Ferona and Feich dove down and clawed at the Gnashing Flora, scratching at the plant's thick vines.

The Gnashing Flora let out a deafening screech that pierced their ears and slightly loosened its grip on both of them. Roya immediately shifted and took to the sky to join her siblings in their defensive attack. It tightened its grip on Seda once more and began forming massive bubbles from its opening.

They slowly floated toward her.

"Avoid the globules!" Ferona shouted as she flew past Seda and clawed at the vine attached to her.

The plant shrieked and flung its vine around while still wrapped tightly around her, leaving Seda disoriented. The globules floated past an arm's length away.

Her mind was overwhelmed with panic, blurring her thoughts and making it impossible to think clearly.

The pearlescent bubbles floated through the air in varying sizes, some popping early and splattering, singing the nearby plant life, sending up small tufts of smoke where they landed.

The flower forced its petals together and pulled her inward toward its large center opening. She looked down and saw the razor-sharp spines fluttering within the opening, dripping with the clear liquid that created the bubbles.

A loud, echoing snarl tore through the air as Elco appeared, soaring high and circling the plant.

He dove down and spewed a stream of red fire from his maw directly onto the vine wrapped around Seda, causing it to wither into dust.

She hit the ground with a thud, and pain surged from her healing ankle. The Gnashing Flora writhed and screeched, flinging its vines into the air as it tried to reach Elco and the Corvids.

It released another massive stream of bubbles into the sky.

The others ran into the clearing, and Seda looked back at them quickly. Cahir ran forward and grabbed her into his arms.

Seren ran past with his sword held high and sliced off a vine reaching for Seda again. The vine shriveled back quickly, and the plant squealed in pain. Kalon, Ojore, Askold, and Benny began stabbing its leaves.

Out of nowhere, a vine snaked out and wrapped around Seren, lifting him and sending a blast of bubbles straight into his face.

The sound of sizzling flesh and screams echoed through the area.

Elco flew down again, preparing another attack when the Gnashing Flora immediately retreated into itself, yowling in pain.

It closed into a large, pulsating pod, dropping Seren's unmoving body to the ground.

What happened? No one had hurt it enough to provoke that reaction. It writhed in pain and screeched into the forest, pulsating with agony.

Seda looked around in confusion and saw Elco land near Seren's body. He blasted fire at the screaming plant, setting it ablaze.

It smoldered into a pile of ash.

Ojore ran toward Seren, and Roya quickly shifted her form to block him, preventing him from going further. "No! Do not touch him! The poison's all over his body."

"I have to see!" Ojore yelled in her face and pushed Roya roughly to the side. He lunged forward onto his knees and bent down toward Seren's lifeless, blistered body, avoiding contact.

Ojore let out a guttural, animalistic roar that echoed through the surrounding trees.

Seda scrambled out of Cahir's arms and ran next to Ojore, ignoring the pain that tore through her ankle. She stared down at Seren's unrecognizable body and softly placed her palm on Ojore's back.

He stiffened, leaped to his feet, and shouted, "This is *your* fault! You're *so* weak, *so* fucking helpless. We're all out here trying to help *you*. And so far we've lost two of our friends, two of *my friends*." His voice caught on the last words.

"Don't speak to her like that," Cahir seethed as he stepped in front of Seda, blocking her from Ojore.

"Or what, Cahir? What will the big, bad Fae do to me that they already haven't? My people have suffered because of your kind... Because of *you*. And now here I am, pretending to get along with scum like you, to save... To save *this thing*." He pointed at Seda. "Some magical creature she is. She can't even protect herself when a fucking flower attacks her! We should be out there searching for what the Rising's meant to do! We need to find the Darkened instead of helping this thing get to the Wisps and dying in the process!"

Elco stalked behind him, letting out a menacing growl at Ojore as smoke billowed from his nostrils.

"Oh, shut the fuck up, you overgrown, disfigured cat! Why didn't you blow that fucking flame where it was needed sooner? Whatever it was scared of, it wasn't you!" He stomped off into the distance, leaving everyone else behind.

Seda dropped to her knees beside Seren.

She looked down at him and watched in horror as his bubbling skin rippled.

He was gone. He was dead because of her. Why didn't she tap into her power? All she felt was fear. It hadn't even crossed her mind to use her power to protect herself or others. All she thought was that she was going to die. She only thought about herself.

She let out a cry as tears started streaming down her face.

How useless and selfish she was. Her mind flashed back to the night when the Jotnar attacked the dome, and she was alone, feeling so hopeless that she curled up into a ball on the shower floor and did nothing. She would have let the monsters eat her back then, just like she would have today.

She was a fraud, powerless, and weak when she had the power not to be.

She cried for Seren, who would still be alive if she had just acted and not halted in the face of danger. His gentle nature and kindness were ripped away from this world, all because of her, all because he was trying to protect *her*.

Elco stepped forward and wrapped himself around both her and Seren's bodies, making sure not to touch the poison. He blocked everyone else's view so she could cry without anyone watching. She buried her face in his mane and screamed as loud as she could, her throat throbbing from the strain, but she didn't care.

She deserved the pain.

Another agonizing scream tore from her lips as she unleashed her anger, sorrow, self-loathing, and outrage at the unfairness of this cruel world.

Dark clouds formed over the clearing, casting a shadow over the area. It started pouring rain with such intensity that Seda gazed up at the darkened sky, letting the rain mix with the tears on her cheeks. How fucking perfect, her first time experiencing the rain was in misery, so ideal for her awful, fucking life.

She held out her palm and watched the drops patter against her skin.

She clenched her fingers into a tight fist.

Purple lightning snaked across the sky as thunder shook the ground. Seda pressed her face back into Elco and screamed. Filled with anger over Seren's death at her weak hands and her lack of courage, she screamed again and again and again.

A giant bolt of purple lightning tore through the area, bursting into hundreds of fragments and scorching the nearby carnivorous plants.

Exhaustion enveloped her, and thunder shook the ground as Elco pulled her closer, allowing her sorrow to pierce him with a sharpened sword he didn't resist.

CHAPTER 35

<u>Roya</u>

The beauty she saw in front of her was unlike anything she had ever experienced in her long life. The magical lightning flashing across the sky, frying hundreds of plants over and over and turning them into smoking piles of dust, took her breath away.

Lightning strikes flashed through the area in rapid succession, making everyone step away from the plants that were long gone.

Seda was *amazing*. She was everything she hoped for. She was devoted to everything that she was.

When Seda's cries subsided and the clouds cleared, Elco slowly untwisted from Seda, releasing her glowing body. She continued to lie on the ground in a tightly curled ball.

Roya dropped to one knee, a hand over her heart, and bowed. Ferona and Feich followed. "My master, my *queen*," Roya whispered.

Cahir ran to Seda and held out a hand for her to take. She

looked up to him and placed her palm into his. Purple ascended Cahir's arm, and he gazed down at it, stunned by the glow they shared.

Seda collapsed into his arms. He gently picked her up and cradled her against his chest as he sat on the ground, with purple glowing through both of them.

"You have some explaining to do," Benny whispered as he stood next to Roya. "You know more than you're letting on." He nodded toward Seda, his brows raised.

"It's for her to figure out, and for us to learn. We're just here to help her along the way," Roya responded as she stood back up.

"What does that mean?"

Roya looked at him, truly looked at him. It had been a really long time since she had been with a man. His hair was a disheveled mess. He was slightly attractive for a human. He was not the tallest, but she wouldn't want a tall man. She also wouldn't want a man stronger than she was.

Ha. That would never happen.

He raised his brows at her again, and she sighed. "Let's say your father was onto something when he wrote that note. Would you like to find Ojore with me? I want to be sure he wasn't just fried to dust after what he said to her."

"You're referring to the Darkened?" Benny asked, obviously not too concerned with Ojore after what he had said, either.

She nodded at him in response.

They both looked up as the last of the clouds dispersed, allowing the filtered sun to return. They walked past the smoking remains of the electrocuted plants and back into the trees. From a distance, Ojore stood with wide eyes, watching Seda cradled in Cahir's arms.

"I cannot believe what I just saw. What kind of magic is this?" he asked as they approached.

"I don't know, Ojore," Benny replied. "She's also figuring this out as she goes. She didn't deserve what you said to her. She's learning. You need to give her the chance to grow and become stronger. She's likely tied to the Darkened somehow."

Roya looked at Benny, at how his brows pinched as he watched his sister.

He isn't so pathetic after all.

She stepped closer to him and brushed her fingertips across his. He glanced down at her hand, then back up at her, a faint smile spreading across his lips. He then looked over at his sister.

"I will apologize. I shouldn't have said those things to her. This really isn't her fault," Ojore said to them.

"Do any of you know what caused the plant to writhe in pain before Elco killed it?" Benny asked.

They looked at each other and shook their heads in unison. Roya had no idea why it would react that way. Nothing had touched it. Surely Elco was about to kill it; maybe it knew its death was imminent?

Benny sighed. "What did you mean about Cahir, and what exactly is the Fae?" he asked Ojore.

THE PURPLE LIGHT from Seda faded, and Cahir sat with his nose pressed against the top of her head, closing his eyes and rocking her gently back and forth as he cradled her to his chest.

As Roya, Benny, and Ojore headed toward Cahir, his body gradually faded away, and a burst of cerulean-colored light sparkled through the air.

Seda fell onto the soft ground with a thud and opened her eyes. They quickly rushed the rest of the way over to her.

"W-What happened?" she rasped to them as she rubbed her eyes to clear her vision.

The three looked at each other in shock.

"Shit," Roya said. "I thought he had more time."

"Where did he go?" Benny asked. "Is this some Fae magic?"

CHAPTER 36

<u>Seda</u>

"What do you mean by 'Cahir disappeared'? Where is he?" Seda asked everyone around her.

"We were coming over to talk to him about what Ojore said, and he just disappeared!" Benny exclaimed.

Kalon stepped forward and sat by her side, and Seda watched him pick at a little white flower with a red center on the ground.

She thought back to her fight with Ojore. He said Cahir was Fae and that Ojore's people were suffering because of it. Seda had known Cahir for years. She trusted Cahir. Why would he hide that from her? She didn't even know what a Fae was. It couldn't be true. Cahir would never lie to her.

"Is what you said true, Ojore?" she asked him.

"Which part?" he asked, his voice rough and his hands twisting together.

"Everything!" she snapped sharply, her brows furrowing.

"The part about him being Fae? Yes. It took me a while to

figure out who he was. And when I did, it really upset me," he started. "But the hurtful things I said about you and about Elco." He glanced at Elco and lowered his head. "Those parts I regret. Those parts weren't true, and I'm truly sorry."

The Fae from her mother's bedtime story growing up? Magical Fae?

She heard Ojore's apology, and it meant something to her, but she was too focused on Cahir to care. She looked up to him and asked, "Who is he, Ojore?"

Ojore looked over in the distance at the smoking piles of ashen plants. "Cahir's really Ael Cutlass, King of the Fae."

Her fragile glass walls shattered, and a painful whirlwind of emotions surged through her. *She never truly knew Cahir.* Who was this person she allowed so closely into her life?

She believed her mother's tales about the Fae were mere myths. But could they truly be real? Or at least partially so? With magic coursing through her veins, Cahir didn't appear too shocked when he discovered this.

How could he? Why would he lie? Where is he?

Her stomach dropped as betrayal consumed her thoughts. She thought they were a team; she believed they were friends; she had started to hope they were *more*.

Bile curdled at the back of her throat. She allowed someone so close in her life, just to be lied to. She was trying to get pregnant... she wanted his children.

Her palms began to glow as anger wrapped itself around her, and she gazed down at them, struggling against her labored breathing.

"None of that, moon-flutter," Elco said from his position across from her. "We don't know why he lied. I've seen him care for you. He must have a reason."

She looked at him and bared her teeth. "What reason could justify him lying to me for years, Elco? To share a home with me! To allow me to inseminate myself to produce his children?"

Her nostrils flared. "Thank whatever fucking god is out there that never happened. Could you imagine?!" Her voice rose, and she threw her hands in the air, releasing the built-up magic from her fingertips.

Elco lowered his head.

"He was not allowed to tell you the truth, Seda," Feich said to her.

Feich, who hardly ever speaks, had no room to say anything. "Who do you think you three are?" She pointed to the Corvids. "You said you followed me around for years, and you *never* showed yourself until all this shit hit the fan! A little warning would have been nice. I don't know, maybe if you couldn't tell me, you guys and Cahir, I mean *Ael*." She rolled her eyes. "Could have written a *fucking letter*!"

Ferona and Roya looked away from her, and Feich anxiously fiddled with his hands.

She stood up and marched around the area, ignoring the pain in her ankle. She wanted the pain for being so foolish. It was a better alternative to the agony eating away at her heart.

She tried to recall the clues she unintentionally overlooked. "When that stupid Rozzer tripped, and he caught the sword with his bare-fucking-hands. I should've known something was strange then. And then he also offered to find Dad when he was taken. I knew he couldn't make a difference, but he *insisted* and went anyway. And then he returned!" She laughed loudly. "He was always gone for 'meetings'. Then he ripped Michael's heart out with his bare hands like he was made of paper!"

She turned to Ojore and commanded, "Tell me what you know about the Fae."

Ojore looked around at the others. "Well, I'll tell you, but there's something I must say first before that wrath of yours comes after me. I know he's Fae for a reason."

Seda looked at him in a what-the-fuck manner.

"I… I'm not human either," Ojore said, placing his hand over his neck and shifting nervously.

Seda threw her hands in the air again, and electricity shot upward into the sky, illuminating the area with a purple flash.

"What are you, Ojore?" she slowly asked in a hair-raising tone.

"I'm a Lycanthrope. Specifically of the bear sort."

"And that *means*?" Her eyes brightly flashed as she focused on him.

"It means that I can shift into a bear."

She heard Benny and Askold gasp.

"And what does this have to do with *Cahir*?" She was quickly losing what little patience she held onto.

"Well, where I'm from, the Lycanthrope and the Fae have had a 'disagreement'. I knew he was Fae the moment I saw him, but I didn't realize who he was until later."

"Is there anyone *else* with any hidden secrets like this?" she seethed, looking at everyone, including her brother.

Benny raised his hands in defense. "Human as they come, Seda. Where do you think Cahir is now?"

"Umbrea, most likely," Roya said as she looked back and forth between them.

"The place he's wanted to take me this *whole time*?" Seda seethed.

"Uh, he did mention that on a couple of occasions," Benny said to her, nervously looking at her eyes and noticing her hands brighten intensely.

"And how do we get there?" she sweetly asked.

Benny bristled and looked away. He had no fucking idea. She looked at the Corvids.

"We have to talk to the Wisps first," Ferona chimed in for the first time. She looked back down at the ground after speaking up.

"And what is it that I need to talk about to the Wisps, Ferona?"

"They, umm. I don't know, Your H..." Roya elbowed her hard in the ribs, and Ferona fell to the ground, apologizing and wheezing.

Seda pulled at her hair in exasperation. "All of these *fucking* secrets!"

She marched over to Seren's body and looked back at the group. "This," she said as she pointed at his body. "I will *never* allow this to happen again. Ojore, you were right. I have failed to protect myself for too long. I will never cower again."

She paused, then softened her voice as she looked down at Seren. "He was the kindest man, and he deserves a respectful service."

THE GROUP LINED up and offered their condolences, each saying something kind about Seren. Seda watched his unrecognizable body throughout the entire thing, never taking her eyes off of him. She would burn the image of him into her mind forever. She would never allow her cowardice to harm another one of her friends again. She had power surging through her veins, and she was going to use it.

In the Camp, she had vowed to herself that the weak Seda of the past was behind her, and she meant it. *Now she just needed to show it.*

When the service was over, Seda bent down and placed a flower on Seren's chest. She said a silent prayer for him, unsure to whom, but it was definitely *not* to Lord Mordred, and then stood up and stared at the group. "Let's get to the Wisps."

They set off north into the trees once more. Seda felt grounded as she limped, her toes squishing into the soft moss and ferns. Kalon quietly walked up to her side from behind and handed her the small flower he was playing with earlier.

He stepped back into his place at the end of the line.

She looked at the delicate white flower in her hand and admired the soft, white petals. They reflected her fragile exterior, but internally, the flower was a vibrant scarlet, echoing the burning embers of her spirit.

She tucked the flower above her ear and continued walking forward into the unknown.

CHAPTER 37

<u>Cahir</u>

"*You've disobeyed us by revealing your Fae form. We've taken the luxury of time away from you, cutting short the time you had left…*"

CAHIR AWOKE, face down, in a large, luxurious bed covered in emerald-colored silks. He jumped up and took in his surroundings.

What the fuck?

He scrambled out of the bed and ran through the lushly carpeted room, knocking into a side table and grabbing a little green-colored box. He looked at the black screen on the front, and a date magically appeared.

Shit! Shit! Shit!

He had been asleep for more than two days. He ran toward the heavy wooden doors and pushed them open. A servant walked by carrying a stack of towels and gasped when she saw him, dropping the laundry.

"Your Highness! You're back!" She bowed deeply, her pointed, delicately green ears darkening at the sight of him, and her full cheeks aflame.

"Call for counsel, *NOW!*" he roared.

She jumped up and ran down the hall, forgetting the towels on the floor. Cahir walked back into the bedroom, slammed the door closed, and paced around. He stared at the reflective, stone walls and punched one, causing his knuckles to bleed. Anger surged through him as he caught his muddled reflection. He ran to the mirror and looked into the glass.

He was Fae again. He examined the whisper of jade-green sheen on his skin, the black tattoos covering his body, and the way his clothing had torn as his size changed.

This can't be happening.

He briskly walked to his wardrobe and grabbed a fresh set of clothes.

What was Seda thinking now? Had the others informed her? She was probably livid, or sad, or he didn't even know what she was feeling. He really needed to talk to her. He quickly changed into his new clothes and looked at himself in the mirror.

Gone were his rounded ears and smooth teeth. Looking back was Ael. Tall with strong features and a massive body. He growled at his reflection and looked away. He really needed to get back to her. Now that his "deal" was over, he could finally explain things.

If he only got the chance to talk to her, she *might* understand his reasoning.

He left the room, kicking the stack of towels the servant had left behind as he walked down the hall. More servants saw him and gasped, bowing deeply.

He needed to speak with counsel as soon as possible. He

made his way down the long halls of the Umbrea Palace and saw his reflection in the shiny, verdant walls.

This form, his proper form, was so different for him now. He spent over five years living as a human. Only once did he use his Fae form. It was a stroke of luck that the rescue attempt even worked that night. His deal with the Wisps to find the stone and her had said that he had to take on a human form and remain one for his duration.

He took a considerable risk that night, changing back into a Fae. What if he couldn't change back? That was a big reason why, when Roya was pressuring him to show Seda, he felt he could not. His magic to transform wouldn't have worked the day Seda was collected at the Wyrd. The Wisps must have blocked it.

And look what it did? The Wisps shortened his time with her as a result.

The ceilings were high and rounded at the top, stretching along the long halls as small birds flew around them, nesting high in the peaks where flowering vines draped. For as long as Cahir could remember, he had a soft spot for the winged creatures, and he had made it clear that they were not to be removed from the palace during his absence. In fact, he noticed how well they thrived.

He made his way into the Throne Room and threw open the double doors, allowing them to smash against the walls.

The counsel, consisting of three High Fae, were waiting for him at the end. They bowed deeply as he walked by. He climbed the ten steps to his emerald gemstone throne and sank into it with a thud.

"Rise," he ordered. They stood up and waited for him to speak.

"My time ran out, I did not get the stone," he sneered and slammed his fist on his knee, not caring if his bloody hand got onto his clean pants.

The council members looked at each other with concern.

"Your Highness, if I may?" an elderly Fae, named Meir, stepped forward.

Ael waved his hand in permission for Meir to speak.

"You have been missed, Sire. We have much to catch up on. Regarding the stone, may we talk about it over dinner tonight? I have instructed the cooks to start."

Meir was Ael's most senior advisor. He was fifteen hundred years old and lived through parts of Ael's father's reign, seeing the destruction of the gods and the rise of the monsters in lower Xyberus. Meir also assisted with Ael's daily responsibilities while he was away.

"Oh, please with the formalities," a sultry Fae named Luelle said. "It's been far too long. What happened, Ael?" Luelle was his 'spy'. As his childhood friend, who knew everyone's secrets in the palace, he gifted her the role when he took the throne. Whenever Ael needed to know something about someone, she always had the answer.

"I ran out of time. We believe Lord Mordred has the stone. I was instructed to help someone named Seda Arbor, but was told I was not allowed to inform her of my intentions or my true nature. I've spent the last five years living as a human with her. She was taken to the Camp, and she started to show some... *powers*." Ael said back to them.

"What powers?" asked Praxis, the third council member, standing beside Luelle. He was his captain.

"I'm not sure, but it's unlike anything we have ever seen," he replied. "Seda has developed a purple power that comes from within. Electric. I've seen her create a storm from the sky and rain down lightning."

The three looked at each other in confusion.

"No one has that power," said Meir. "I will see what I can research in the library. May I please be excused?"

Ael nodded at him, and the older man bowed again before walking away and closing the doors behind him.

Luelle stepped forward, and Ael raised his hand to stop her. "Before anything, I need you to go to the witch. I need a way to check in and communicate with Seda."

Luelle bristled, her face flushing red. "You know that old hag doesn't play nice! Last time she chased me out with a broom and a few zaps to my ass when I asked her something."

"I *need* this, Luelle. I left on bad terms, and she's in danger. I don't understand how she fits into all of this. Tell the witch I've sent you," he replied.

"Can you go back?" Praxis asked.

"No, I cannot. I'm forbidden from finding Seda unless she comes to me."

"What kind of horseshit are the Wisps playing at?" Luelle asked.

Ael looked at both of them. "I wish I knew."

Luelle and Praxis left the Throne Room quietly. Ael stared around the room. He forgot how large it was, how opulent. Two birds chirped from far above, and he looked up at them. They were fluttering around the few hanging vines.

Oh, Seda. I can explain. Please come to me, he thought as he sat on his emerald throne.

CHAPTER 38

The days passed as they walked through the misty redwoods. Every time they encountered what appeared to be Gnashing Flora, Seda used her magic to electrocute them to dust. It didn't always work when she tried. At times, it would sputter out and only scorch the plant; other times, it would shake the earth so violently that they all had to leap back. If only she could better control her power and understand how it worked.

She realized she had to think about what angered her to wake the source. She would practice by thinking about Joro and how unjustly people are treated, about Esper and how her life had ended so terribly, and about how Cahir had spent years lying to her.

She thought about him often, and her mind warred with itself each time. One part of her felt his betrayal deeply, angering her, and another part of her tried to think of reasons he might not have been forthright.

She was still so confused. How had her mother known about

these stories of the Fae? And Ojore was actually a bear? The Corvids existed. What else was out there? Who were the Wisps?

Her bare feet grew used to traveling the forest floor. She looked down and noted how dirty they were.

I no longer care.

Shoeless, she felt liberated, and the damp earth beneath her toes made her feel grounded. She thought back to her time in Joro, when she would never have allowed herself to become this dirty. She was always meticulous about showering and keeping herself clean. She felt dirty for fifteen years and was constantly scrubbing her body raw.

No more. Seda now preferred to have that dirt caked between her toes.

Feich walked by her side, not saying much. She looked over at him, taking in his magical beauty. He walked with a stiff posture, standing tall and proud, his eyes scanning the area with a wary glance, as if he could see through objects to detect any signs of danger. She felt comfortable around him.

"I apologize for my verbal attack toward you and your sisters," she fiddled with her dress. His eyes darted to her, and he nodded.

"So, can you tell me anything about you guys?" she asked him as she stepped over a large mossy log, a small red mushroom growing from the top.

"Well," he started, "We've lived for hundreds of years. We have waited for you for a long time. When you arrived, we instinctively knew you were here. We were unable to locate you, so we consulted the Wisps for your current location. All Corvids know who you are, but most are hesitant as you are not ready."

Well, this was the most information she had gotten from them. Maybe she needed to talk to Feich more. Curiosity was eating at her to know them, so she asked, "How many Corvids are there?"

"Thousands of us, living amongst the trees and caves of the

high mountains. Roya's been our chosen leader for as long as I have known. Our father came prior."

"How do you guys communicate with each other since it's just the three of you here?"

"We call it the Corvid Whispers. We can communicate telepathically amongst each other as needed."

"Is this why you don't talk much?" Seda asked, intrigued. She blushed, realizing how rude that sounded, and looked away. "Sorry."

"No need. I'm a man of few words. I also don't say much to my kin unless necessary." He smiled at her, his light skin radiating in the filtered sunlight through the trees. "They nag too much."

Seda laughed loudly and stepped over a group of small red mushrooms. She looked down at them, noting their colorful tops with yellow spots.

"Ouch!" Askold yelled from ahead of the group. He dropped one of the mushrooms he picked up, his fingers turning red.

"Don't think those are edible, Askold," Kalon said from his side, shaking his head. "Watch out, everyone, these mushrooms bite back when touched, and I see a lot more of them in the distance. They seem to be getting larger also." He walked back to Seda and offered her his arm. She accepted it as he guided her around the large swaths of mushrooms, avoiding them with her bare feet.

Elco was flying with Roya and Ferona, playing through the air. She looked up and smiled. Elco was free to fly again and enjoy the freedom it brought, no longer being chained and caged. She wondered about his past and where he came from. They imprisoned him for more than a thousand years. This beautiful, magical creature endured horrors no one should see for far too long.

Seda accidentally stepped on and crushed a mushroom. Pain shot up through her foot and leg. She hissed and nearly lost her balance, but Kalon caught her in his arms. "I think it's safe to say you might want a ride until we pass this."

She smelled his sandalwood scent as he smiled down at her. She blushed, flinching from the pain, but was grateful for the offer. He picked up her dirty foot, examined the bottom, and gently squeezed it. "You have a blister, but it doesn't look too bad."

She held onto him as her foot throbbed. The warmth of him crept into her, and she shivered as she thought about Cahir holding her the same way.

"Are you cold?" He looked down at her, and his beautiful seafoam-colored eyes seemed to slow down time. He looked at her like he saw the person she was meant to be, not the weak Seda of the past, but the strong woman she longed to become, almost as if he understood her true potential.

She shook her head and looked away from him, breaking the trance she felt she was in.

Thoughts of Cahir circled back through her mind. He must have had a reason for lying to her for all these years. Allowing her to inseminate herself with him artificially *enraged* her. At what point did he realize things were going too far? Did he ever think that? Did he even feel guilty for lying to her? She wondered what he was doing now.

She desperately wanted to talk to him again, even if it was for closure. And honestly, to even see if what everyone was saying was true, because what if it wasn't?

"What are you thinking about?" Kalon asked as he was stepping over dozens of mushrooms on the ground. "You look lost in thought."

She thought about what to say. Should she be honest? Would she find comfort in sharing her thoughts with this man, especially so soon after one had lied to her?

"I'm thinking about closure," she replied.

"Hmm." His full lips thinned, and he said, "The most

dangerous liars are the ones who think they're doing it for the right reasons."

She looked back up into his bright eyes, surrounded by dark eyelashes, as he gazed down the path. "Have you ever been lied to before by someone you care about?"

He looked down at her, and her heart fluttered. Then he smiled at her before glancing back up to watch his steps. "Yes. I've been lied to, and it broke me." He sighed. "Want to hear something honest?"

"Yes," she replied anxiously. She did want to hear something honest. She wanted honesty from everyone. She was tired of the mysteries.

"Sometimes forgiveness is the hardest part, but it loosens the chains we strap ourselves with when we carry our anger." He took a deep breath and continued, "And... I think you're the most stunning and powerful being walking this planet. I believe you're more than you even see about yourself." He kept walking through the trees and the mushrooms, then stopped and looked up.

Seda blushed. No one ever said that to her before. It was very flattering that someone could see qualities in her that she didn't recognize in herself.

She looked up at what Kalon was staring at, and Benny had his hand raised in the air, stopping everyone.

"Look at these," Benny said as he pointed.

Seda noticed that the mushrooms had grown larger the farther they walked. The ones around her were as tall as Kalon, and in the near distance, they were as large as the oak trees in the Heath Forest.

"Oh my," Askold whispered in awe. "Have you ever seen anything like this before?"

Elco circled, trying to find a place to land that was free of the red-topped mushrooms. Finding that he could not land on the ground, he perched on top of a tree that bent to the side and stared down at Seda. "This is the Amanita Copse. The last time I saw this place, it was not nearly as vast as it is now. They're very dangerous if you come into contact with them. They don't move or bite, but they're poisonous if touched. Tell your friends not to touch the large ones. The larger the mushroom, the more potent the poison." He took off into the sky, and the force of his weight lifting made the tree swing back and forth.

She reiterated what Elco said to Kalon, who called out to the group. The group continued forward carefully and began searching for a place to rest.

THEY KEPT WALKING for another hour when Seda felt something in her underwear. She let out a groan out of habit. None of her attempts at getting pregnant had worked out, so her period was always a letdown each month.

Her whole life, she was told that having periods was shameful and that it meant you weren't loyal to Joro.

"I need to find somewhere private, please," she said to Kalon, who was still carrying her.

"Is everything alright?" he asked, his eyebrows rising as he looked down at her.

She ground her teeth and looked away. "Yes, I just think I might have started my... *period*." She winced as she said the last word.

She averted her gaze from him, her face feeling like it was on fire.

He set her down, and she carefully stepped around the smaller mushrooms, finding a spot behind a large one for some privacy. The rest of the group all stopped and looked at Kalon.

"What's going on?" she heard Askold question.

"Seda needs privacy for a moment. Let's take a short break,"

Kalon replied. She listened as everyone set down their items and talked among themselves.

Seda peeked around the corner of the mushroom, being careful not to touch it, and looked to ensure no one was watching. When it seemed safe, she bunched up the skirt of her dress and slid her underwear down her legs.

The red spot stared back at her.

Sadness surrounded her as the last insemination failed. She deeply wanted to have a baby, and the monthly cycles of hopeful waiting were draining. Perhaps motherhood wasn't meant for her, a thought that made her heart ache.

She looked around, realizing she had nothing she could use to keep herself clean. There wasn't even a damn moss ball she could use. There was no way in hell she would use a mushroom. What was she going to do?

Crap! Crap! Crap!

She heard a tearing sound, then someone cleared their throat from the other side of the mushroom. Seda jumped, quickly pulling her underwear back up her legs.

"Yes?" she nervously called out.

"I have something for you. Are you decent?" Kalon asked.

What could he have for her? It's not like he carried cotton pads in his pack. Did he?

"I'm decent," she replied.

He walked around the corner and smiled at her. Her eyes moved down his body of their own accord. A long, tension-filled moment passed between them as Seda's eyes roamed down his bare chest, and she noticed it rise with a deep inhale.

Heat crept up her cheeks as she stared at his strong muscles, olive skin, and the black tattoos that slithered from the moth tattoo on his neck, down to his hands, around his chest, and hid below his belt line. She really hadn't seen many tattoos before. Occasionally, people in Joro would visit Barrio to have small pieces of art applied to their bodies. But they were usually pricey and flashy, so not many, aside from The Rising members, had tattoos that she'd seen.

She cleared her throat and ran her hand over her neck. "Why aren't you wearing a shirt?" she asked, inwardly groaning at herself for ogling.

He held out his hand filled with scraps of material to her. "Here, thought you might need something for that." He nodded toward her stomach. "I have another shirt in my pack."

"Oh... thank you." She fidgeted with the skirt of her dress.

He smirked at her as she took the cloth from his hand, their fingers brushing against each other for longer than usual.

She looked back up at him, her gaze meeting his as his eyes flickered between hers.

"You didn't have to tear your shirt. I could have torn the bottom part of this awful dress," Seda said breathlessly.

Honestly, she hadn't even thought of that until this moment. That probably would have been a good idea. But then the thought made her cringe—this dress was already scratchy against her skin. It would have been awful if it were down there, too.

"Wouldn't be the first time I sacrificed a shirt. Don't worry about it," Kalon said to her as he waited for her approval. She nervously looked down at the scraps of his shirt.

"You know... It's natural. There's no need to be ashamed, Seda," Kalon said, his brows knitting together and his smile fading.

She was at a loss for words and reluctant to discuss this with him, so she quickly changed the subject. "Why didn't you give me the shirt from your pack?"

He stared at her for a long moment, then his smile returned.

"This one's softer," he replied, giving her a wink as he turned around and walked back to the group.

She watched him walk away, admiring the defined muscles of his back and his firm...

Stop looking!

When he was gone, she shook her head and pulled her underwear back down, placing two of the scraps there. Then she put the rest in the small pocket of her dress. She pulled her underwear back up, feeling a bit better, knowing she had something to keep herself clean.

Her mind whirled; she had hoped that the last insemination had worked. But, with all the recent events, it was better that it failed. She couldn't be pregnant on this journey, and she also wasn't entirely sure how she felt about Cahir. He wasn't even human. Could that even have worked?

Maybe that's why it continuously failed.

She sighed and walked around the mushroom.

Kalon was putting on a replica of the shirt he had just shredded.

He extended his arms for her to fall into, and she side-eyed him.

"Not as soft, huh?" she asked, gesturing toward his shirt.

"Not as soft," he replied with a guileful smile, and picked her up, carrying her deeper into the mushrooms.

CHAPTER 39

<u>Ael</u>

"The witch gave me this," Luelle said as she held out a clear stone the size of his palm.

"What is it?" he asked her, picking up the piece of transparent stone and holding it up to the warm light streaming through the large domed windows of the Throne Room.

"She said you speak the name of who you want to see, and it will show you their image. She also said that the next time you want something, you should come and ask her yourself. And *then* after she handed me that rock, she threw the broom at my head and screamed as if *she* was the one in pain." Luelle rubbed the back of her head.

"I wanted to be able to speak to Seda, also. Can this do that?" he asked, ignoring her complaints.

"Just the image in real time," Luelle responded, dropping her hand. "Sheesh, at least show some *concern* for my well-being after sending me to that old hag. She's truly terrible. Next time, send Praxis. I'd love to see him with a bump on the head from a broom."

The doors swung open, and Praxis marched in and bowed deeply.

"Speak of the stinky devil," Luelle mumbled.

Praxis ignored her but fought a smirk. "Sire, the Lycanthropes have gathered at the western wall. It's been quiet while you were away. They may have learned of your return."

"Have you been in contact?" Ael asked as he slipped the stone into his pocket.

"No, Sire. We await your command," Praxis said as he stood straight, awaiting orders. Praxis was nearly as tall as Ael, his height giving him a natural presence amongst the guard. His black hair was shaved into intricate designs along the sides, revealing his tall ears, adorned with iron cuffs.

"Make contact, find out what they want," Ael ordered and waved his hand in the direction of the doors. Praxis left the room and closed the doors behind him.

"Ael, may I be excused? I have a hot date with curves I'd like to get to," Luelle said to him, foregoing formalities. She rarely called him by his titles unless others were around.

He chuckled, the sound low in his Fae form, and waved toward the door again, excusing her. Luelle walked out, her long flaxen hair pulled back into a tight ponytail with curls at the end that swayed with each step.

He watched the ponytail leave.

When the doors finally closed, he anxiously pulled out the stone and looked at it. His heart raced, and he drew a deep breath to steady himself.

"Seda Arbor," he said to the stone.

He anxiously watched. Nothing happened for a few moments, and Ael was about to curse the old witch for her trickery when it began to shine brightly, lighting up his palm.

He stared at it intently as Seda's image appeared. She looked exhausted from her journey. He sighed in relief, seeing that she was alive and safe, and his eyes caught on arms wrapped around her body.

Frantically, he looked closer to the stone. The image panned out, and Kalon came into view, holding her the same way that *he* had her on the trip.

What the fuck?!

Memories of her soft body pressed against him as he carried her through the woods, of their day waking up in his bed together, the countless times they shared laughs as he slowly broke down her walls, showcasing that beautiful, kind, strong woman within.

He struggled to remind himself that Seda was free to make her own decisions, but the fiery dragon of jealousy churned deep inside him. He took a deep breath, and his magic billowed from his nostrils, spreading across the face of the stone and creating a fog around the moving images of Seda and Kalon. He wished he could hear what they were saying. He was determined to watch this fucking stone all night long if he had to.

Even if it meant seeing things he'd regret.

He was watching it intently, unblinking, checking if Kalon moved his hands anywhere that was questionable, when a knock came at the door.

He quickly pocketed the stone. "Come in."

An elderly Fae woman with gray hair and a stern face entered the room. She bowed. "Your Highness, we welcome you back to Umbrea. I've selected five of our top women for your selection." She rose and waved her hand toward the door.

Five beautiful Fae women, wearing little more than a vibrant array of see-through lace scarves that clung to their naked bodies, walked in and bowed deeply before him.

"You may have as many as you like, Sire," the woman said.

CHAPTER 40

Everyone gradually moved forward through the towering mushrooms that blocked out the sky. As the mushrooms grew larger, the smaller ones became scarce on the ground. Kalon carefully set Seda down once the small mushrooms had disappeared, and Elco, Roya, Ferona, and Feich followed on foot with them. They stepped over glowing moss balls that shone brightly, gently illuminating the darkened area.

Seda gazed at the ghostly white stems that grew into wide-brimmed, velvety, red caps, admiring their wonder.

Benny held up his fist at the front of the line again. Everyone stopped. He slowly turned around to face them, putting his finger over his lips as a sign for silence.

Seda looked around nervously as she felt a tingling at the back of her neck. She kept peering into the dark clearings between the mushrooms, hoping to see something, anything. The sensation of being watched weighed heavily on her skin.

"I smell something," Elco told her.

Seda sniffed and looked at him in confusion, then glanced

around their surroundings. She didn't smell anything except the damp soil and the earthy scent of the mushrooms.

A fleeting shadow blurred past them in the darkness, causing Seda to hold her breath as her heart raced.

"Did anyone else see that?" Askold asked as he drew his sword.

Ojore sniffed the air. "I smell food."

Seda inhaled deeply through her nose, but still couldn't smell anything.

Another shadow darted through the stems, and everyone suddenly turned toward it.

"Show yourself!" Benny demanded of the shadows.

A soft giggle echoed through the darkness.

Not again. Not more monsters.

Seda promised herself she would act the next time they faced new fears. She looked inward and drew on her anger, focusing on Cahir, and her arms started to glow in the dim light.

"*STOP!*" a loud voice echoed through the mushrooms. An older man, no taller than five feet, with a long, gray beard, stepped out from behind the large stems. He wore a crown made of the painful mushrooms on his head. "What magic is this, human?" he asked. He was a stout, broad man dressed in earth-toned clothes that stretched over his belly.

"I thought you said humans don't have magic, Papa?" a small boy, no taller than two feet, said. He ran up to him and hugged him from the side.

The older man looked down in alarm at the little boy and reached out his hand toward the group. He unleashed a spray of thorny vines that shot out in all directions, trapping everyone. The thorns were as thick as Seda's arm and sharper than needles at their tips. She gasped and stepped back, pointing her hands at the older man. Elco growled deeply, and warmth spread through the area. The Corvids moved quickly toward Seda.

Kalon gently placed his hand on Seda's arms, softly pushing

them back down. He looked at her and shook his head, saying, "There's a child."

Seda looked at the small boy, at the innocence shining in his eyes as he watched eagerly. She dropped her arms to hang loosely at her sides, the magic still flowing through them, casting a ghostly glow around the area.

"Sorry, everyone. My grandson wasn't supposed to be here. You know how kids are. I had to be cautious in case you have bad intentions," the old man said as he protectively wrapped his arms around the little boy. He looked back down at his grandson and said, "You're right, little Orion, humans don't have powers. She looks human. But… I've never seen a human display any magical abilities, and I've never seen a magical being with purple power before." He looked back up at the group and said sternly, "Who are you, and what are you doing here?"

Benny moved closer to the edge of the thorns. He held up his hands protectively and said, "We're travelers heading north. We do not wish to have any conflict."

The old man hummed thoughtfully and then clicked his tongue. "You seem to be travelers consisting of a Lionne, Corvids, a Lycanthrope, humans, and… more."

"We wish no harm to your family or people. We want to pass peacefully," Benny added.

A small, round woman with full cheeks like ripe peaches, wearing a dusty-colored dress with a worn-out hem, approached the older man. "Father, is this how you treat travelers in need of warm food and soft beds? Look at them! They could use a bowl of soup in their bellies." She crossed her arms over her heavy chest and harrumphed loudly, her matching crown of mushrooms shifting on her head.

"I'm the leader, Lucja. It's my job to make sure we're safe," he said to her, his eyes narrowed and fixed on the group with a wary gaze.

"Hobberwash! Release these people from the prison you

built. Just look at the poor souls. They need our help!" she demanded.

"We do not help. Ever since the gods fled, my dear," the man replied.

"Then it's past time. We're due for a little fun around here." Lucja placed her hands on her hips and tapped her foot impatiently.

He eyed Seda and Elco suspiciously, then turned back to Benny. "How did you find us?"

"We don't know our exact location, sir. Like I mentioned, we were heading north and stumbled upon these mushrooms, so we kept moving forward," Benny replied.

"These mushrooms have shielded us since the monsters won the war," he stated.

Since the monsters won the war, that was the truth. No sugar coating it.

Seda stepped forward and said as powerfully as she could muster, "I apologize for calling upon my power. We do not wish to harm anyone who does not wish to harm us. These are my friends, and I promise that if you bring us no harm, none will be returned." She smiled to herself, pleased with how she handled that perfectly, without a single stutter.

He gazed at her curiously, then glanced down at her hands, noticing that the purple was fading. He looked doubtfully at Elco, his lips pressed into a thin line.

"Tell him I wish the same, please," Elco said to Seda.

"My friends all wish the same," she told him. "Even my friend, Elco." She nodded her head toward Elco as she continued to look at the older man.

A long moment of silence as the older man considered her words. Then he sighed and snapped his fingers. The thorny vines disappeared without a trace.

"Wow," Askold said in awe. "How did you do that?"

"My name's Chief Vidar. Follow us," the older man said. "I'll tell you along the way to our village in the Amanita Copse. Please do not make me regret this. I do wish to please my daughter, and my kindness only goes so far."

Vidar led the way through the large mushrooms, with the group following quietly.

"So what are you guys?" Askold asked as he jogged up to Vidar. "That was pretty cool back there. I've never seen anything like it. Well, honestly, all of this is new to me. I'm human and don't have any powers, which sucks."

Vidar looked at him and sighed again. "We're called Vatte. We have lived deep within the redwoods for thousands of years. When the gods left, and the monsters took over the lower half of Xyberus, we migrated into the Amanita Copse. No monsters come here because these mushrooms are incredibly toxic, as I'm sure you have experienced." He looked at Askold, noting his blistered fingers.

Askold wiggled them in the air. "Not too bad."

"Well, you must have touched a small one. The bigger the mushrooms are, the worse they are. Be sure not to touch these at all. We do not have a remedy for the burn as we are immune to them."

Seda was listening with rapt attention as the group followed Vidar, Lucja, and a skipping Orion through the mushrooms. Small twinkling lights in the distance caught her eyes as they walked forward. She looked at Elco and asked, "What do you think about all of this?"

"I've heard of the Vatte. They were once a thriving community, rich in earthen magic. This is my first time truly meeting them, though," he replied.

Seda looked around in wonder as they approached the twinkling lights. Small homes with thatched roofs made from ferns, rounded wooden doors, and circular windows were erected haphazardly around the area. Strings of lights, made from the little glowing balls they had stepped over earlier, were strung between all the buildings, lighting up the area. Hundreds of Vatte were outside doing various tasks. They washed their clothing in a stream, cooked over small fires, fixed crumpled rooftops, and chatted with each other happily as they drank from small, round cups made from carved wood. The most interesting part was that they all did these tasks with magic. The water moved on its own, and the ferns for the roof were magically placed.

No one was over five feet tall, leaving Seda appearing awkwardly tall. Everyone wore the same earth-toned garments, men with pants and tops, and women in dusty-colored dresses. When they saw the group, they all paused their tasks and watched, leaving their magicked items floating in the air. Children pointed at them as they passed, halting the games they were playing.

Vidar led them to the center of the small village and climbed onto an old redwood stump, waving his arms. The stump grew another ten feet taller, lifting him toward the sky.

The villagers hesitantly approached the area, watching Seda and her friends.

"My people, we have travelers tonight. They wish to seek shelter and food. It's been a *very* long time since we last had guests, and Lucja wishes for us to celebrate and host. Please show them as much kindness as they show us. Let's show these people how the Vatte like to party!" Vidar shouted from the stump.

The Vatte all jumped and clapped excitedly, their peach-like cheeks glowing pink with delight, their previous tasks now long forgotten. Music began playing around them, coming from small stringed instruments carried by several Vatte. The sound was so new to Seda, so unique and so beautiful.

"Get more mead!" someone shouted, and Seda looked around, trying to find the source of the yelling. She had never tried mead before. She heard about it in Joro, but only the critical members of society living in Cascade had access to it.

An excited bubble grew in her belly.

Orion ran up to her and grabbed her hands. "What's your name, beautiful, magical, purple lady?" he asked her as he hopped around her in circles. "My powers haven't come in yet. I have another hundred or so years. It's hard being so young and so unfair!"

"I'm Seda. It's nice to meet you, Orion," she said to him. He grabbed her hand and pulled her into the center of the floor, where others were already dancing to the music. He jumped around and danced as the space filled with more Vatte. Seda looked around, a little embarrassed to be dancing. She didn't know how to dance, and her body felt awkward as she tried to mimic the other Vatte's movements. Her ankle still hurt, but she ignored the pain.

She caught sight of Kalon watching her, and she nervously waved at him. He had his hand over his mouth, trying to stifle a smile as he watched her with eyes full of delight.

A small man approached her and handed her one of the small wooden cups. She peered into it and saw the thick, golden liquid within. She took a hesitant sip, and the sweetest taste she had ever experienced exploded in her mouth.

As the sweet honey and caramel flavors laced her palate, she let out a moan. She took another deep sip, enjoying the fiery sensation as it moved down her throat.

The Corvids shifted into their raven forms and flew around the area, their wings flapping with the beat of the music, creating a gentle wind that blew everyone's hair around. The Vatte cheered and clapped at them, spilling mead from their cups. More and more people and group members began drinking and dancing, including Seda. The air was thick with a substance the Vatte were smoking, and it smelled strong, with an earthy aroma. She felt so free, so *alive*, no longer caring if she looked silly as she moved her body.

The Vatte brought out food and handed Seda a small bowl brimming with vegetable soup and flatbread on the side. She found a place to sit down and sip the broth. Warmth spread through her body, and the spices burst in her mouth. She had never tasted soup as delicious as this before.

She glanced over at Elco and saw children playing around him, placing flowers into his silky mane. He pretended to paw at them like a large cat with mice, with his long, spiked tail flicking around.

Dizziness swirled in her mind from the mead as she sat on the log watching the others. Kalon approached from behind and sat beside her, his arm brushing against hers. She looked down and saw that he had rolled up his sleeves, and the hair on his strong, muscular arms was standing where it touched hers.

He took a sip from the soup he was holding, and Seda watched his Adam's apple as it moved on his throat. Blurry images of him and the Vatte surrounded her as the laughter and smells of the environment lifted her spirits. She felt happy and carefree. She smiled at him and giggled when he looked at her with a questioning expression, causing her to drop her bowl of soup onto the ground accidentally.

Kalon quickly picked it up.

"Would you like more?" he asked her, offering his own bowl.

"I donnnn't think so," she slurred and hiccuped.

"The mead's strong here. Do you feel okay?"

She looked in his direction, and his fuzzy image came into view. "I feeeelll great." Her words grew more muddled and slurred the longer she sat. She reached out and gently took the ends of his braid in her hand, twirling it around her fingers.

Kalon sat back, chuckled, and looked at her as she played with the ends of his hair.

"You are sooo handsome," she said, foregoing her usual filter, her honesty spewing out like a broken hose.

Seda sighed. Her filter no longer mattered, not at the moment. She felt free from her usual chains of reservation.

She should find more mead. That sounded nice.

She looked around at the glowing balls of light and the cheerful people nearby. "So beautifulll..." she said, feeling at peace for the first time on their journey.

Kalon remained silent, and Seda glanced back at him.

"Yes. It is," Kalon whispered, his eyes flickering between hers.

Heat blossomed in her chest and pooled into the depths of her stomach. She felt transfixed, her eyes locked onto his, gazing into a sea of obscurity.

"May I?" he asked as he held out his arm in invitation.

"Yess," she said sheepishly. She let go of his hair and dipped her chin down, trying to hide her pink cheeks. He wrapped his arm around her shoulders and pulled her close. His warmth and size made her nestle in closer.

She immediately thought about how Cahir would hold onto her the same way and recalled his dimpled smile. She would never get to experience that with him again. The safety and sense of home she had felt with him were now lost forever.

She let out a small sob. She felt Kalon pull her closer, and she buried her face in his chest, inhaling his sandalwood scent as she wiped away her tears. "He lied to me, Kalon. What if he's in danger?"

Kalon tensed and then said, "That man's not in danger. He's a king, Seda. He likely has multiple women in his bed right now."

Seda felt a strange, ugly feeling grow inside her. She hadn't considered that. She thought about Cahir with another woman pressed into him, his arms wrapping around her, making her feel safe just as he did with her. She felt the burning fire of anger race out through her chest, and the hints of purple lit up her fingertips.

"Whoa, whoa…" Kalon began as he gently placed his warm hands over hers. "None of that. He's fine, Seda. We'll find the Wisps and figure out what to do next. Have you seen Benny?"

She didn't know why she had that reaction. She pulled her powers back in and looked around for her brother, but things were blurry. She shook her head.

"Let'ssss go find him. Walking around might help," she said as she fumbled to get up. She was wobbly, and Kalon held out his arm for her to take. He guided her around the area, looking for her brother. She absentmindedly ran her fingers up and down his strong, veiny arm, playing with the goosebumps that appeared along his skin.

They stumbled and laughed as they tripped over people lying on the ground and dancing haphazardly. When they couldn't find Benny, they walked along the edge of the village. They heard rustling in the nearby bushes and moved closer, curious to see what was making the noise.

Benny popped his head out, facing away from them with his hair a disheveled mess. A thin hand with sharp, blue nails popped up from the bush and pulled Benny back down. They heard moaning and kissing from the bushes.

"Oh! Oh wow…" Seda whispered in shock. She did *not* want to see her brother engage in those activities. Such behavior was not allowed in Joro's public places, and watching Benny interact with Roya made her wonder why anyone would want that. Her only experience was deeply traumatizing.

She turned away quickly, facing the dancing Vatte in the distance.

Kalon laughed. "I see he's doing *just fine.*"

He looked at Seda, and she made sure not to meet his eyes. The sounds they were making rang through her ears, and she grimaced.

They walked back toward the Vatte, and nausea washed over her from both the mead and the sounds from her brother. "I think I need to lie down. I don't feel so good."

They found Lucja, and she led them to a small house. She opened the door, and Seda looked into the room. Small furniture lined the walls, and a short sink was in the corner. She looked at the single bed and at Kalon.

"Will you stay with me?" she asked him quickly, before she thought better of it. She really did not want to be alone.

He nodded, and Lucja left the room. As they stood in silence, Seda's nerves flared. This wasn't like being alone with Cahir. She played with her hands, running her fingers through her hair. Maybe asking him was a mistake. She sat on the side of the small bed, and Kalon sat beside her, making the bed creak loudly, his body pressing into hers as they sat in silence.

He looked down at her with a gentle smile. Seda's heart was pounding as he gazed into her eyes, as if he was looking into her soul and seeing something she couldn't quite understand.

He softly traced his finger along her hand, and she looked down at it, then back up at him, noticing that his eyes had darkened. She held her breath as he gently reached out and cupped the back of her neck with his large hand, making her feel small.

Leaning in close, he whispered into her ear, "My little lunita."

His breath sent a shiver down her spine, and she gasped as he pulled back, his fingers grazing her necklace and leaving a trail of tingling sensations on her skin.

His eyes found hers again.

Ever so slowly, he leaned down to kiss her, his full lips brushing against hers. A spark of her magic sizzled between their lips, connecting them both.

His kiss was soft, tender, and almost as if he were asking for approval. She felt desire pool within her, and she kissed him back, unsure of what to do, but let him lead the way with his gentle, passionate touch.

Time seemed to slow, their lips exploring each other with tender promise.

Images of Cahir flashed through her mind, and her body stiffened. She quickly placed her hands on Kalon's chest to stop him.

He pulled back gently, a flicker of pain crossing his eyes before it disappeared. Seda noticed it.

"Your heart truly does belong to him," he breathlessly whispered, letting her go.

She didn't feel prepared to move forward; she needed to talk to Cahir first. Not that she and Cahir were a couple, but they had been *something*. Right?

She believed Kalon recognized her potential, almost as if he knew exactly what to say, like he understood her better than she did herself. Plus, she felt undeniably attracted to him, but she couldn't help picturing Cahir sitting there, his gaze and lips fixed on her, not Kalon's.

He got up, then lay down beside the bed. Seda remained seated, unsure of what to do next, and even hesitant to breathe too loudly. A long moment of silence followed as he settled onto the floor next to her, gazing up at the ceiling.

Thoughts of Michael and Alexi's angry faces flashed through her mind as they hurt her. She curled her hands into fists, trying to forget the day, telling herself this was not the same. Not all men took what they wanted without permission.

Kalon seemed different. He genuinely appeared hurt by her rejection. He stayed respectful and paused when she asked him to stop.

"I'm sorry," she finally whispered, consumed by shame that left her feeling like she couldn't breathe.

"I'm patient." He closed his eyes.

She recalled the warmth of his lips on hers, and a spark of

heat spread through her again. She had never been kissed before, and the experience was *electrifying*. Part of her yearned for more, and she struggled with the desire to reach out to him, but confusion overwhelmed her mind.

She shouldn't feel that way. What would Cahir think if he knew they kissed?

Kalon was right; her muddled heart tangled with another.

She pulled the covers back, crawled under them, and closed her eyes as she thought about Cahir. That morning, as they woke up together and he pressed into her, she flinched, and he pulled back.

Cahir was the one who apologized, not her.

She missed him. One warm tear slipped free and ran down her temple, leaving a damp spot in her hair as memories of him flooded her mind. She missed and loved her friend, and she wanted to talk to him to try to understand his side of the story. He had to have a reason.

Her eyelids grew heavy as she thought about his smile and the way he would push those disgusting eggs at her and make her laugh, how the rice was probably still stuck to their apartment walls, and how they always laughed after every argument.

Her final thought before drifting off to sleep was that she wished Cahir were in the room with her, not Kalon.

The same black snakes and a sense of comfort intertwined through her dreams, caressing her body and soothing her broken heart.

CHAPTER 41

<u>Ael</u>

When the women left earlier, Ael exhaustedly went into the kitchens, grabbed a bottle of wine, and took it back to his room. He popped the cork and took a deep drink from it, skipping a glass.

Regret consumed his soul as if he were drowning in a vast ocean, unable to surface, pulled down by the vines of his own mistakes.

He climbed into his oversized, rumpled bed and removed the stone from his pocket. It was a massive bed, and his already imposing size seemed tiny by comparison. He really missed his small, twin-sized bed back in Joro, mostly because Seda was always around. The apartment bedroom never felt empty, unlike his lonely room here at the castle.

He really needed to talk to her; it dominated his thoughts.

"Seda Arbor." He looked into the translucent stone, waiting with bated breath for it to glow brightly, nerves tightening in anticipation of what might appear.

Please be okay.

Seda was lying in bed, staring at the ceiling and quietly crying. His heart sank when he saw her upset. What was she thinking about? He wished he could be there with her to kiss away the tears escaping her eyes.

Where was she? The room and decor didn't look familiar to him. Where was there an inn along the route north? The only one he knew of was with the Lycanthropes, but their journey wasn't along that path, and there was no way they made it that far.

He noticed a form lying on the ground next to her and sneered when he saw it was that fucker, Kalon. What was he up to? He didn't trust him, and it wasn't just because Kalon clearly wanted Seda. He was trying too hard and obviously hiding something, but Ael had no idea what it could be. Still, he was glad he was on the floor and not in her bed.

He kept drinking from the bottle as he watched Seda fall asleep. When her eyes finally fluttered closed and her breathing changed, he decided to check on the others.

"Roya Corvid," he said. When the image of Roya and Benny appeared, he quickly looked away. Roya was running her nails through Benny's hair as his face was between her pale legs.

Well, I'll be damned. Benny actually did it.

He wanted to know where they were, so he called out Elco's name instead. Elco was sitting beside a fire, with flowers woven into his mane, and was gnawing on what looked like a deer's leg. A group of very small children was curled up against him. An older man appeared, leading most of the children away from Elco. The wind stirred his long, gray beard, and then Ael noticed the giant mushrooms in the background.

Interesting. I didn't know anyone lived there.

The Amanita Copse was deadly and hidden deep within the northern redwoods. No one dared to go there anymore. He glanced back at the image of Elco and noticed other small beings in the distance.

No way, he thought as his mouth fell open.

The Vatte had been missing for a thousand years. Everyone thought they all died when the monsters took over the lower half of Xyberus, and the humans hid inside the dome. That was them, though. What a clever place to have made a home. No Jotnar would ever venture there, and since the Vatte were small people with earth magic, they could build and navigate through the mushrooms easily. The fact that Elco made his huge, scaled ass in there made him think they must have adapted the area for their village.

He directed the stone back to Seda and watched her sleep. Her closed eyes moved gently, and a small smile played on her lips. What was she dreaming about?

He didn't care if others thought it was creepy that he was watching her. Fuck them. If she were dressing or bathing, he would look away out of respect for her. But since she was sleeping peacefully, he decided it was okay to invade her privacy and make sure that fucker Kalon didn't try anything while she slept.

Not that he had any power to do anything. But he would find him if he did, and the thought of ripping his dick off his body made a wicked smile spread across his lips.

He reflected on the women from earlier—how they had all tried to sit on his lap and lick his sensitive ears. He considered taking them to release the tension from years past.

He had closed his eyes while listening to their gentle moans, imagining it was Seda caressing him tenderly. A warm tongue had traced his neck and made his cock stiffen. He opened his eyes, and a restrained moan escaped from his parted lips as another grabbed it firmly through the fabric.

He jerked back, overwhelmed by revulsion as he regained awareness.

He sent them all away and didn't watch as they pouted and walked off, their sheer, flowing scarves slipping down their bodies. He heard the Madame in the hall scolding them all for not having success.

He only wanted her.

Seda is mine, he finally admitted to himself.

He loved her before, he loved her now, and he would love her forever—he loved her more than words can express, even beyond life itself. She was his closest friend and his whole heart, igniting his soul with a fiery passion he would willingly let consume him forever.

He would turn the world upside down for her, starting with Kalon or any man who believed they could have her. He wanted to *squeeze* their hearts as he had done with Michael's.

And he would enjoy doing that for her *over and over and over again.*

He dozed off with the stone pressed against his heart, ravaged by vivid nightmares of Kalon and Seda locked in a passionate embrace with their bodies twisted in a tangled web of desire.

"WE SHOULD HAVE A BALL," Luelle said to him over breakfast the next morning. "You know, to celebrate your return. I haven't worn a fancy dress in years. Plus, a ball is the perfect place to hear gossip." She was picking at her pancakes, using the fork to lift them and plop them back onto her plate.

"I don't want a ball," Ael replied as he munched on a piece of bacon. "I hate balls."

"It would be wise, Your Highness, to host such an event for your return. The people would love to see you and celebrate with you. It will bring up morale to the kingdom," Meir said from his spot next to Ael. "I agree with Luelle."

Luelle smirked at Ael in a 'I told you so' manner. Ael rolled his eyes.

"What do you think, Praxis?" he asked him, knowing the answer.

"Don't care about balls. At least not those balls. I rather appreciate my own, though," Praxis said and smirked. Ael chuckled, and Praxis continued, "Whatever you want, sire. I'll have the guard on duty when it happens."

"You're disgusting!" Luelle sneered as she dropped her fork on her delicate china plate, cracking the edge. "No one here wants to think about your saggy, sweaty balls."

Meir was glaring between the two, clearly baffled by their lack of manners toward Ael. Ael tried to conceal his laughter with his hand when he saw Meir's reaction, and his eyes began to water.

"My balls are *not* saggy, thank you very much. But they're rather sweaty. Wanna help me air them out?"

"*Sire*," Luelle said sarcastically, but acknowledging his title because Meir was there. "Please tell your chief to shut the flying-fuck up. I'm going to puke." She stood up and wiped her mouth with her napkin, pretending to gag. "You know what, I'm going to leave. I'll be back later. *Sire*, will you have a job for me soon? I've been bored with you being away. Everyone's been so dull, and I'd like a little fun."

For Luelle, fun was either hooking up with strangers, fighting with Praxis, or gathering information and gossip for Ael.

Praxis wiggled his eyebrows at her, and she growled at him, looking like a ferocious rabbit, and stormed out of the room.

"Your Highness," Meir said as he tried desperately to change the subject. "I will coordinate a ball for two nights from now. Also, I've been researching the library and haven't found anything on magic that uses purple. I'll continue my search and let you know what I find. Would you like anything else from me before I make my way over there?"

Ael shook his head and thanked Meir for trying. Meir bowed and walked out of the doors, leaving Praxis and Ael behind.

"Sire, it's good to have you back. Luelle's more feisty with you here. She was a boring mess when you were gone. Also, I don't know why she complained about my balls. She's played with them countless times," Praxis said as he chewed through his scrambled eggs.

Ael laughed. "I did miss you guys. She can go find some poor soul to consume for the night while she awaits some drama to unfold." Ael took a sip of orange juice and asked, "What's the word on the Lycanthropes at the wall?"

"We tried to make contact, but they disappeared before the guard arrived. I figure they just went back home," he took another bite of his eggs.

"I need to make peace with them. If what's happening in the southern parts of Xyberus reaches here, we shouldn't be fighting among ourselves, even if I don't give two shits about those people. I will make time after this ball to go down and visit them," Ael said.

Two servant women walked in and collected the dishes. One pretty young Fae appraised Ael from head to toe, her eyes taking on a sly, suggestive glint.

He looked away.

Praxis noticed the exchange and waited for them to leave before saying, "Sire, you used to accept offers like that so willingly. I heard that you sent away the Madame and her women last night, as well. Is everything okay?"

Ael sighed and admitted, "I'm no longer available for them." He fiddled with the clear stone in his pocket and wished he were alone to watch Seda like the creep he knew he was.

CHAPTER 42

<u>Seda</u>

The sound of birds chirping woke Seda as she looked around the room. Her head throbbed from drinking mead the night before, and the rising chirping seemed to press against her temple. Maybe mead and her didn't mix so well.

At some point during the night, Kalon left the house, leaving her alone. She glanced over at the partially open door. She wondered whether anyone else had entered the small home, or if he had simply left the door slightly ajar.

There was a knock at the door, and Seda sprang up. "Come in," she called to whoever was on the other side. She winced as it felt like her brain was throbbing from the movement.

At least they knocked while the door was open.

With her mushroom crown hanging loosely on her head, Lucja walked in carrying a tray of food for her. "Good morning, dear. Thought you might like some food after all that mead last night. You were not feeling too hot there at the end."

"Thank you, Lucja. I really appreciate all of your hospitality," Seda said to her. She had never in her life been treated so sweetly by strangers. This small woman invited her into her home, threw a party, let her drink mead for the first time in her life, and was now bringing her breakfast in bed.

"Oh, I do wish you had fun," Lucja responded, her face brightening at the compliment. "We never get travelers here. And it's been so long since we got to host a party."

Seda sat at the edge of the bed and accepted the tray of food. Her eyes widened as she saw the plate loaded with fresh berries, pancakes, jam, and fried eggs. "I've never had a feast like this before in my life, Lucja! This looks amazing!"

"Dig in, sweetie. Best while it's still hot."

Seda immediately dove into her plate, starting with the pancakes. "Yummm," she moaned as the flavors hit her tongue.

She loved how the butter melted in her mouth, its taste and texture unlike anything she'd ever had before. This breakfast was a completely new experience, and she'd heard that people in Cascade often enjoyed meals like this.

It wasn't fair that they were so lucky.

Seda took another bite of her food, and Lucja smiled brightly at her. Her peachy cheeks lit up her happy face.

Now that Seda could see the room fully illuminated by the filtered daylight, she examined the space more closely. Her eyes fixed on a painting of what seemed to be young twin boys hanging crookedly on the wall.

Lucja saw her staring at it and said solemnly, "That's father and his brother."

Seda studied the painting. Something so oddly familiar about the young boys stood out to her, but she couldn't place it.

"Is his brother here?" Seda asked her.

"No. My uncle left our world a long time ago. My dad doesn't mention him anymore," Lucja replied. "Oh! I almost forgot, we might have some clothes that would fit you, but they might not be the right size. I noticed you didn't bring any other clothes when you arrived, and you're wearing that worn-out dress." Lucja looked at her dirty garment. "Sorry if that was too blunt, but a lady should have clothing without holes. We once had a Vatte who was five feet two inches tall. How tall are you?"

"Five-six," she answered as she looked down at her gross gown.

"Well, we can try. If not, I can magically adjust it to fit depending on the material. No harm in trying. Let me find those, and then you can try them on. Please find me when you come out of here. I'll likely be near the coffee pot, recovering from the mead myself."

Lucja left the room and closed the door behind her.

Slowly, Seda finished her plate of food, scraping up every last bit of blackberry jam with her fingers and licking them clean.

She stood up, set the plate aside, and reached into her other pocket, the one without the cloth, for the chewable datun to clean her teeth. She picked up her plate again and walked out of the house to find a place to set her dirty dish, locate her friends, change the cloth in her underwear, and find Lucja for the clothing.

She spat out the datun as she approached a small woman washing dishes in the stream, her magic at work. The woman graciously accepted the plate and placed it into the cool, flowing water. She gave Seda a slight nod and asked how she slept. They exchanged polite small talk, and when Seda asked, the woman offered her a bar of soap for her hands.

Seda left the area feeling welcomed and accepted by the community. She strolled along the stream until it hit the edge of town, then slipped behind a tree to switch out the cloth in her underwear. Afterward, she washed the dirty ones in the water, pocketed them again, and washed her hands.

She looked around and saw Elco asleep with Orion, both

leaning against a small home. She walked over to him, and he lifted his head at her.

"There you are, my moon-flutter." His eyes sparkled at her sleepily.

"I see you've made another friend." She nodded toward Orion, who was using Elco's long, silky mane as a blanket.

"I really like this one. Orion reminds me of the innocence of my kin's younglings." Elco looked down at Orion, and a quiet purr came from his throat. "I saw you went to bed last night with Kalon following. How was that?"

Seda's cheeks turned red at the insinuation. "Nothing big happened, Elco," she lied. "He's *just* my friend."

"Just your friend, the same as Cahir is?" he asked.

Seda looked down at her hands and nervously shifted her feet. She felt foolish. Cahir, or rather, Ael, would have been upset with Seda for allowing or even seeing another man enter her sleeping area and for kissing him. She also thought about how she had fallen asleep wishing it were him there last night, not Kalon.

"No, not like Cahir," she admitted.

"What's Cahir to you?" he pushed.

"Honestly, I'm not sure. Cahir was my best friend for years, and he was the only one I had. He was also my very first true friend. He always treated me with kindness and respect. But now I'm confused, Elco. He betrayed my trust by lying to me, but I still miss him so much." Her voice hitched. "And I don't know what to do."

She sighed heavily and rubbed her eyes, attempting to prevent the tears from falling.

Elco hummed thoughtfully. "We must get you to Umbrea so you two can communicate. And in the worst-case scenario, at least you could have closure. I'd suggest not rushing into anything else until you know how your heart feels after."

He looked at her with gentleness in his red-glowing eyes.

She sat beside him and Orion and snuggled into his mane as well. His purr vibrated against her body.

"I'm really fond of it here. I'll stick with you through this, Seda. I'm yours, and I'll do my best to make sure you have everything you need. But I do wish we could stay." He looked down at Orion.

She turned and hugged him, saying into his silky fur, "You deserve all the happiness."

"No, Seda, I don't. I've done many horrible things. I don't deserve to live in peace or remain with these kind people before us, despite my wishes."

Seda disagreed, knowing Elco had a kind heart and that his experiences at the Camp weren't his fault—he had to eat to survive.

They sat in silence, listening to Orion snore. Lucja approached, holding a cup of steaming coffee in one hand and a pile of clothing in the other.

"Oh, look, there's Orion! And Seda, I've found some clothes for you to try. Would you like to come back with me to the house?" she asked.

Seda said goodbye to Elco and followed Lucja, who carried the clothing in her arms. When they entered the room, she placed the items on the bed and looked at Seda intently as she examined her body. "We can make this work, dear. I will need to modify a bit, but this will do."

"Which do you suggest first?" Seda asked as she looked through the earth-tone clothing options.

"Well, I'd suggest a dress for a beautiful lady like yourself, but since you're on foot through these woods, pants might be a better choice." She held up a pair of light-brown pants and a matching top with a lace-up front. She noticed Seda's hesitation. "Don't worry, dear, I'll turn around, and the door's locked. No one will come in."

When she turned around, Seda removed the scratchy dress she wore and pulled the pants up her legs. They were a little tight, reaching her mid-calf. She then tightly laced the top and sighed with relief, glad to have her breasts supported. "I'm ready."

Lucja turned around and smiled. "Already much better. Let's fix those pants." She waved her hands through the air, and the pants' natural fibers lengthened, weaving around her calves and down to her ankles. The pants also stretched slightly, and Seda took a deep breath, feeling she could breathe more easily in them.

"Now for shoes," Lucja said.

"Oh, no, I'm okay without shoes." Seda enjoyed the sensation of her bare toes in the dirt she had been walking through.

"The terrain north of here becomes icy and rocky. Are you sure?"

Seda reconsidered; the idea of losing her toes to frostbite or slicing them on sharp rocks sounded horrible. "What do you have?"

Lucja walked into a small closet and pulled out a pair of men's lace-up boots that would reach Seda's mid-calf. "These might actually be big on you. They used to belong to my husband. He's now with the Mother Goddess, bless his heart, and I know he'd love to see them used again."

Seda thanked her and pulled them on.

"Hmm, leather I cannot modify as it does not grow from the ground. Do the boots fit okay, dear?" Lucja asked.

They were a bit big on her, but not overly so. She nodded and thanked her again. Then they both left the house and went their separate ways.

She caught sight of the Corvids circling overhead and then glanced over at Benny and Askold, who were sitting by a small campfire. She made her way over to them.

Benny caught sight of her and turned red. "So, uh… how was your night?"

"Not as eventful as yours." She poked his shoulder and grinned.

Just as Benny was about to speak, his mouth dropped open, and Askold burst into laughter. "Benny's shacking up in the birdhouse," he said.

Benny closed his mouth and blushed. "Zero regret." He shrugged.

"Nice outfit, Seda!" Askold said, eyeing her approvingly. "Sweet boots. I would wear those. No more hitching rides from strong men, huh?"

Seda laughed. "No more hitching rides."

She also wasn't comfortable asking Kalon to hold her again after what had happened the night before.

"I think we should gather everyone and see about heading out soon," Benny suggested.

Seda and Askold nodded, and the three of them walked off to find the others. They found Ojore wrestling with two Vatte behind some trees. They were attempting to jump on him from behind, and he was maneuvering around them, showing them how to defend themselves.

"Ojore! We leave in fifteen minutes," Benny shouted, and Ojore saluted back before being tackled to the ground by the Vatte.

They gathered the others, except Kalon, and discussed their plan to move farther north.

"Has anyone seen Kalon?" Ferona finally asked. Seda's mind kept drifting to him, but she didn't want to be the one to ask. "We have circled the area multiple times, and he's nowhere outside."

They all looked at each other and shook their heads in unison. Where could Kalon have gone? Was he in another house?

She wouldn't hold it against him for wanting to sleep some-where else.

"He was in my room last night, *sleeping on the floor*," Seda made sure to include, purposely leaving out the kiss. "And when I woke up this morning, he was gone. I've not seen him since."

They found Vidar and Lucja and asked if they knew whether Kalon was in any of the homes.

"I last saw him early this morning, walking south of town with something that sparkled in the light as he moved," Vidar said. "I'm not sure where he headed. Maybe he was looking for a private spot to take a bathroom break?"

Without hesitation, Seda raised her hands to her neck to check for the chain, but she found nothing. She frantically unlaced the top of her shirt, and Askold exclaimed, "Whoa, there, Seda! Keep those laces on, please. For our own safety from a jealous king."

She looked at him angrily. "My necklace is gone!"

"What necklace?" Askold and Ojore asked at the same time.

"*MY NECKLACE!* The one I've had since I was a child. It sparkles!" The men looked at each other in confusion.

"Are you sure you didn't leave it in the house when you got dressed?" Benny asked.

Seda ran back to the house and flung the door open, letting it slam shut behind her. She searched everywhere for it. She couldn't remember taking it off the night before, but she also didn't remember having it or seeing the sparkles light up the room when she changed not long ago.

Feich was the first to burst through the doors. "Did you find it?" he asked her while frantically looking around for it. The others piled into the room as well.

"No! Last night we kissed, and I pushed him away. But I felt him run his fingers along my chain."

Feich's eyes widened as he continued helping Seda look for the moonstone necklace.

"Do you think he took it?" Benny asked.

"Yes! He took it, Benny!" She ground her teeth together, and rage bubbled through her veins. Her hands glowed, illuminating the room.

Kalon stole her necklace. Why would he do that?

CHAPTER 43

The Monster King

The Monster King exhaled sharply as he finally pulled himself out of the nightmare that haunted his mind during daylight hours. He reached across his desk and grabbed his veilroot smoke, lighting it with a match. He inhaled the weed and exhaled slowly, letting the drug soothe his nerves.

It had been weeks since his last episode. He almost thought maybe, just maybe, these nightmares were finally over.

A knock on his door made him look over.

"Come in," he said, rubbing his sweat-slicked forehead.

Jason walked in and stared at him, unaffected by the thick smoke.

"The Jotnar wish to meet," Jason said. The Monster King took another drag of his smoke and blew it out, creating small circles in the air.

"Those imbeciles always want to meet, and yet they haven't fulfilled their side of the bargain. I continue to provide them with fresh meat and have nearly met their quota. Yet, the dome still stands," he replied before taking another drag. The effects of the veilroot only slightly calmed his growing agitation. "I'm losing my patience with them."

Jason stood tall in front of the mahogany desk, awaiting the response to provide to the Jotnar, and the Monster King grumbled. "Fine! We'll meet here at the camp in two weeks. I want to make that blubbering idiot of her son feel some pain to remind her who's really in charge around here."

The Monster King stood from his desk and strode across the plush carpet toward the door. He pushed it open so forcefully that it slammed against the wall. He then flicked his veilroot smoke onto the ground outside and stepped into the courtyard to take in the view.

A man had been tied to a post, and the Rozzers were whipping him across his back. Fresh blood dripped onto the sandy ground, and the Dragors kept licking his back whenever they had the chance.

The Monster King smiled brightly. He enjoyed watching new torment, loved ruling with an iron fist, and above all, relished being the man everyone here feared.

Jason stepped beside him and observed the tortured man with a look of boredom. The man's screams each time the whip hit his back caused the Dragors to hiss in excitement.

"Have you heard if your source has retrieved the stone yet?" Jason asked.

"Not yet, but they should have it soon," he replied. The stone was part of a set of keys he needed to collect, and once he had all of them, nothing could stop him.

"Have you decided what to do with Lord Mordred?" Jason asked him curiously, raising his brows and leaning in toward the Monster King.

"*That fucking puppet,*" the Monster King seethed. "He tried to get in my way. He was the reason why Seda and that fucking Lionne were able to escape to begin with." The Monster King spat on the floor and kicked a plume of sand into the air. His anger was flaming, and Lord Mordred was at the center of it all. "I gave that man so much to live for. I let him lead and be prayed to, just as he always wanted, and this is how he repaid me. For now, he's going about his days like nothing happened. Like I don't know he was behind it."

Jason's face returned to its usual bored expression.

"I think..." The Monster King looked toward Jason and smiled. "I think we will introduce a new lord to Joro. Joro needs a lord who *has respect*. We'll plan a celebration, imprison Mordred, and put you in his place. Everyone will believe he's dead, and I can punish him as I see fit." He chuckled, admiring his creativity.

Jason bowed deeply. "I'm here to serve, my king."

A bound and gagged woman was dragged across the sandy ground toward the Monster King by a Rozzer and roughly thrown onto the dirt.

As he circled her, the Monster King gazed down, taking in her appearance. She tried to kick at him, but he quickly moved out of the way and nodded toward the Rozzer. "She'll do. Bring her inside."

The Rozzer dragged the woman into the Monster King's office, her muffled screams following her as she went through the door. The Monster King smiled and looked at Jason as he adjusted his pants. "Schedule that time with the Jotnar. We will meet again and craft a plan for Mordred. His 'death' needs to be *exciting*."

He left Jason in the courtyard and went back into his office, then shut and locked the door.

CHAPTER 44

<u>Seda</u>

"We need to go after him, Benny!" Seda yelled after her brother refused her request for the third time.

"We can't, Seda. I'm sorry. We need to head further north. If he left at three a.m., he'd be well south by now. He has a nine-hour head start," Benny replied as patiently as he could.

"Seda, your brother's right. We need to get you to the Wisps," Roya delicately said from her side.

She looked at Roya, and her anger flared. She was mostly angry with herself for trusting someone so closely only to be betrayed… again.

"I've had that necklace for as long as I can remember. Mom said I was carrying it when she found me. It's gotta mean something, Benny! Why else would Kalon steal it? What would he need it for?"

"Seda, let me fly south to find him," Elco suggested from the side of the group.

Seda looked at Elco. "The last time I let someone I care about leave me, they didn't come back for days, and I couldn't eat without fearing they wouldn't return."

"I'll do as you wish, Seda. But know that I can fly much faster than any of you can walk. I could catch up to him and bring him back here so you can do with him as you please," Elco replied.

That did sound nice. Maybe she could fry Kalon's insides and make that silky hair of his crispy?

"Alright, but if you can't find him by nightfall, please come back to me," she said, her voice heavy with a sigh as she ran her fingers through her hair.

"If we leave now, we can probably get to the Wisps early tomorrow," Ferona suggested.

Seda nodded. "Fine. But if anything happens to you, Elco, I will haunt you even after your death." She approached him and gave him a firm hug. "Come back to me, please."

"I'd expect nothing less." He huffed warmth into her hair and then pulled away. He headed to the southern part of town and stopped, turning around to look at Orion. Orion ran up to him, and Elco nuzzled the little boy closely. Seda could see Orion crying, and her heart ached for them.

Elco does deserve happiness.

When they ended their embrace, Elco quickly headed south and found a clearing in the Amanita Copse to take off into the air.

"Thanks, Seda. I know that necklace means a lot to you. We'll get you to the Wisps and then figure out how to get it back if Elco cannot find him," Benny said to her.

She flipped him off angrily and left to thank Lucja, Orion, and Vidar for their hospitality.

IT TOOK them hours to traverse the northern Amanita Copse, but slowly the mushrooms began to thin and shrink, giving way to the majestic, pillared redwoods once more. The air was fresh and laced with thick fog again, and the ground creaked with their steps through the deepening snow.

Seda was deeply grateful to Lucja for warning them about the shifting terrain they were traveling through and for insisting that she wear the leather boots.

Her thoughts drifted to Elco, and she hoped he was safe. He had promised to return at dusk. She looked up at the slowly setting sun, knowing he would keep his word.

Benny was right next to Roya the whole time, gently touching her hand or offering her help to cross tall logs. She gave him several scathing looks at his offers of help, but would always accept them and wear a slight smile afterward. The three Corvids took to the air once they were able to do so again, and played through the tops of the trees, landing on branches and staring down at the group, dropping snow onto their heads below and laughing through the air at their own trickery.

"The sun's setting quickly," Ojore noted as he looked toward the reddening sky. "We should stop soon, Benny. It's about to get really cold, and we should start a fire."

"Just a little further. The snow's too deep here."

They continued until they came upon a large river, like a silver monster itself; the waters were rapid and volatile, and appeared to be a hundred feet in width. Chunks of ice and forest debris rushed through the current.

"How do we get across?" Benny asked loudly to the Corvids as the loud waters drowned out all other sounds. "Do you see a way?"

"No. We must pick a direction and travel the length. It's bound to thin eventually," Roya shouted back and flew up into the air, flying west.

The group followed.

It was pitch-black, and the group was struggling to get around. Seda unleashed her power, lighting up her arms to help them navigate the fallen trees and the muddy, treacherous shoreline. Benny raised his hand to halt the group and yelled, "The waters are still too wide. We need to set up camp and keep going in the morning."

Ojore and Askold set down their bags on a dry patch of land near the shore and began gathering loose sticks to build a fire.

Not far in the distance, a low, throbbing hum vibrated through the darkness, rattling the trees and sending snow cascading to the ground.

Everyone froze, the silence hanging heavy in the air, overwhelming even the crashing waters.

"What was that?" Askold asked.

The low hum shook through the trees again.

Roya and the Corvids flew down from the tree tops and shifted forms, surrounding Seda. "We cannot see what that is," Roya shouted over the raging river. "It's too dark around here."

They extended their claws, ready to strike back at anything that came at them suddenly.

Something vast and menacing slipped through the trees behind them and crashed into the water.

"Whatever it is. It's in the water now," Ojore said as he slowly turned toward the rapids with his sword drawn.

"Don't make any sudden movements," Roya advised, her eyes slanted as she peered into the darkness.

whoumm-whoumm-whoumm

Seda felt the cold realization that another monster was hunting them. She immediately activated her power, and the purple glow surged up to her shoulders, lighting up the fierce waters ahead.

She practiced for this. She would be brave. She would help protect her friends.

A quick movement and loud splash in the water startled

them. Everyone turned toward the sound. They searched for the source, but it had disappeared.

whoumm-whoumm-whoumm

"This fucker's playing with us," Ojore yelled.

"Everyone, be prepared for this thing to come out!" Askold shouted.

Like a fierce storm, a silver stream of wet flesh erupted from the water and surged toward Seda. She fired her magic at it. Purple lightning erupted from her palms, but she missed the object, hitting a nearby tree instead.

Feich quickly stepped in front of Seda after her failed shot and sliced through the tip of the flesh with his claws.

Their ears were filled with a loud, grinding roar.

The air thickened as a slippery nightmare emerged from the water, its pulsing silver form now visible.

The monstrous creature, with eight long, waving tentacles, let out another deafening roar in the purple glow of the darkness. It slammed its limbs into the river, sending icy water crashing into the group. It had a single, opalescent eye and a snapping beak at the center of its face.

The Corvids soared into the air and began attacking the beast. They scratched at it with their long claws, causing red blood to trickle into the rushing water. Their strikes were precise and swift. The beast shrieked and reached out to grab them, narrowly missing.

Askold and Benny used swords to cut into the massive tentacles extending onto the shore, causing more thick blood to gush out.

Blue light flashed, and Ojore transformed into a massive brown bear.

Askold did a double-take as he thrust his sword into the creature's tentacle. Ojore charged forward, biting down on the slick limb and tearing off a thick chunk.

Seda gathered her strength once again. She concentrated her

anger over Kalon's theft and unleashed her furious storm on the beast's round, gelatinous head. Lightning hit it, sending electrical shocks rippling through its soft, silky skin. Its limbs jerked outward, and the electric current traveled through the surrounding waters and onto the snow on the shore. Askold, Ojore, and Benny scrambled onto a log as the purple electricity nearly struck them.

"No, Seda! Not with the water!" Ojore yelled.

She didn't know what to do since her only weapon was her power. She looked around for something to use or grab, and her eye caught a pointed stick in the snow. She picked it up and held it as she'd seen the others grip their swords, sturdy and poised for action.

The beast's screeching grew even louder now, clearly pissed off by Seda's magic. It ceased its convulsing as it narrowed its eye on her. It flung a tentacle in her direction, and she prepared her stick to defend herself.

Feich quickly swooped down from the air and slashed at it, but the beast didn't flinch from his strike. It wrapped its tentacle around Feich, squeezing him tightly.

Feich immediately went limp and vanished. The beast pulled its tentacle toward its beak and snapped a few times, biting itself in the process.

It roared in anger.

With loud caws, Roya and Ferona swooped down from the air, clawing at the beast's face and eye. The beast squinted and flung its tentacles around itself. They almost got hit by the flying limbs when a roar echoed from above.

As Seda looked up, Elco came into view, and she let out a relieved scream. He made it back safely and could help with this beast.

Roya and Ferona moved out of the way as Elco narrowed his angry, red eyes and charged down from the sky, opening his mouth to blast molten fire directly into the center of the monster's face.

With a screech that pierced the air like a blast of metal, the beast's body burst into flames, burning like oil-soaked wood.

A large plume of snow fell onto Seda from the tree above, and she quickly scrambled out of it, watching as the monster's skin was engulfed in flames.

Elco soared back into the air and spun around, preparing for another attack.

With a loud thud, the monster's body hit the shoreline, reduced to a charred mass. The air was filled with the smell of burnt fish, mixing with the smoke.

Everyone froze and looked around, unsure if the fight was over.

As Roya and Ferona reached the shore, they cried out for Feich and frantically searched for him, struggling to make sense of what they saw. Soft moans began to escape their lips as they searched for him. As Roya bent down to gather his black feathers that had scattered on the ground, her piercing screams burst out, overwhelming the river's furious waters.

Both Corvids collapsed to the ground, holding onto each other and crying as they rocked back and forth, their pale bodies intertwined like delicate spider silk.

Seda approached Roya and Ferona and hesitantly embraced them both, grief over their brother's loss heavy on her heart. She held them for long moments, listening to their cries.

"It's the way he would have wanted to go," Roya finally said as she watched the flowing water in front of her and wiped her nose. "He died protecting you. He served well. *He did well.*"

Seda didn't understand why they wanted to protect her. She felt guilty that their loved one was dead because of her. She angrily wiped her eyes with both hands and gazed out at the river as the quiet of their grief lingered in the air.

"Should we eat it?" Askold asked of the charred beast, breaking the silence.

"What the fuck, Askold!" Ojore shouted at him.

"Moon-flutter, I'm sorry for your friend, and I don't want to take you away from this moment, but that was a Mungder, and where there's one, there's another. Its mate will be looking for it soon," Elco said to Seda.

Seda gasped and looked at him, "You said another will be coming?"

"That's it! We need to cross this fucking river as soon as possible! Can you ask Elco if he would be willing to carry us over?" Benny asked as they all gathered to pick up their belongings.

Elco glared at him and growled, smoke billowing from his nostrils and slowly melting the snow on the ground. Benny raised his hands in surrender.

"Elco, *please*. We need to cross. We traveled down this river for miles, and it never narrowed enough to cross anywhere. Can you please help?" Seda begged.

He looked at her, then at her glowing arms. He growled again and flew up into the air with a huff, his wide wingspan blowing icy wind around them.

"Guess not," Benny said, then let out a scream as Elco dove down and grabbed him and Ojore by the scruff with his front paws.

He lifted them into the air and flew across the river, dropping them roughly on the icy ground. Then he returned for Askold, who covered his head with a yell, and gently picked him and Seda up. He carried them across the river, set them down gently, and landed behind them, letting out a low growl as he looked at Benny.

"Why couldn't he have picked me up at the same time as Seda?" Ojore grumbled, massaging his leg where he'd fallen and shifting back into a human. He was naked and quickly rummaged through his bag for some clothes.

"I won't ask again," Benny said in defeat. "Thank you, Elco."

Seda turned around and looked at her fierce friend with awe and love. "Elco, we would have all died back there. Thank you for coming when you did."

"I didn't find Kalon, Seda. I came back as you asked when it got dark," he replied.

Seda's heart sank. She sat on the ground and drew a picture in the snow. "Thank you for trying."

He nuzzled his nose into her and reminded her that they needed to get moving.

Ferona and Roya flew ahead and stayed in their Corvid forms, avoiding the others. Benny looked up, and Seda noticed the sadness on his face over their loss as he watched them fly ahead.

Another hum echoed in the distance, and no one hesitated, quickly heading north through the crunchy snow and among the tall trees. Those on the ground stayed close to a grumpy Elco, letting his warmth help dry their soaked clothes.

CHAPTER 45

Ael

"Preparations are ready for tomorrow night, Sire," Meir said to him as they walked through the long halls of the Umbrea Castle. "We just need to get you fitted in your suit."

Birds chirped far above, and Ael looked up at them again, enjoying their playfulness through the vines. His head throbbed. He'd had the same nightmare the night before and was feeling drained.

"I agreed to a ball, I did not agree to wearing a suit," Ael replied casually.

"But, Sire…" Meir objected.

"His *Highness* doesn't want to wear a suit, Meir… drop it," Luelle said as she came up behind them and squeezed herself in the middle, wrapping her arm around Ael's side.

"I, on the other hand, can use a seamstress. Meir, can you send them my way, please?"

Meir furrowed his thick, bushy eyebrows at her, but remained silent.

"Fine, I know of a good one anyway," Luelle answered for herself with a huff.

As they walked through the halls, everyone bowed deeply at Ael. A little Fae boy ran out of a side door, carrying a wooden toy bear, and crashed into Ael, falling to the ground and dropping the toy. As the little boy began to cry, his mother rushed from the doorway, saw that her son had bumped into the king, and begged for his forgiveness.

Ael looked down at them in confusion. He was nothing like his father during his rule. When had anyone in his court been this scared of him? He knew he demanded respect, but he tried to rule with care and compassion.

"It's no problem. Are you okay?" Ael asked as he bent down to look at the boy. He picked up the wooden toy and handed it back to him. "Here you go. Be careful running these halls, child. There are usually people carrying important things around."

He extended his hand to the little boy, who accepted it.

The mother thanked Ael for his kindness, then grabbed her son's arm and dragged him back through the doors, scolding him as she went, and glancing back over her shoulder at Ael.

He sighed. "Is there anything else I am required to attend within the next few hours?" he asked Meir and Luelle.

Meir shook his head.

"Then I'll head back to my room and get some rest. I'll see you later when the petitions arrive for review."

Luelle and Meir bowed, and he walked down the hallway toward his chambers. He closed the large doors and eagerly reached into his pocket, saying Seda's name and waiting for the stone to light up.

After a few moments of waiting with no image appearing, he tried again. After the stone failed to work on his third attempt, his heart dropped in fear that something had gone wrong.

It took four more tries before the stone finally flickered, and he caught sight of Seda walking through snowy terrain. Then, the image vanished, replaced by the witch's crazed face. She beckoned him with a finger to come to her, and the stone went blank.

That fucking tricky witch!

He snarled like a beast and turned toward the doors, throwing them open and marching down the hall. He ignored the chirping birds above. At least Seda was alive.

She's getting closer to the Wisps.

As AEL and Praxis made their way to the witch's cabin through a field of lavender, they watched the magical green essence float around them like fireflies on a warm summer night. Umbrea was known for its surplus of magic that flitted through the air. The essence allowed their gardens to grow large and healthy, producing the best fruits and vegetables in Xyberus. Umbrea traded produce with Tuath for meat, as the Lycanthropes were known for their skilled hunting and ranching.

"What do you plan to say to her?" Praxis asked him.

"I need to know what she wants me to do to fix this damn stone," Ael said as he stepped over a low log fence separating the forest from Umbrea's gardens.

The witch had been around for as long as Ael knew. She was the oldest living Fae in the realm and had traveled the world. He'd heard tales of her from her younger days, that she was a gifted oracle with magic that surpassed traditional Fae powers.

It was probably all those nasty potions she liked to brew.

She experimented with crystals, monster parts, herbs, and chemicals. No one dared to ask her what she knew or how she had come to know it. But it was widely known that she kept her spells within her Book of Light, which she kept hidden.

"Last time, she wanted you to find her the eye of a Mungder

to give you information. Do you remember how hard that was to get?" Praxis shook his head. "That asshole almost took us both out. I can only imagine what it will be this time."

"I'll drag her the entire head of a Mungder if she wants it. I want the stone to work," he replied.

They strolled through a grove of towering pines and spotted a small plume of smoke rising from the witch's fireplace in the distance. As they drew closer, the small cabin came into view, its stone facade, straw roof, and warped windows standing out. A gravel path lined with herbs and flowers growing from the soft earth led the way to the cabin's wooden front door.

Ael banged on the door, a little too hard. "I have come as you called."

Shuffling noises and clinking pots echoed from inside the cabin, and then the door swung open, sending the magical essence swirling around the air.

The witch's silver, ragged hair hung down to her crooked knees, which bent awkwardly as she walked. Her nose was as crooked as her knees, and her beady, green eyes stared out at Ael with a lifetime of wisdom.

"About time you showed up, letting that miserable girl take your place. Totally unacceptable!" She flashed a wicked smile, revealing a mouthful of sharp, yellow teeth.

"But Luelle loves to visit you, Tahti," he replied.

Tahti peered around Ael, taking in Praxis before fixing her gaze back on Ael.

She growled at him. "Only you can enter. He's not welcome here." Her rough voice grated like fingernails on a chalkboard, sending a shiver down Ael's spine.

"I'll be out here when you're done," Praxis said nonchalantly, as he turned and leaned against the side of the cabin.

Ael watched him for a moment, then turned and looked at Tahti again. "May I come in, please?"

She turned around and hobbled inside with a cane. "Come in and close the damn door."

As he walked in, he smelled the pungent aroma of herbs and spices, with a faint hint of chemicals underneath, and saw the organized chaos around him.

Tahti had an assortment of jars containing body parts of creatures submerged in a light-brown liquid, rows of dried herbs hanging from the rafters, pots and pans stacked against the far wall, buckets of crystals lining the kitchen, and a small, tidy bed tucked in the corner. In the middle of the room, an iron cauldron filled with bubbling, neon-green liquid cast a plume of smoke that rose through a brick vent in the ceiling.

Tahti turned to him, and her green eyes glazed over to solid white.

Great, I love this part, he thought.

"Where's the dark stone? Why didn't you retrieve it *or* Seda?" she asked. "You failed."

"I know who has it."

"We need them both. All of Xyberus is at risk. The dome will fall soon." Her white eyes focused on him.

"I'm waiting for her to come to me before going back for it."

Tahti continued studying him with unblinking eyes. "You've fallen in love with her." It was not a question.

"I have," he finally admitted aloud. He truly loved Seda. In all his centuries, he had never met and cared for someone as deeply as he did for her.

"We need her, King Ael. She's the final key, and she *needs* that stone, amongst others."

"You don't think I already know that?" he snapped, losing his temper with the crazy woman. "She's all I can think about. I refuse to use her in any way that can harm her!"

She stared at him without saying a word for long moments. Ael glared back, refusing to show any submission to this ludicrous woman.

Her pointed ears twitched, and she lunged to her side, grabbing a squeaking mouse with her sharp teeth and knocking over the pots, causing a loud ruckus.

Praxis banged on the door. "Are you okay in there, Sire?"

"All is fine, Praxis," he replied. He heard Praxis grumble then lean against the wall, patiently waiting.

Tahti chewed on the mouse, blood dripping down her chin, and slurped up its tail with her lips. She refocused her attention on Ael.

"Seda Arbor is the key, King Ael. There's no way around it. You need to take her with you back to Joro to retrieve the Dark Stone."

"I refuse!" he shouted. "Seda's suffered enough in her life! She deserves happiness… *here*. With me."

"You won't find happiness unless you do. It's the only way."

Ael changed the subject. "I want that stone you gave Luelle to work again, please. Fix it for me."

"There's no point. You'll see her soon. Not worth the magical resources."

"Are you *fucking kidding me*?" he seethed, running his hand through his hair in frustration. "When will Seda be here?"

"Soon."

Ael growled and struggled to ask softly, "Will she arrive okay?"

"She'll arrive in a plume of mist and flame. Get prepared, King Ael. *This is your warning.*"

She blinked, and her eyes changed back to their natural shade. "I've said what I said, now get out!" she shrieked at him, pulling her hair with her wrinkled palms. She screamed as if she were in pain and grabbed her broom, hitting him solidly on the head as she chased him out the door and slammed it shut.

"Sire, that appears to have played out as expected," Praxis said, his eyes shining with delight.

Ael rubbed his throbbing head, which now stung even more

from the broom's blow. "I should've known she would be of no use. Spit out things I already knew."

But he didn't know everything she said before today. She informed him that Seda would be here 'soon' and that she would appear in a 'plume of mist and flame'.

What did that mean?

CHAPTER 46

The terrain changed as the group gradually hiked uphill, their legs sinking knee-deep into the snow and often slipping on sharp, icy rocks. They walked for a couple of hours after the fight with the Mungder, trying to put as much distance as possible between themselves and the monsters in the river.

They hiked until Askold dropped to his knees, covered in snow, and begged them to stop. The dark landscape was barren, and finding materials to build a fire was impossible. Everyone huddled close to a growling Elco for warmth, who let them get near because of the circumstances, reminding them that it would only happen this once.

Doubt crept into Seda's thoughts, and she looked to Roya and Ferona. "Do you know if we're heading in the right direction?"

The two Corvids hadn't spoken since the Mungder attack.

When they were a safe distance from the river, they held a small service for Feich and laid flowers on the ground where they had been growing through the snow. Ojore prayed to the Mother Goddess, and the remaining Corvids kneeled near the flowers as they kissed the icy ground.

Ferona looked at Seda with swollen, red-rimmed eyes. "We're on the right track. The Wisps will be at the top of this mountain."

Roya didn't glance at Seda and stayed focused on the dark horizon. Seda drew her knees to her chest and peered around at the dark ridge behind her.

"Are there monsters here?" Benny asked. He sat next to Askold, who had fallen asleep the moment Elco agreed to protect them from the cold. Benny looked at Roya with concern and then turned to Ojore, who was sharpening his sword.

"Except for a possible Jotnar, there are no fearsome creatures on Mt. Ebenveil," Ojore replied as he set his sword aside and looked up at the twinkling stars. "The Wisps are worrisome enough."

Seda looked at him. "What do you know about the Wisps?"

He paused briefly, picking up his sword again, and then continued, "The Wisps are the most magical creatures that still live on Xyberus. They're said to have been the divine servants of the gods. When the gods left, the Wisps stayed behind. No one knows why. But anyone who goes to them looking for answers usually has to give something in return. That's enough to scare me. I have no intention of asking them any questions."

"And yet I still have to," she whispered.

Roya looked at her, breaking her focus on the darkness from which they had come. "The Wisps have been waiting for you, Seda. They do not intend to harm you." She turned her gaze back to the dark landscape.

What could they want from her? Did they have answers about this mysterious power and why Lord Mordred targeted her? She had so many questions, but after what Ojore said, was it even safe to ask them? What could she offer? She had nothing to give them—no money or treasures.

Her thoughts drifted to Cahir and Kalon, thinking about how they'd both betrayed her in their own way. Kalon had taken her necklace, likely knowing it held meaning for her. He'd also taken her first kiss! He must have been insulted that she'd pushed him away, so he stole it as a kind of revenge? What else could be the reason?

As for Cahir… she couldn't understand why he'd lied to her. What would a king have to gain from lying to a human and living with her for five years?

What Kalon said about Cahir spending time with women just wasn't possible, even if he were a king. They'd been together for years, and he'd never had a relationship with anyone.

Or did he? What were all of those meetings about?

She thought about how he would always return from them looking disheveled. There were whore houses down in the Barrio. Did his meetings end there?

Her anger toward them intensified the more she thought about it, and having to wear scraps of Kalon's shirt down there made her blood boil. She should have asked Lucja for some fresh cloth or pads, but completely spaced it when she realized her necklace had been stolen.

She looked over to her brother.

Benny sat next to Roya, who didn't flinch or give him any scathing looks. He rested his hand on her knee and looked off into the distance with her.

So much had happened lately, and Seda had learned a lot about herself and her world. She realized she had not only discovered that surge of power inside her but also found her voice, restored her diminished confidence, and gained the potential to become the person Kalon had pretended to see.

She was Seda, not just a girl with white hair and pale eyes

who endured trauma, but a woman who was healing, brave, and loyal—*and she loved herself.*

THE SUN WAS RISING as Seda opened her eyes. She had fallen asleep leaning against Elco, but not before she ducked behind him to change out her stupid cloth from Kalon, and his front paw had pulled her closer for the night. She reached up and played with a strand of his mane that was tickling her face. He purred, and the vibrations ran through her body.

"What will you say to the Wisps?" Elco asked her, pulling her out of her continuous murderous thoughts about the two men and back to the Wisps.

Seda had trouble sleeping, lying awake late, and thinking about the questions she wanted to ask them. She had no idea where to start or if questions were even allowed.

What exactly did the Wisps look like? Were they large creatures?

"I honestly don't know," she replied with a sigh.

They stayed silent as Seda wove a few small braids through his mane, savoring each other's peaceful company until her friends started waking up.

That night, Benny had fallen asleep with Roya held tightly in his arms. The two of them looked so peaceful together. Despite being complete opposites in every way, they fit perfectly together.

Askold lifted his head and looked around. "Elco, that was the best night's sleep I've had on this entire trip. Thank you."

Elco didn't respond. "What did he say?" Askold asked her eagerly.

"Uhh... he said you're *very* welcome," Seda replied, and Elco growled in response, causing Seda to press her lips together to hide her smile.

Someone approached, and Seda glanced up, spotting Ojore making his way up the mountain with a small sack.

"What do you have there?" Benny asked as he rubbed his eyes.

Roya slowly opened her eyes, and her vacant gaze drifted back across the distance.

Ojore opened the pack, and a cricket hopped out. Ferona leaped at it, grasping it with her claws.

"Uhh, that's *grizzly*," Askold grimaced.

"That's not all," he said with a crooked smile, opening the bag wider. Inside, more items came into view: fresh winterberries, mushrooms, apples, and even more crickets.

"How did you find all of this?" Benny asked him.

"Let's just say I have a great sense of smell." Ojore laughed at his own joke.

"I *bearly* believe that," Askold said, and Ojore looked at him with pursed lips.

Seda perked up, suddenly feeling very hungry. Ojore held out the bag, and she accepted it, pulling out an apple and a small handful of berries, trying hard to avoid the moving crickets inside. She handed the bag to Benny, who took out his items and offered the bag to Roya, but she shook her head.

Ferona grabbed the bag from him and reached in for the crickets.

Everyone ate silently and watched the sun rise in the distance until the Corvids exchanged glances with furrowed brows.

"What's up?" Benny asked them.

"It can't be," Ferona whispered as she looked at Roya. "There's no way he survived."

They both shook their heads, rubbing their temples.

"What is it now?" Ojore grumbled. "What did the other Corvids say?"

The Corvids exchanged silent glances.

"Come *ON*… Just tell us!" Ojore raised his hands in frustration.

Roya cleared her throat and smiled warmly at Benny and Seda. "The Corvids say your father's alive. They saw him walking through Joro."

Both Benny's and Seda's jaws dropped, causing a berry to fall from Benny's mouth.

Seda couldn't believe he had survived the Camp. She saw all the men gathered that day… but her father… *wasn't there.*

"Are you sure it was him?" Ojore asked. "What if they got it wrong? I don't remember the last time a man made it back from that place."

"They know who Jason is, Ojore," Ferona deadpanned. "They saw him. He's alive."

Ojore, Askold, and Benny sighed in relief, but Seda felt confusion churn in her stomach, as if she were trapped in a maze of wavy mirrors.

How had he escaped the Camp? Was he injured, like so many others, after being in that place? Was he with her mom now?

"Well, is he okay or what?" Benny snipped at Ferona.

"He's fine. No injuries… *nothing.* Same as he was before. They saw him smiling and walking to the Gardvord with your mother."

"Can you ask them to continue checking, please?" Seda asked eagerly. This didn't make sense. She couldn't believe it. If her dad was taken to the Camp, he had to have injuries. There was no safe way out of that place.

Maybe his role was significant enough to earn him freedom? Seda smiled as a faint flicker of hope grew in her chest.

Both Corvids nodded, their brows furrowed, as they gazed out at the horizon. Then, they relaxed their expressions and stood up.

"We should head out," Roya said, shifting into her Corvid form and taking to the sky.

"I suppose we should get up now," Askold complained, stretching and reaching for Seda's hand to help her stand on her aching legs.

The group climbed the steep, snowy slopes of Mt. Ebenveil. Seda appreciated the rest she got the night before, but her nerves tingled more as they pressed on. She kept trying to think about what to ask, what to say, and how to say it all. She had so many questions, but was also afraid of their answers.

What does all of this mean?

The mountain grew steeper and foggier the higher they climbed, forcing them to take several breaks to catch their breath. The group supported each other as they navigated tricky inclines and steep rocks hidden by the haze and snow. Elco and the Corvids had taken to the sky, but they couldn't travel far because visibility was poor. Elco offered to carry Seda the rest of the way, but she declined, not wanting to arrive before everyone else or leave her friends behind to hike alone.

They reached the top of the mountain by midday. Seda pulled herself over the last rock and stood on unsteady legs, wheezing for breath.

She gasped, taking in the breathtaking view and the warmth surrounding her.

The mountain's peak was free of snow, as if the frigid weather from below couldn't touch its surface. The peak was shining in the daylight, and the green foliage glistened with dew. The fog had transformed from its usual white haze to a gentle pink.

It was still hard to see, but she could spot fluttering cerulean shapes in the distance, moving between the blooming trees.

"Are we here?" Seda asked Roya as she landed beside her and shifted into her human form.

Roya nodded. "Those are the Wisps." She pointed her finger at the fluttering shapes. "We're right here. Go on…"

Seda hesitantly stepped forward on her weak legs and then paused to look back at her friends.

Benny was smiling reassuringly at her, while Roya and Ferona appeared tense. Ojore and Elco scanned the area for danger, while Askold fidgeted nervously.

"You've got this, Seda. They called on you," Ferona encouraged.

Seda turned around and slowly moved into the dense, pink fog toward her answers.

As she approached, she noticed the fluttering shapes were coming from tiny, butterfly-winged pixies, with sparkling dust swirling around them.

Their small, nude bodies danced through the air, circling her.

How tiny they were! She had expected giant, mythical creatures, but the Wisps were so delicate and beautiful. She felt a powerful sense of love blossom through her heart.

"Hello. My name's Seda," she nervously announced, raising her hand in a hesitant wave.

"*We know,*" they said in unison, their high-pitched, ethereal voices echoing around her. "*We've been waiting for you, child.*"

If Seda wasn't anxious before, she definitely was now. They all spoke as one, confirming that the Corvids were right: *they were waiting for her.*

"What is it you wanted to talk to me about? Can you answer my questions, too?"

"*Your journey is not complete, child. You have more to learn. We are sad to see that you are not ready. Time is running short. You must return when all is unlocked,*" they echoed around her.

"Unlocked what? My power? I've found my power. Can you tell me what it means?"

"*The winged powers,*" they replied. "*But...*" They paused as Seda's heart thrummed like a caged drum.

"But what?"

"*You'll need their help to succeed. Return to us once you have all four stones and are in harmony with them. The heavens, the earth, and the dreams must unite alongside The Mother Goddess. Place the stone of protection into the magical door you were shown, and return all to the tree in which you were born. We will grant your wish when you come back,"* they said.

"What wish?" she asked.

They didn't answer.

Seda's mind spun. They described a magical door she was shown...

Her adrenaline suddenly surged, and her eyes widened as she realized what it was—the door Roya had led her to beyond the Gardvord.

But what was the stone of protection? She recalled the door wouldn't open, and there was a mark beneath the rounded opening.

It was perfectly shaped like a crescent moon, just like her moonstone.

Her heart raced with excitement. She had to find Kalon and get her necklace back. She *knew* it was important.

The pink mist began to swirl around her in a tornado of fog, with the Wisps blurring in the whirl. She felt dizzy as her hair knotted above her head. She watched the Wisps turn into blue ribbons flying through the air around her.

"Wh—" Seda tried to ask, hearing Elco's roar behind her.

Blackness swept her under, dragging her into the darkness of sleep.

"There she is..." the familiar, deep voice said in her dreams. "Do you remember yet?"

CHAPTER 47

<u>Luelle</u>

"Ouch!" Luelle growled at the seamstress who stuck a pin in her side, likely on purpose. This was the third time she had poked her while being fitted for her dress.

"I'm sorry, madam," the young seamstress said with an innocent look. Her large, blue eyes sparkled with mischief, and golden curls fell into her face as she knelt to finish hemming the bottom of the gown.

Luelle fought the urge to kick the woman.

The seamstress bit her lip and then shyly asked, "So you and the king are close, yes?" Her eyes shifted back to Luelle as she tried to hide her eager anticipation.

"Yes. His *Majesty* and I have been friends since childhood," she replied with an annoyed huff.

"I've heard he's been rejecting ladies and will not take any women to bed." She went back to pinning the dress for Luelle, her pointed ear tilted toward her.

"How curious… what else have you heard?"

Finally, some gossip.

The seamstress perked up and said in a low, conspiratorial voice, "Well, just between you and me, I heard he rejected the Madam's ladies the other night. What a gentleman he is." She released a deep sigh as if she admired the king for being such a good man, and continued, "As you know, it's time for him to choose a wife. That's what Advisor Meir announced when King Ael left, remember? Upon his return, he would select a wife. Some women were planning to make themselves more known to him tonight, myself included. Do you think he's being honorable by not taking those filthy whores?"

"Oh yes… King Ael's *very* honorable." Luelle rolled her eyes as the seamstress looked down. She didn't remember Meir making this announcement. How had it slipped past her?

Maybe she really wasn't the best spy.

"Are you also planning on trying for the king's hand in marriage?" she asked Luelle as she placed a pin in her mouth, pretending to focus on her stitch.

Luelle burst into laughter, causing the seamstress to jump back in surprise and drop the pin from her lips. "I'm sorry. But *no*. King Ael and I do not see each other that way. You can stop poking me with the needle now. I'm not competition."

The seamstress's cheeks turned bright pink, and she went back to finishing up the dress. It was beautiful. The deep, wine-colored silk ran to the ground and hugged her curves. The breasts were trimmed with vines with little red flowers, and the slit ran up her thigh.

"You look stunning, madam," the seamstress said, stepping back to take in her work. Luelle turned to face the full-length mirror.

"This is perfect," she replied. She ran her fingers up the vines that acted as straps over her shoulders and admired the work. "I will make sure to call you next time. As long as you promise not to prick me again with those damn needles."

The seamstress looked away, appearing ashamed. "I'd love the work. Do you think you could put in a word for me to the king?"

"I'll be sure to say something to him," Luelle answered with a smile. She was definitely *not* putting in a word for her, but she would complain and warn Ael that tonight he would be bombarded with floozies.

Luelle changed back into the boring gown she'd arrived in and thanked the girl as she left the room. She stepped out into the long hall and watched as the Fae scurried around, getting ready for tonight's festivities, hauling decorations, food, and other supplies.

She turned a corner and glanced back, checking to see if anyone was watching. Seeing it was clear, she pushed a luxurious tapestry to the side and walked into a dark corridor hidden away from view.

The dark hallways used to serve as the servants' passages before Ael ruled. When he took the throne, the servants were treated with greater respect and weren't forced to hide from the upper-class Fae of Umbrea. As a result, they hadn't been used regularly in over two hundred years.

They were perfect for Luelle. Most had forgotten their existence, and she used them to navigate the castle in private, eavesdropping on conversations and observing suspicious individuals who had no idea she was watching them.

For the past few years, the castle had been pretty dull without Ael, and she was hoping to hear something exciting now that he was back.

She made her way through the long, narrow hallways, passing by the backs of paintings and furniture, where she could overhear dull conversations. She rolled her eyes as she peeked through a gap at a large man, chatting about all the food he planned to eat later.

She continued walking and paused when she heard moaning

from the other side of a painting. She gazed into the tiny hole, curious to know who was now fucking whom.

There was a Fae woman with shoulder-length, curly, dark hair and large breasts on full display, on top of someone in bed. She was quickly rotating her hips, and the bed was thumping against the wall, her breasts bouncing with the movement.

Who was with her?

She looked more closely into the hole and saw a gray, scruffy beard emerge.

Disgusting!

Meir flipped the woman over and took her from behind, his tiny, hairy ass clenched together as he thrusted himself into the woman.

Luelle backed away, deeply disgusted by the sight—one she would painfully never forget—but she heard Meir say, "I'll make you a queen, my Neoma."

That caught her attention, and she promptly stopped in her tracks.

She hesitated before glancing back into the hole once more.

"You do this for me, and you'll help rule," Meir said.

Do what for him? She usually never watched over Meir. *He was an uninspiring advisor,* constantly in the library and strictly adhering to every rule, even when they were foolish.

"I want to be a queen." The woman let out a soft moan as she pretended to come undone under Meir.

Meir slammed into Neoma a few more times and then grunted. He fell to the side of her on the bed, his tiny erection sticking up in the air.

Well, no wonder she faked it.

"Do you promise me?" Neoma asked as she stroked his wiry, gray chest hairs between her fingers.

"Yes. It'll happen soon."

Luelle bit her perfectly manicured nail as thoughts ran

through her mind. Not only was Meir in cahoots to find Ael a wife, but Meir was now making promises to a mysterious Fae.

That was definitely interesting. Why would he care so much?

Certainly, the kingdom would welcome a queen and potential royal children roaming around, but Meir was old and never showed any concern about that.

She needed to watch him more closely, even if it meant seeing that small, disgusting penis again.

She stepped away from the wall and continued down its dark passages. She had been hoping to spend some time with someone before tonight's festivities, ideally someone without a penis, but after Meir's show, she felt nauseous.

She chose to go to Ael and share what she had heard, feeling excited to see the drama unfold.

CHAPTER 48

<u>Ael</u>

Ael sat in the dining room, trying to eat a late lunch, when a prickling feeling at the back of his neck made him look over at a servant with messy hair who hovered too close.

"Can I help you?" he asked with an annoyed huff.

She bit her lip, her eyes hooded, and said, "I can offer other services if you'd like, Sire." She reached out and ran her finger up his arm.

Disgust immediately churned inside him, and he twisted away from her, narrowing his eyes. "*Never* touch me like that again," he seethed. "Leave this room *now*. Send in Fran. I need to speak with her."

The woman's face paled, and her eyes glossed over with tears. She quickly ran out of the room and closed the door behind her.

What's happening? This was the third woman today who tried to throw herself at him. Was he really that much of a whore before he left Umbrea for Joro? He reflected on this, recalling that he'd had a few relationships with women, but nothing like the attention he was getting now.

The large curtains to his left shifted, and he looked over, assuming it was another servant lurking for him in the unused passageways. "I don't *need* anything right now. Please leave."

Luelle peered out and smiled at him. "Ael, that was *very* entertaining. I promise you I'm not here for that, though." She pretended to shiver in disgust and put her index finger in her mouth, making a gagging gesture.

"Thank gods it's you, Luelle. What's going on?"

"I have some *interesting* information regarding this problem you seem to be having." She sat in the chair next to him, grabbed a red grape from his plate, popped it into her mouth, and chewed slowly.

Her eyes sparkled as she waited for Ael to ask her for more details.

"Go on..." he said, knowing how badly she wanted him to show interest. He watched her patiently as she slowly chewed on the grape.

She smacked her lips and sighed. "Turns out Meir's behind this whole thing with these women throwing themselves at you. Apparently, when you left, he had planned that upon your return, you would select a wife to be your queen." She rolled her eyes and continued, "Many women are trying to get your attention, like that servant just now, like my seamstress, and like the big-breasted Fae with dark curls I just saw him fucking and making sweet promises to about becoming a queen."

She plucked another grape from his plate and took a bite, her brows raised and her eyes sparkling, as she waited for his response.

"Meir did what?" Ael erupted, leaping to his feet and pounding his hands on the table, his magic bursting from his palms. He ground his teeth together. "Why would he think I'd be picking a damn wife when I got back?"

Luelle shrugged. "Don't know. Haven't gotten there yet. I'll try to find out, but if you ask him directly, I want to be there for that little showdown." Luelle smiled deviously and popped another grape in her mouth, this time chewing it quickly.

Ael clenched his fists. He never told Meir he would choose a wife. He didn't want a random woman in his bed; he wanted someone he loved by his side. His mind flashed to Seda, and he pushed the thought away. He hadn't thought that far ahead yet. Umbrea would have a hard time accepting a human as queen, but if she accepted him, they would just have to fucking take her.

A problem for another time.

"Where's Meir?" he asked.

"Not sure, he was in some room fucking that woman. How many guests are staying here tonight? I didn't recognize the woman he was with. I assume she was some noble's daughter."

Someone knocked, and the door swung open. Fran, the head housekeeper, entered. "You called for me, Sire?" She bowed deeply. Flour covered her tall, curvy figure and blue dress.

"Tell your staff to stop touching me and to *stop* throwing themselves at me. It's unacceptable to touch *anyone* without permission." Ael watched her with such intensity that she fiddled with her apron.

"Yes, Sire. It will not happen again. I will also speak directly with Suza, the servant who was just here. Is there anything else I can assist with?"

"How are things looking for tonight?"

"We're getting close. The ballroom's almost done being set up."

Ael dismissed her with a wave of his hand, and she quickly bowed and left the room, closing the door behind her. He looked at Luelle. "Let me know if you find anything else regarding this and Meir."

He angrily marched to the door and left, leaving Luelle to finish his grapes.

***

As Ael entered the ballroom, the sound of stringed instruments suddenly ceased. The crown he hated wearing because it reminded him of his father, weighed heavily on his head. He only wore it on special occasions, and Meir had *insisted* he wear it again tonight, along with this stupid suit.

Ael really didn't want to be at this fucking ball, preferring to have some alone time away from prying eyes. His mind drifted to Seda. He needed a plan for when she arrived. How would she appear with 'mist and flame'?

It didn't make sense.

Meir spoke from the dais and extended his hand toward Ael, "Presenting King Ael, ruler of Umbrea."

The hundreds of Fae in the sparkling ballroom bowed deeply as Ael approached the throne at the room's northern end.

The glittering essence drifted in and out of the open windows lining the fifty-foot ceilings, and the tall, reflective walls glowed with candles lit from a grand chandelier, adding to the magical atmosphere.

The music resumed as Ael took his seat. Meir sat in a small, wooden chair beside him. "This is a lovely event, Sire. All of Umbrea's finest are within these walls tonight."

Meir surveyed the crowd and waved toward a woman with dark, curly hair. The woman wore a revealing emerald dress with a long train that trailed behind her on the floor. The neckline dipped below her navel, and her ample breasts struggled to stay in place. She approached the throne and bowed deeply, causing her cleavage to slightly reveal the edge of her nipple.

Ael caught Meir's gaze and saw him watching with a hungry

look as it slipped out. He remembered what Luelle had told him, and he definitely didn't want Meir's sloppy seconds.

The woman stood, and Meir cleared his throat and said, "Sire, please meet Neoma. Second daughter of Lord Ephron from the northern Umbrea mountains. She's traveled far to be with us tonight."

"And where is Lord Ephron? I haven't seen him in decades," Ael asked in a bored tone.

"He—" Meir started.

Neoma interrupted Meir in a sing-song voice, "He was unable to make it this evening, Sire. But he sends his regards. It's wonderful to have our king back in Umbrea. This is my first time in the castle." Her eyes sparkled in awe as she took in the room.

Ael looked at her and sneered at her impudence, but his expression softened slightly as guests watched the exchange. "Thank you for coming tonight, Neoma. I hope you find your stay welcoming."

He glanced over the crowd and saw a line of women forming behind Neoma. "I need to talk to you, Meir. You have some explaining to do."

"What about, Sire?" Meir asked nervously, looking back at Neoma and the girls lining up behind her. Neoma glanced over her shoulder and spotted the other women. She then turned back to Ael and took a confident step forward.

"I have a gift for you, Sire," she said to him quickly. "May I?"

Ael hesitated before nodding to her. She slowly approached him and raised her leg from the slit in her dress, revealing a sparkling garter with a red ribbon.

Ael reached out to push her thigh away when, in the middle of the ballroom, a cloud of pink fog erupted into a tornado, with flames dancing around the swirling storm.

His hand clenched on Neoma's thigh.

The wind blew fiercely in the ballroom, causing Neoma's loose top to blow open and her breasts to spill out.

Guests gasped at the sight of the tornado and quickly backed toward the walls, trying to get as far as possible from the fog and flames. The stringed instruments fell silent, their notes snapping suddenly, and the grand chandelier swayed like a pendulum.

Ael froze and watched as the ballroom tables caught fire and the glassware shattered onto the ground.

As the fog lifted, a deafening roar erupted from the center.

Elco appeared, cradling Seda in his arms, his massive bat-like wings spread wide, like an eclipse shielding her glow from those behind him.

Seda shimmered like moon dust around the room.

Ael's heart skipped a beat, and he felt a surge of excitement as he caught sight of her. She was stunning, like a goddess descended from the stars.

Seda opened her eyes, and her glowing amethyst irises narrowed on Ael.

His hand was still firmly wrapped around Neoma's thigh, and he quickly pulled it away when he noticed her watching.

Praxis and a few guards stormed in, powering up their magic and drawing their weapons as Ael shouted, "*STOP!*"

Everyone in the room froze, watching in eerie silence. Elco roared again and shot flames upward, turning the stone ceiling red with heat.

The people in the ballroom screamed in fear.

"Elco, *STOP!* We will not harm you or Seda!" Ael held his hands out to the guards, stopping them from advancing. Murmurs began to spread through the room as everyone looked between their king, this mystery woman, and the monster inside the castle.

Seda dropped to the floor and rose gracefully, her shimmering moonlight hair spreading around her, her glowing eyes flickering between Ael and Neoma. Neoma's breasts, still exposed from her gown, caught Seda's eyes, and they flashed brighter as she looked at them.

Her gaze snapped back to Ael in anger, her nostrils flaring, and her purple arms began sparking with electricity.

"You lied to me!" she snapped at him as everyone murmured around her display of power. "You *LIED* to me!"

She was here. Ael *finally* had her in Umbrea after all this time, and he was *never going to let her go.*

He stood from his throne, and Luelle approached him. "She's magnificent. You've got your hands full, Ael," she whispered into his ear with a chuckle.

Yes… and I'm going to love every fucking moment of it.

Dark clouds gathered and churned violently against the ceiling. A flash of lightning and a deafening crash of thunder shook the chandelier, causing the candles to fall and clink against the marble floor.

Seda raised her hands as she aimed them at Ael, and lightning erupted from her fingertips.

CHAPTER 49

<u>The Monster King</u>

"Gag him," the Monster King seethed to the Dragors as they forced down Mordred, who was screaming profanities at him, onto the floor. He was sitting at his desk and peered over the tabletop to see him.

Mordred's once pristine black robe was now shredded, and he had a bruise on his cheek. The Dragors wrapped a soiled cloth around his face and into his mouth, muffling his stupid whines. He was fighting back, but his attempts were weak in comparison to the force of the monsters.

The Monster King smiled.

"You tried to interfere," he said to Mordred, who responded with a muffled slew of curses. "You assisted in the escape of the Lionne and Seda. *I NEEDED THEM!*"

He picked up a bloodstone knife from his desk and let it glint in the sunlight filtering through the window. Mordred flailed and kicked the scaly skin of a Dragor, causing him to fall backward. The other Dragors pushed him down tightly against the floor, pressing his face into the rug.

"It's been a long time since I've been allowed to scar that face and body of yours. What used to be so handsome, Mordred, is now just a shattered mirror of what it used to be." He approached him with a bright smile as Mordred's body jerked slightly, beads of sweat streaming down his forehead.

The Dragors held firm, allowing the Monster King to approach with ease. He pressed his knife to Mordred's face and slowly sliced off a chunk of his forehead, allowing his emerald-colored blood to flow into his eyes. Mordred's muffled shrieks echoed into the room, and the Monster King laughed loudly.

He grabbed the chunk of Fae skin into his fist, held it to his lips, and licked it. He groaned in pleasure when the earthy taste hit his tongue, and his cock hardened in his pants. He took the skin and put it in his mouth, chewing slowly to savor the flavor.

When he swallowed, he looked back down at Mordred. "I know why you did it. I know why you let her escape."

Mordred's eyes widened, and he tried to shake his head.

The Monster King let Mordred's desperation fill the air before continuing, "She's your child, the Fae bastard of a wanna-be-king."

The Monster King was thrilled by Mordred's muffled curses. He knew she was his. He could tell by how the bitch looked when he saw her. "But who's her mother, Mordred? She does not have your coloring. When were you able to sneak in a fucking love affair without me knowing? I need her back to open the door."

He walked around him again and sliced off the last bit of his left ear that remained. Mordred screamed in pain and thrashed his legs around, his blood now dripping down his neck and soaking into his robe. He threw the piece of flesh into his mouth and chewed it loudly.

"Un-gag him, I want him to answer!" The Monster King screamed as Mordred's blood splattered from his lips.

The Dragors quickly released the cloth from his face, and

Mordred screamed, "She will come for you! Your days are fucking over!" Mordred laughed maniacally, as if he held a secret the Monster King didn't know.

The Monster King angrily backhanded him across the face, whipping his head to the side. "I only want to hear *answers* from you! Tell me what I need to know!"

"I will never tell you anything. Never again," Mordred sneered. "My life changed all those years ago. All because of you!"

"Then I will take your *fucking fingers next!*"

The Dragors firmly held him down and pried open his clenched hand, spreading his fingers out.

The Monster King laughed as he regarded Mordred's scarred skin and wide eyes. "Oh, look how far you've fallen, when all you had were dreams of success. Now, just a broken husk of an ugly man."

He bent down closer, first running his fingers over Mordred's bloodstone cuffs, emitting a snicker, and then dug the knife into his pinky finger, having to force through the bone with a crunch.

Mordred's screams pierced the room.

"We will continue to do this until you have none left, then we will move to your toes." The Monster King laughed menacingly as he lifted the finger to inspect it. "You can avoid losing more by just telling me what I need to know."

"Fuck you," Mordred answered through ragged breaths.

The door opened, and Jason walked in. The Monster King looked at him, smiled, and then looked back at the Dragors.

"Place him in the same cell where Seda stayed. Let him rot where her blood and pain once were, so he can think about how his plans never work. *They never have.*"

He threw the finger onto the floor next to the Dragors, and one grabbed for it quickly, chewing on it and groaning as bloody chunks fell from his mouth.

"Jason. Let's get cleaned up. You have a special Wyrd and an announcement to make to those blubbering citizens. First, though, I need a woman here. Go find me one."

Jason said nothing as he turned around and left the room.

As the Monster King watched Jason leave and Mordred hauled away, he bit his nail. He desperately needed Seda and the Lionne back, or else Somnium would haunt him forever. She was the key he needed to free himself from Somnium's torment, the key to finally killing him and taking complete control.

The Monster King wanted to be the most powerful and feared in all of Xyberus, and only one person still stood in his way… *Somnium*.

EPILOGUE

<u>Somnium</u>
(A very, very long time ago)

An elderly man tossed and turned in bed, tormented by disturbing dreams of infidelity. His body was overheating, and sweat dripped down his forehead. His wife shook him awake, and he sat up abruptly in bed.

The connection collapsed.

Somnium chuckled as he gripped the arms of his dark throne. He closed his eyes, searching for his next victim and relishing the torment he inflicted on the sleeping beings of Xyberus. His lips curled into a wicked smile as he sent out dark dreams of agony, fear, deception, and pleasure. Images of writhing bodies, sinful lust, and psychological distress were among his favorites now. He delighted in their anguish, inhaling the air around him deeply and exhaling through his unholy lips. He laughed as he focused on a young woman, sending her images of fear-inducing snakes.

"Immortal Somnium." He lost his connection and seethed

with anger. His gaze fell to a shadowy snake, and he let out a low growl.

That one was going to be good.

"What is it?" His eyes locked onto the snake, making its body shimmer with changing opacity.

"Someone's here… they wish to see you." The shadow flickered, awaiting a response.

He glanced across the polished tiles in the long, empty room toward the double doors and spotted a young woman.

He snorted in disgust. What did a fucking Fae want from him?

She stood in the doorway, watching him with wide eyes. He saw her eyes widen even more as he looked at her through his mask, and his covered lips curved into a smile.

Fucking good. Be scared.

He studied her closely, noticing she cowered between the rooms, clearly frightened of what monster was concealed within.

"What do you want?" he shouted, his voice reverberating off the worn, hollow walls and the cracked bone mask that covered his face.

She hesitated as she entered the room and caught her dress on something, causing her to stumble. As Somnium watched her collapse to the floor, his seafoam-colored eyes sparkled with delight at her unease.

She quickly rose and cleared her throat. "I've traveled far…"

She nervously glanced around, her eyes briefly resting on the empty throne beside him. The dusty throne, covered in spider silk, would have matched his own if it hadn't been vacant for so long.

Anger erupted within him, and he snarled as he stood, his black snakeskin armor rattling with the movement. "What do you want?!"

She quickly glanced back at him and cleared her throat again. "*Kalon de Somnium*, I'm an oracle, and I've come to tell you that the tree has fallen, the Mother Goddess's stone is now dark, the guardian has been captured, and the gods have been banished. We must wait for the return of yanantin."

Following the events of years past, Somnium had grown tired of the war against the monsters and gods and instead chose to spend his time alone in his realm, Noctrya.

Did this imply that his heart, his love, his *everything*—the reason he continued to breathe each day—would return?

For the first time in decades, a faint hint of optimism wove the first mending thread through his shattered heart.

He smiled and began thinking of ways to torment that pathetic man who pretended to be a monster king, and he would do it for *her*.

He closed his eyes and started to scan the minds of the beings of Xyberus. He would find her, even if it took a thousand years...

He would find her.

Seda's journey continues in *CORVID WINGS*, the next book in the series, *The Amethyst Wrath*.

Coming in 2026.

ACKNOWLEDGMENTS

The journey of writing this book wouldn't have been possible without the support of these fantastic people:

My husband, who continues to support my creative journey, never blinks an eye when I mention a new idea. Initially, I owned a small boutique, and after that, I launched a cake business. Now, my childhood dream of becoming an author is finally coming true. I dedicated many hours to this story, and he was consistently supportive. I love you so much!

My daughters, who constantly remind me of the importance of following my dreams.

My youngest, so loving and caring, wants to read my book, to which I, of course, must say no (maybe when she is older).

My oldest, who is passionate about creative writing and art, is gradually working on her own book. She reviewed my first chapter during my initial draft and identified significant gaps I needed to address!

My sister, who was my first reader of the story, provided invaluable feedback when something didn't make sense or was off the mark. She cheered me on to keep pushing forward, even when I felt discouraged along the way.

My best friend, who cheered me on throughout the writing process, often said she kept forgetting it was someone she knew who had written it as she read.

My biggest fan!

My beta readers and developmental editor were invaluable, offering a wealth of constructive feedback.

My friend and coworker. We were talking about childhood dreams one day, and they asked me… Why not? Why not write a story? What's stopping you?

They were the initial push that made me start, and once I did, it was like a tsunami consuming my life. Thank you so much for that.

My father, who passed away from cancer just days before I started writing this.

I must admit that I disassociated and started writing because I missed you intensely and couldn't handle the pain.

We love and miss you, Poppy. You will forever remain in our hearts.

Thank you all for your support and love. <3

ABOUT THE AUTHOR

Dee Mannine is a debut author who loves storytelling and enjoys reading fiction, particularly fantasy, romance, and dark gothic genres. She works full-time in the tech industry, but her genuine passions are in the arts—such as painting, drawing, and baking. She has two daughters who love anything that sparks their creativity, which helps keep her motivated on her personal journey. Dee has been happily married for 10 years and lives in beautiful Northern California, running a small homestead with her husband. She has always had vivid dreams and ideas, so she chose to write some of them down, turning them into this story.

Find out more at:

deemannine.com

TikTok: @author.dee.mannine

Instagram: @author.dee.mannine

Character art illustrations created by:

Anas Arzaq — Instagram: @anasarzq